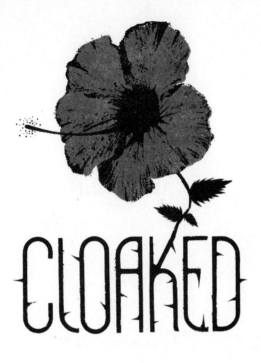

CLOAKED

Also by
ALEX FLINN

BREATHING UNDERWATER

BREAKING POINT

NOTHING TO LOSE

FADE TO BLACK

DIVA

BEASTLY

A KISS IN TIME

CLOAKED

ALEX FLINN

An Imprint of HarperCollinsPublishers

HarperTeen is an imprint of HarperCollins Publishers.

Cloaked
www.harperteen.com

Library of Congress Cataloging-in-Publication Data
Flinn, Alex.
Cloaked / Alex Flinn. — 1st ed.
p.   cm.
Summary: Seventeen-year-old Johnny is approached
at his family's struggling shoe repair shop in a Miami, Florida,
hotel by Alorian Princess Victoriana, who asks him to find her
brother, who was turned into a frog.
ISBN 978-0-06-087422-3
[1. Missing persons—Fiction.   2. Magic—
Fiction.   3. Animals—Fiction.   4. Characters in
literature—Fiction.   5. Shoes—Fiction.   6. Princesses—
Fiction.   7. Miami (Fla.)—Fiction.   8. Key Largo
(Fla.)—Fiction.]   I. Title.
PZ7.F6395Clo 2011   2009053387
[Fic]—dc22   CIP
                                                                          AC

Typography by Sasha Illingworth
11 12 13 14 15   CG/RRDB   10 9 8 7 6 5 4 3 2 1
❖
First Edition

For my daughter, Meredith

Special thanks to Toni Markiet, Jayne Carapezzi, Joyce Sweeney, Dorian Cirrone, and George Nicholson

Few people know how to take a walk.
The qualifications are endurance, plain clothes,
old shoes, an eye for nature, good humor, vast curiosity,
good speech, good silence, and nothing too much.
—Ralph Waldo Emerson

1

There once was a shoemaker who worked very hard, but was still very poor. . . .

—"The Elves and the Shoemaker"

I've never seen a princess before. And it looks like I won't be seeing one today either.

Let me back up: I come from a long line of shoe people. My grandfather called us cobblers, but that sounds more like a dessert than a person. My family's run the shoe repair at the Coral Reef Grand, a posh hotel on South Beach, since before I was born—first my grandparents, then my parents, now my mother and me. So I've met the famous and infamous, the rich and the . . . poor (okay, that would be me), wearers of Bruno Magli, Manolo Blahnik, and Converse (again, me). I know the beautiful people. Or, at least, I know their feet.

But, so far, I haven't met a single princess.

"She should be here any minute." Ryan, one of the college guys who works as a lifeguard, interrupts me as I rip the sole off a pair of Johnston Murphys a customer needs by eight. "My friends texted me that her motorcade's down Collins Avenue."

"And this affects me how?" I do want to go see her, but I have to stay at my post. Can't afford to miss a customer.

"It affects you, Johnny, because anyone, any normal seventeen-year-old guy, would rip themselves away from the shoe counter if a hot-looking princess was in the lobby."

"Some of us have to work. I have customers—"

"Yeah, shoes are important."

"Money is."

Ryan doesn't usually talk to me. Like most guys my age who work here, he's only earning money to gas the convertible he got for graduation or maybe to buy clothes. I notice he has on a new Hollister polo that's tight in the arms, probably to show off the muscles he's always flexing.

Me, I work here to support my family, and the only workout I get involves running penny loafers through a Landis McKay stitcher. Even though I'll be a senior in the fall, I won't be off to college next year. No money. I'll probably be repairing shoes until the day I croak.

"Don't you *want* to see her?" Ryan looks at me like

I've admitted I'm wearing Pull-Ups or have gills. He flexes again.

Of course, I want to see her. I've been drooling over pictures of her on the covers of the *Miami Herald, Miami New Times, Sun Sentinel,* and *USA Today* newspapers that face out in the hotel coffee bar across the way. One tabloid claims she's mated with an alien, but most of them show a hard partier who frequently disgraces her family and her country. She's in Miami for some important, top-secret business, which probably involves consumption of many drinks with "tini" at the end of them.

Oh yeah, and I know she's beautiful.

And I, who have the most boring life of anyone, should at least get to see her, so that when I die of an aneurysm, trying to rip out a tough stitch, at least I'll be able to say I once saw a princess.

"Mr. Farnesworth doesn't want us out there, gawking at her. Besides, what if someone shows up and I'm not here?"

"Some kind of shoe emergency?" Ryan laughs.

"Yeah. It's always an emergency when you can't wear your shoes. I can't do it." I try to say it with finality, the way Mom used to say, *We can't afford it,* when I was little, and I knew there'd be no more arguing.

"What's up?" My friend Meg sidles up toward me.

I'm glad to see Meg, who works the coffee counter next to our repair shop, but I know she's going to be angry because her brothers, who worked last night, didn't clean up at all. Like me, Meg works for her parents, helping out even during the school year. She's my best friend, and usually the only friend I have time for. In middle school, I had a sort of crush on her. I even took her to our eighth grade dance. She wanted to make some other guy jealous, but for a moment on the dance floor, I thought there could be something there. But that was a long time ago.

Anyway, Meg will understand why I can't go with Ryan.

Ryan flexes and looks Meg up and down, like he does every girl. "I was trying to talk Johnny here into taking five minutes off from the fast-paced world of shoe repair to go see Princess Vicky's motorcade. This guy never wants to have any fun."

Meg makes a face and lays her hand on my arm. "And why, exactly, would John want to see Eurotrash?"

"Hello?" Ryan says. "Because he's a seventeen-year-old guy with normal male urges, and she's got—" He holds both hands out from his chest.

"Really pretty eyes," I complete his sentence.

Meg rolls her own brown eyes. "And the IQ of a single-celled creature."

"Anyway, he's not going." Ryan just has to keep putting the boot in. "The boy is in love with shoes."

"'The shoe that fits one person pinches another.'" This I say with a wink to Meg. She and I collect quotes about shoes. I've been waiting for the opportunity to use that one. "Carl Jung said that."

"Carl who?" Ryan asks.

"A Swiss psychiatrist," I say. "Ever hear of Jungian—"

"Whatever," Ryan says. "So you're really not coming?"

Meg glances at me. "I can tell your customers you'll be right back, if you want to go. But I'm sure—"

"Can you? Thanks." I know Meg expected me to turn her down, but I really do want to go. Not that I'll ever get closer to Victoriana than watching her check in from behind a potted palm. But still, it's a brush with adventure, and adventure is something I get none of.

"Gotta go!" Ryan holds up his phone. "Pete at the door just texted that her limo's in view."

"You've got connections," Meg says to Ryan.

"It's the name of the game." Ryan moves closer to her. "Maybe you and I could make a connection sometime—like, say, Friday night?"

I'm sure Meg will say yes. Most girls turn into puddles of drool around him. But she doesn't even smile. "No, thanks. You're not my type."

Ryan looks as surprised as I feel. "What's your type? Other girls?"

Meg shrugs, glances at me, then shrugs again. "Why don't you go ogle your princess now?"

"You're sure you don't mind covering for me?" I know she does.

"Just go before I change my mind."

Ryan glances back at Meg as we walk away. "She's hot for you."

"Yeah, right."

"She is. You should go for it. She may not be that good-looking, but you can't be too picky."

"She turned you down flat." I glance back at Meg, who's still watching both of us. She flips her chin-length brown hair back from her eyes, and for a second, I remember that night in eighth grade. But when she sees me looking at her, she holds up her hands like, *What are you looking at?* "Nope, she and I are just friends."

Still, I wave to her before I make the turn toward the lobby.

2

The lobby is bustling like the *Calle Ocho* street carnival, but without the salsa music. A housekeeper leads six swans on their morning waddle around the hotel fountain. Another removes a cover from a parrot cage. The Miami sun streams through the thirty-foot-high windows at the front of the room, hitting the marble floors so they look like pure gold. It also makes it hard to see because the manager, Mr. Farnesworth, glances right in my direction. I think he's going to come over, but then, his head snaps back, and I see why. Every bell-hop in the place is entering, each carrying two Louis Vuitton suitcases. I skitter sideways, as quick as a crab, and stand as I'd planned, behind a potted palm, imagining what must be in those suitcases. The shoes. Prada, Stuart Weitzman, Dolce & Gabbana, Jimmy Choo, and Alexander McQueen!

Ryan's right. I'm not normal. No one else would think of shoes at a time like this.

Among the suitcases, I notice a dog carrier. Now, needless to say, the Coral Reef doesn't allow dogs, but I guess you don't tell princesses that. It's a large carrier, and I peer through the bars, expecting a standard poodle or an Afghan. But, instead, I see a bloodhound's black-and-brown face and sad eyes staring back at me.

"Hey, boy," I say.

The dog growls.

"Nice going." Ryan has also taken up residence behind the palm. "He sees us."

He means Farnesworth, who's taken his eyes off the door long enough to march over to our palm. "You! Where are you supposed to be?"

"We're on break," Ryan says.

"Be on break elsewhere. I don't want you bothering the princess."

"*Excusez-moi?*" a voice interrupts. "You are ze hotel manager?"

Farnesworth turns and takes a step back, then a second, onto my foot. I try to jump back. It's her!

Farnesworth, still on my foot, stutters, unable to form

words. I wonder if they'll send a cha
after him when he pees his pants.

"Uh . . . ," he manages.

I bow, pushing Ryan down with
not to stare at her shoes, but from this
thing I can see. Roberto Cavalli.
V-strap platforms with a woven leath
tectural heel.

"'Allo?" She's still trying to make contact with
Farnesworth, who's panting like he just jogged down the
beach. Sweating too. She leans toward me and gestures that
I can stand. That's when I get my first good look at her.

I've seen lots of pictures, but none of them prepare me
for the real thing. Her beauty shocks me, which is saying a
lot, considering I live in South Beach, where hot is the new
average. She has long white-blond hair that curls down to her
perfectly proportioned hips. Even though she emphasizes
her body with fitted clothes and a short skirt, her huge eyes,
which are bluer than the ocean outside, make her look all
innocent, like a Disney princess.

"Nice dog," I manage.

Oh, I am such an idiot.

She nods and opens the cage. The dog scampers out,
looking for something to sniff, but at a signal from the princess, he comes right back and sits behind her. She strokes its
head, then turns to me.

"Is he"—she nods at Farnesworth—"not right?"

...ay, usually."

...esworth's mouth tries to move. "You . . . you're . . ."

...am Victoriana."

People are like shoes. Some are like sneakers or flip-flops, while others are like high-heeled pumps. Princess Victoriana is like the shoes she wears—not very practical, but beautiful.

Farnesworth finds his voice. "I didn't expect you to . . . I mean, I thought I'd be dealing with your lady-in-waiting or . . . something."

"She is back zere." She gestures behind her at a woman with short hair, a plain skirt, and what looks like the Alorian version of Aerosoles. "Slow." She looks at Ryan and me. "And zese . . . zese are some of your employees?"

Mr. Farnesworth recovers with a look of complete contempt. "Oh, them. Don't worry. I won't let them bother you." He flicks his hand at Ryan. "Surely your break is over. And you . . ." He glances at me.

"*Non, non.* Zere is no need to leave. I will be here, maybe some time, and I would like to know zose who offer zeir services." She looks at Ryan particularly. It's news that she's staying a long time. Actors sometimes stay awhile if they're filming a movie, but visiting dignitaries are usually here only a day or two. She looks again at Ryan. "What is your name?"

He grins, used to attention but still flattered. "I'm Ryan. I work at the pool. Maybe if you're there sometime,

I can rub lotion on your back."

"Maybe, maybe not." The princess maintains eye contact an instant longer than required, and I can tell she's sizing Ryan up. I fantasize she doesn't like what she sees. She turns to me. "And you? Who are you, and what do you do?"

Words fail me. Why does she want to know about me?

"Say something!" Farnesworth hisses, thumping me on the back. Like he was so eloquent!

I say, "I'm Johnny. I . . ." And the second before I say it, I'm ashamed of it. "I repair shoes. My family runs the shoe repair here." I gesture toward the hotel shops.

"Shoes!" She claps her hands like it's the most wonderful news she's ever heard. "I love ze shoes! I have a suitcase of zem!"

I laugh. Of course she does. She's a princess.

"You laugh at me? You think my love of shoes is—'ow you say—shallow?"

"I didn't—"

"Maybe I am. But I believe zat ze shoes, zey are magical, like in 'Cendrillon'—'Cinderella' to you—or *Ze Red Shoes*. I believe in magic. Do you?"

I gape at her. "Uh, I guess so." One of the swans from the fountain walks by, and the bloodhound starts to bark, not a mean bark, but a soft, steady bark, like he's talking to it. Victoriana places her small hand in front of the dog, and he stops.

"Where I come from in Aloria," Victoriana says, "zere

is magic. Sometimes good, sometimes not so . . ." She stops and shakes her head, obviously realizing she sounds nuts and should change the subject. "You must never be ashamed of shoes, and to work for your family is honorable. I, too, am in ze family business. It is not always easy."

I nod, thinking it seems pretty easy to me, traveling around and going to parties. But maybe it isn't. Staring into Victoriana's eyes, she doesn't seem to be the girl from the newspapers and the tabloids, the party girl who cares only about clothes and drinking. Instead, her eyes are sort of sad, like she feels trapped in her life, just as I am in mine.

Farnesworth must decide that's enough from me, because he offers her his arm. "Your check-in has already been taken care of. I can show you to your room."

The princess looks at me an instant longer before saying, "Very well." She ignores Farnesworth's arm and starts toward the elevator. Farnesworth trots behind her.

Ryan and I head in the opposite direction. When we reach the hallway that goes to the pool, I turn to Ryan. "God, I think I'm in love."

"Yeah, whoudda thought? A princess who's obsessed with shoes. Shame you're not better-looking. And shame you don't work at the pool like me. I'll probably get to see her every day in a bikini."

"Yeah." I'll never see her again. Princesses don't get their shoes repaired. They send the servants out for new ones.

He starts to whistle, then stops, maybe seeing how

seriously depressed I am. "They're looking for a new life-guard. You should apply."

I shake my head. "Can't."

"Can't swim?"

"Nah. I'm a great swimmer. But my mom needs me to work in the shoe repair. It's just the two of us."

"Cut the cord. You're what, seventeen? Time to make your own decisions." He shrugs. "Suit yourself."

I glance at the elevators. Victoriana's boarding the one that goes all the way to the penthouse. She's scratching the dog's ears. I picture myself with them, flying all the way to the sky.

3

A buyer came in, and liked the shoes so well that he paid more for them than usual. With the money, the shoemaker was able to purchase leather for two pairs of shoes.

—"The Elves and the Shoemaker"

"Hey, this place looks a lot better than when I left." I pass the coffee shop on my way back to the Johnston Murphy shoe emergency. It's crowded with conventioneers, but last night's ketchup stains have been wiped from the tables, the straw wrappers and napkins that littered the floor are gone, and the floor itself sparkles like the beach sand outside. Meg and another employee are pouring coffee and plating croissants. "How'd you get it clean so quick?"

"It was like this when I got here," she says. "So you saw Her Royal Highness then?"

I nod, eyes still scanning the shop. "She seemed nice."

14

"Nice looking, you mean," Meg says. "Not like you actually spoke to her."

"I did, actually." I still don't believe it myself. "She has a dog, and she said that repairing shoes was . . . honorable."

Meg makes a noise halfway between a laugh and a snort.

I glance around. Even the honey squirter is wiped clean, and the sugar shaker actually glitters. "It was *not* like this last night. Sean and Brendan left it a total mess. I figured you'd flip when you saw."

"You were here last night when they closed?" Meg asks. When I nod, she says, "And you're back again by seven?"

"Six. It's not a big deal."

"It is a big deal. You can't work sixteen-hour days."

"We need the money."

Meg nods. She gets it. Summers are tough. During the winter, we usually hire an extra employee, but in the summer, when not as many people stay at the hotel, the bills pile up. It's summer now, but I'm not going to the beach or sleeping in. What Meg doesn't know is that my mother took another job, so I'm all alone.

" 'Our incomes are like our shoes; if too small, they gall and pinch us, but if too large, they cause us to stumble and to trip,' " Meg says. "John Locke said that."

"I think I could handle a too-large income right about now." I look down. "There was a puddle of milk under that table."

"Mopped it."

"Before, you said it was clean when you came in."

"I was lying. I didn't want you to know that I'm a cleaning genius. If it gets around, they might want to hire me as a chambermaid, and I'd miss the glamorous world of coffee. Now, can we drop it?"

"If we can drop talking about how I shouldn't work double shifts."

Meg frowns and puts her hand on my shoulder. "I'm sorry. I just . . . wish I could help."

I shake off her hand. "You could give me an espresso."

"Got it." She gets out a cup.

I head for my counter and start working on the sole of the shoe I left. It's not that I don't agree with Meg. But I need to work here. We can't afford what someone else with my skills would cost, so I have to. Losing our family business would be too much of a blow for my mother to take.

At least I did most of the repairs last night. Maybe after this one, I can work on what's in my secret box, the one I keep under the past-due bills.

I take it out for a second, just to look. Inside is a prototype for a ladies' high-heel kelly green sandal, skeletal structure, hidden platform for comfort as well as style. I made it.

Most of our customers are businessmen in town for meetings. They travel so much they don't notice that their seven-hundred-dollar Esquivel loafer is wearing thin until the day of a big meeting. Since they're desperate, we can charge fifty and up for a rush job. They can afford it.

I hardly ever get ladies' shoes. The kind of women who stay here throw out shoes if a strap breaks, even if they've only been worn once. But sometimes, a maid or au pair will bring in one of her employer's trashed Giuseppe Zanottis or Donald Pliners, hoping to make it over for herself. That's how I learned that those strappy sandals can sell for hundreds of dollars.

And the thing is, it would be fun to make them. They come in every color and texture and style. The really good ones are like art. I know shoes, and if I had the materials, I could make shoes just as good as those expensive ones. Better.

So that's my dream, to become an internationally known shoe designer, instead of just a shoe boy in a hotel. I may repair soles right now, but in my soul, I know I can do more.

It would be nice if I could go to college to learn to market what I design. But, for now, we need to keep the rent mostly paid.

"That's hot." Meg comes up behind me with the coffee. "Where'd you get it? Some rich lady?"

I slam the box shut. "It's nothing."

"It's not nothing. It's gorgeous. You made it, didn't you?" She inches her hand over to the box. "Come on. I've seen you drawing shoes and stuff when you think no one's looking. I, of all people, won't make fun of you."

I relent. She's right. I know all her secrets, like this one time when we were twelve and she had a crush on a lifeguard.

She went to the pool after work, her bikini top stuffed with cotton balls, only to forget about them when she jumped into the water.

I was the one who alerted her, let her walk behind me until we were out of the sun god's sight, and went back and explained to him that the cotton balls he was picking out of the drain trap were mine, for a bunion.

No, Meg wouldn't make fun of me. I slide the sandal toward her and walk over to the auto-soler with the loafer.

"I love it." She traces the strap with her finger. "Can I try it on?"

I did make it in a size six, Meg's size. So, on some subconscious level, I was probably looking for a model. Still, the idea of someone, some actual person, wearing them is scary.

"Please. My feet are really pretty. I've been told I could be a foot model."

"Right." I laugh.

"True. Someday, you'll see an ad for toenail fungus cream, and it'll be me." She holds up the shoe. "I love this design. I want to wear it."

"You can't afford it. This is going to be a five-hundred-dollar pair of shoes."

"Oh, at least a thousand, I'm sure."

"Not for people like us who shop at Tar-*jay*." But I'm flattered she likes them so much, so I say, "Oh, okay."

She makes a big deal of taking off her own sandals (Mossimo, store brand of Target, $14.99 in faux leather). She does have cute feet with red nail polish that matches her T-shirt. She slips the shoe onto her foot, then stops to admire it before holding it out to me. She says, all wide-eyed, "'But you see, I have the other slipper.'"

I know this quote. "Right. Disney's *Cinderella*."

"Any girl would feel like Cinderella in these shoes." Meg slips on the other shoe. Then, she stands and struts the hall-way between our shops, strutting and dancing like a runway model. "Meg is wearing a new design in emerald green by that exciting new designer, Johnny Marco."

"It's kelly green."

"Kelly green. It has a platform and a four-inch heel."

"Three inches. The platform makes them seem higher."

"Three inches." She twirls again. "I love them. But I guess I should take them off."

"I guess." But I like looking at them, so I say, "Are they comfortable?"

She uses her announcer voice again. "Like walking on the beach." She kicks her feet onto my lap. The fluorescent lights glint off the green leather, and it's magic, just like Victoriana said. "Are there others?"

I reach into the box and hand her the folder at the bottom, the one with all my designs. "Just here."

She flips through, admiring. "Oh, you have to make this one."

"That's the problem. I can't afford the materials right

now. But I have a plan." I point to the sign that says, ITEMS LEFT MORE THAN 14 DAYS WILL BE DONATED TO CHARITY. "I figured I could put them on eBay, make some money, and still donate part of it to Goodwill. I ended up making a pretty good profit. But sometimes, people leave just a single shoe. I couldn't sell those or donate them, so they ended up trashed. But then, I got the idea of using them for parts. Open that drawer." She does and takes out a bag of scrap leather pieces, all different colors. "You know those really expensive handbags that are made from bits and pieces of other expensive handbags? I'm going to do that with shoes."

Meg claps her hands. "That's genius. I always knew you were a genius."

"I have almost enough for another pair."

"When do you find time for this?" She touches my arm. Her hand is icy cold, and I shiver under it. She sees me flinch and removes it. "I thought you were just staring into space, drooling."

"Hey, I'm a surprising guy."

"Excuse me. Who do you have to kill to get some service around here?"

My first customer of the day is a businessman in an Italian suit. A rude one. He's drumming one set of fingers on the counter. With the other, he holds a Cole Haan black blucher oxford. Retail: About two hundred dollars, low-end around here. He wiggles the loose heel. "If it's not too much trouble, maybe you could fix this. I need it right away."

20

I reach past Meg for it. "Of course, sir, but I have other jobs ahead of you. I'll have to charge you for a rush job." I'm lying.

"Yes. Anything. I have a life-changing meeting in an hour."

Life-changing. I wish something life changing would happen to me.

I examine the shoe. The heel's worn down an inch, and it doesn't look like the original either. This guy bought a pair of expensive shoes years ago and has been using them to try to impress clients ever since. I'm guessing if I examined his suit, it would be going threadbare too. I think about giving him a break on the repair. But then, I remember the bills stacking up, Mom crying over them yesterday. Besides, he was a jerk. "Sixty dollars," I say.

"Sixty? In St. Louis, I paid—"

"This is South Beach not St. Louis, and you need it in a hurry." But I relent. "Okay, fifty. I'll have it done in twenty minutes."

Fifteen minutes later, I send him on his way. "Good luck!"

As soon as he leaves, Meg's signaling to me to come over. Between customers, she says, "I had an idea. If you could get Princess Victoriana to wear a pair of your shoes in public, everyone would want them. You could charge a thousand dollars a pair!"

"Yeah, and if a frog had wings . . ."

But then, I think it's an inspired idea. I've been around enough rich people to know that what they really want is to look like richer people.

"'My shoes are special shoes for discerning feet,'" I quote Manolo Blahnik, the shoe designer. "Maybe you're right. Who better to wear them than a princess?"

"Who better," Meg agrees.

"But one problem. How do we get her to wear them?"

"Give her a pair. You said she seemed nice. Maybe when she sees how amazing they are, she'll wear them. And then, if she gets photographed falling drunk out of a limo, it will be in your shoes. You've got to talk to her again."

Suddenly, I hear a commotion coming from the lobby, a commotion that could only mean another Victoriana sighting. I run to check it out.

Not her. Only her dog. Her dog, three bodyguards, two hotel employees, six swans-a-swimming, and a partridge in a pear tree.

"No luck?" Meg says when I return.

"No luck," I say, "but I'll keep trying."

4

All I can think about the rest of the day is Meg's idea of getting Victoriana to wear my shoes. I'm excited for the first time in, maybe ever. It's a busy day, not much time to sit and dream, but that's a good thing too. As I pull off each heel tip, sew each rip, I scheme about how to make it happen. At six, I decide to close for an hour, for dinner. Mom should be home, and I want to tell her about it. Meg's already left, but her brother Sean says he'll let customers drop off their repairs at the coffee shop. If we even have any.

It's raining when I leave. Even so, I bike home feeling totally pumped.

As soon as I reach the apartment, I know something's wrong. The lights aren't on, and neither is the air-conditioning. My mother sits on the sofa, fanning herself.

I say, "Hey, you'll never guess who I saw today."

"Oh, Johnny." My mother has on a T-shirt that says, "Love that dog!" It's from her second job, a hot-dog place. She walks over to the window. "Sorry it's so hot. They—"

"Turned off the power. Got it." When she nods, I say, "How much do we owe?"

"Five hundred. It was either that or rent. I got some ice from Mrs. Castano. That should keep the food cold until payday if we don't open the refrigerator too much."

I mentally add up today's repairs. Not even close. Now, I'm sorry I gave that St. Louis guy a ten-dollar break.

But Mom smiles, like she's used to it. She *is* used to it. It happened last summer too.

Me, I don't ever want to get used to it. When I was little, we made it a game, like camping. But now, I know it's not a game. I wonder how long it will be until we can't pay any bills and lose the business too.

"So tell me," Mom says. "Did you see the princess?"

"Yeah." I try to smile, but suddenly, it doesn't seem that cool. I mean, what's a princess anyway? Just someone who won the birth lottery and gets to do nothing and have everything while the rest of us poor slobs sweat. Literally. It's so hot I'm actually shivering from it.

But Mom wants to hear about it. "How did you see her?

Was she beautiful? Was she drunk? Did she have a million servants?"

"Yeah, we—Ryan and I—saw her check in. I thought Farnesworth was going to swallow his tongue. And she had a dog, a bloodhound."

Mom laughs. "Your father always used to want a bloodhound." She glances at the bookshelf, at the eight-by-ten wedding photo she keeps there. I glance too. She's gotten out some candles, the white ones in a jar that they sell at the supermarket during hurricane season. We keep them around for when the power gets shut off. She's arranged them around my father's picture, so it looks like a sort of shrine.

My father sounds like a jerk. When I was two, he went out fishing and just never came back. For years, my mother looked for him, hired seedy private investigators to run his driver's license and Social Security number, see if he's working anywhere, searched online. Nothing. It's like this book I saw in a used bookstore once, called *How to Disappear Completely and Never Be Found*. It told you all about how to fake your own death and then assume a new identity.

Unless he actually is dead.

"You know," I say to Mom. "Someone once told me that you can get a person declared dead if they've been missing for seven years. Then you could get Social Security."

"He isn't dead."

We've been down this road before. "How do you know that?"

"When we were in high school, he used to bring me flowers every day and braid them in my hair."

I stare at her. "And that has *what* to do with this?"

"When someone is your soul mate," she says, "you know when he's dead."

I shake my head. It seems to me like if they had this huge love affair, he wouldn't just leave. But she won't listen. "We could really use the Social Security about now. Do you want to lose the business and work at Love That Dog forever?"

"Tell me more about the princess," she says, obviously wanting to change the subject.

"She's into shoes. Meg says I should try to get her to wear one of my designs. But I guess it's stupid." I didn't think it was stupid an hour ago, but I wasn't sweating like this an hour ago either. Now it seems crazy to think someone like Victoriana would want anything to do with someone like me. I mean, sure, she was nice. She's been trained from birth to be nice. It's easy to be nice when you have everything handed to you.

But Mom's thrilled to be talking about something other than how broke we are. "What a wonderful idea. Meg's right. This, her staying at the hotel, is your chance. It's meant to be."

The heat beats on my head until I see red and black spots before my eyes. I want to go back to work where, at least, it's cold and sterile and quiet.

"How can you believe that . . . fantasy? The reality is, Dad's never going to come back and I'm never going to see the princess again. Nothing good is ever going to happen. That's what's meant to be."

She doesn't say anything, just picks up a magazine and fans herself with it, covering her face, and I feel instantly bad. She didn't ask to be poor. She didn't ask for my father to leave her. She's done her best. I want to apologize, but I'm too hot, even to speak.

Finally, she says, "If I didn't believe, there would be nothing left."

I take a deep breath. "I'm sorry. I know. Look, I'm going to go back to the hotel to work. You should come too. It's cool there. If we stay until dark, we'll only have to sleep here. Then the heat won't be so bad."

But she shakes her head. "You go. But let me make you some eggs. I can light the gas stove with a match. We should eat the food before it goes bad."

I nod. So much for magic.

5

For the next week, I try to run into Princess Victoriana again. It should be easy, right? Considering she's staying at a hotel where I spend sixteen hours a day (more than usual, due to the lack of air-conditioning at home), and it's not like she can keep a low profile. I try to make friends with the paparazzi in the lobby but quickly find that they're only talking to me 'cause they think I know Victoriana's schedule.

I don't. The only thing I know is that every morning at eight, a servant leads the bloodhound down Collins Avenue, and almost every day, the papers carry a photograph of Victoriana, partying the night away at the Mansion, the Opium Garden, or some other SoBe club.

I do find out where the dog goes anyway. The next day, the *Herald* carries an article with photos of the dog, sniffing around the Port of Miami.

There's a quote from Victoriana, saying, "Where my staff takes my dog for walks is none of my fault. In Aloria, I can walk him myself, but here, I am hounded by reporters."

There's a photograph of the dog, with the caption, "Hounded?" The "People" column carries another shot of Victoriana dancing on a table.

I start sleeping in the shop, slumped over the counter, thinking maybe I can see her when she comes in from one of her benders, but I never do. I swear, sometimes, I wake to see her standing behind the potted palms or even by Meg's coffee shop after it's closed for the night. Obviously, sleep deprivation is making me hallucinate.

But one day, she comes to my shop.

Yeah. She really does. And she's drunk.

That, in and of itself, isn't a big shocker. The shocker is she's drunk enough to speak to me.

"*Scusez-moi,*" she says as I rush to my feet from my stooped position. "I am an emergency."

Before I can breathe, much less speak, a second voice, then a third, interrupts her in French. Two big bodyguards cast a shadow over my whole field of vision, blocking her.

She starts scolding them. "*Non! Non!*" A small white

hand insinuates itself between the mountains of meat. She says something in French, then adds, "I must speak wiz him myself."

She pushes them apart, like an ice pick going through Mount Rushmore. The two guards obviously don't want to part, but they have no choice. She's their princess.

She lifts her sandal onto the counter. It's olive-colored snakeskin, retails for over a thousand dollars, and has a broken strap.

None of that's what I really notice.

What I notice is, it's still on her foot. Attached to her leg. On my counter!

"Lovely, no?" she says.

"Yes." The word is barely an exhale. Then, I get that she means the shoe. "Yes, lovely. Donna Karan, from Italy. I saw it in *Vogue*, her spring collection."

"I need your help." She blows *mojito* fumes—rum and mint leaves—on me with the "h." "Zees, zey are my favorite, and now . . ." She stares forlornly at her foot, like it's an injured puppy. ". . . ruined."

"Okay." I reach for the shoe, my instincts kicking in despite my nerves. Then, I stop at the evil eye her guard's giving me. "Um, I can help you. I can fix it."

"Oh, *merci*!" The princess claps her hands, almost falling back as she does, but the guard catches her. "And you will have zis finished by ten thirty tomorrow? I have a luncheon with ze mayor at noon, and I need to dress well in time of it. It is most important."

For a second, she doesn't sound drunk at all. She sounds like she's talking about something more important than a shoe. Like world peace.

But then, she sways again, and I doubt she'll even be awake by ten thirty, much less capable of walking on five-inch stiletto stilts. Still, I say, "I'll have it done," already trying to think of a way to ask her about trying on the shoes, *my* shoes.

"You are my hero!" She leans farther forward, flexible for one that drunk, and kisses me on the cheek. Then, she removes her shoe. She slides her foot off the counter, stumbling backward into the guards. When she recovers, she says, "Tell him my room. I forgot."

The guard says something in French.

"*Non.* I want him to deliver it. He is handsome."

Handsome. A princess thinks I'm handsome and is inviting me to her room? Impossible.

I chuckle, a chuckle the guard silences with another glare. "She is in Penthouse B."

"And here!" The princess is leaning over the counter, so I can once again drink in both her blue eyes and the smell of secondhand *mojito.* She hands me a wad of bills. "For the rush."

It's three hundred dollars. "No, it's too much . . . let me . . ." I start to give most of the bills back. It's not unheard of to get big tips around here, but I feel bad taking advantage of the obviously drunk, even though I can already feel the air-conditioning.

"*Non.* I know it is three hundred dollars. It will be well worth it if you give my shoes on time and personally deliver. *Personally deliver.* I am certain you understand." She goes to touch my arm but accidentally *brushes my chest. "Oui?"*

She looks up, and I realize she expects a response. Like, waiting for me to actually speak even though she just touched me and my mouth is hanging open. I close it, then open it again.

"Um . . . *oui*? Thank you. I'll, um, be there at ten thirty."

"No earlier. I need to get ze beauty sleep."

I don't just fix the strap. I test the heels and replace the heel tip. I wish I had the other shoe, to make it even more perfect. I polish and buff and check for loose stitching. This princess isn't going to trip over her shoe—not on my watch. I remember what she said about an important meeting with the mayor, and I try to decide what it could be about: Some crucial matter of diplomacy, maybe a treaty between our countries? And I'll have saved the day with my perfect repair of Victoriana's favorite shoe. Maybe I'll get a medal. Or a knighthood.

Who am I kidding? Miami's not at war, and I'll be happy if I get to look at the princess for an extra five minutes. And maybe, when she sees what a great job I did with the repair, she'll agree to wear my shoes. When I finish them.

At nine, I go to the pool to find Ryan. He snuck in late. Now, he's on his lifeguard chair, shirtless and already asleep.

"Too much partying last night?" I ask.

He jumps awake. "No such thing as too much. You should come sometime."

I shrug. "No money. So, I notice you've chosen to go shirtless today."

He makes his chest muscles move side to side. "Enjoy it?"

"Nah, I was just hoping since you're not using your shirt, maybe I could borrow it."

"And cover it with sweat. Don't think so."

"Please." I explain about Victoriana and the shoe. "I can't show up in a grungy shirt I've had on all night."

He grins. "Got an idea. How 'bout I deliver the shoe. I'm better looking anyway."

"Not going to happen. She asked me to. Besides, you're working now. You've been working since . . . eight twenty-five. Doesn't your shift start at eight?"

"You're blackmailing me?"

"Such an ugly word. I just want you to loan me your shirt, as a friend, just like I'm keeping your secret, as a friend."

"Fine." He takes the red Hollister polo out of his gym bag. "I get it back by eleven."

"Deal." I take it and start toward the lobby. "Thanks."

Next, I find my friend Marisol, one of the chambermaids. I talk her into letting me use a shower in one of the rooms where the guest has checked out. I shower and wash my hair with their shampoo. Ryan's shirt hangs on me in places, and I wish I had cologne or, at least, clean underwear. Still, I look good.

I know it's crazy, getting all worked up about a princess. But, hey, a guy can fantasize. I mean, here I am in South Beach, fun capital of the world, and all I do is repair shoes and dream dreams I can't afford. Why shouldn't I at least try?

6

It takes nearly five minutes for the elevator to reach the penthouse floor. I knock and hang around like a stalker until another Mount Everest of a guard asks what I'm doing there.

"I was . . . I work at the hotel. I'm bringing the princess's shoe." I hold it up.

"I take zis!" The guard plucks it by the strap and starts to close the door.

"But I . . . she . . ." I slump over. She's probably still asleep. Can it really end here, my one big chance?

His hand's on the doorknob. "You have been paid?"

I nod. "But—"

"Zen go on your way." And the door slams.

That's that. I head back for the elevator. It was stupid, me thinking I could talk to the princess about anything but her broken strap. I mean, who am I? Some poor slob who works in a hotel. I should be happy I got to meet her at all. Someday, I'll probably tell my grandchildren about it. And they'll assume it's dementia setting in.

But still, I feel like going downstairs and banging something with a hammer until it's obliterated. Victoriana said she wanted me to deliver the shoe personally. I went to a lot of trouble. It's not right that the guard is keeping me out. He's not any special person. He's only a guard, just like I'm only a shoe repair guy. He's no better than—

"*Pardonnez-moi?*" Mr. Everest is back.

"What do you want now?"

"It is ze princess who wants. She says I must ask you to come into her suite."

"So she *did* want me to deliver the shoes in person?"

"*Oui.*"

"So I was right? I wasn't just lying to get to see the princess?"

"Yes, yes. Is zat not what I just say?"

I'm savoring this. "So I was right, and you were . . . what's the word I'm trying to think of here . . . ?"

The guard's face is purplish. "Leesen, you leetle pipsqueak. If you do not wish to see ze princess, I will be happy to tell her you left ze building."

"Okay." I follow him into the suite.

I've never been in the Royal Suite before, but it's bigger than our apartment. Flowers decorate every flat surface, so it looks a little like a funeral, without the body. There's even an aquarium with a small shark swimming between the anemones. The guard leads me through one room, then another, until finally, we reach a sitting room, decorated in blue and white to blend with the cloudless sky outside its glittering French doors. The princess sits in a big wicker chair. She's dressed all in white, golden hair flowing down her shoulders, wearing the shoes I've repaired. I notice, with satisfaction, that the left shoe is a bit shinier than the right.

She doesn't look hung over. She doesn't look like she only got four hours sleep. She looks like a marble statue of an ocean goddess. If I ran into her at Walmart, I'd still know she was a princess. I stop, then bow low.

"Please." She gestures me up. "Please, zis is not needed."

I stand. She says something in French to the guard. He shakes his head but leaves, muttering something and glaring at me. The door closes, slightly louder than necessary.

I am alone with the most beautiful girl I've ever seen. Please, God, please, don't let me say anything stupid.

"'Allo, Johnny."

I start at my name, that she remembers it.

"Did I get it wrong? You are Johnny, *non*? Ze boy who watches me?"

"I don't . . ."

"It is nothing to be ashamed. Everyone watches. But I have to sneak to watch zem."

"Sneak?" So she *was* there, all those times I thought I saw her. But why?

"Sit." She gestures at a chair.

I do, tripping over my own feet as I go, almost falling into her lap. "Sorry."

"It is all right." She stares ahead, saying nothing, like she's waiting.

"The shoe, it's okay?" I have no idea why I'm here.

"Shoe?"

"The one I repaired? I should have asked you for the other one, so I could polish both, so they'd be perfect. I could still." I'm babbling. I'm babbling. Make me stop.

She glances at me, then her shoes, and finally, it seems to dawn on her what I'm talking about. "Oh, *oui*. Ze shoe is lovely." She lowers her voice. "Ze shoe, it was—'ow you say—a ruse."

"A ruse?" I whisper.

"*Oui*. A ruse. I broke ze strap in order to speak wiz you, and I pretend to be drunk so ze guards would not suspect my duplicity."

"You pretended to be drunk? But you reeked of *mojito*."

"I had *one*, and I kept ze mint in my pocket to chew."

"But you were stumbling and acting, um . . ."

"Crazy?" She rises and stumbles across the room in perfect imitation of a drunk. When she comes back around, she slumps against my chair. "Zis, I do all ze time."

"But why?"

"Many reasons. For ze press, mostly, so zey will see me as harmless, someone to be ridiculed and never suspect ze turmoil in my country, ze turmoil"—she touches her chest—"in here."

"Wow." Meg will freak when she hears this. "So . . . ?"

"I needed to speak wiz you about a matter of ze utmost importance. I wished to see you"—she glances at the door—"alone."

She places finger to lips, then tiptoes to the door and pulls it open. A guard falls into the room. Victoriana barks several sentences to him in French. The guard retreats, and this time, Victoriana stands by the door until she's sure he's far away before pulling it shut.

"What did you tell him?" I ask.

"Zat if I catch him eavesdropping again, it would mean not only his job, but also his children would be kicked from ze Alorian soccer training team."

"Harsh."

"A princess needs her privacy." She walks to the French doors. "Let us go out."

"Isn't that dangerous?" I picture sharpshooters, waiting on the beach, or the Zapruder film of the Kennedy

39

assassination we saw in history. "Couldn't someone . . . ?" I mime a gun.

Victoriana shakes her head. "*Non.* Sadly, ze person who is ze greatest danger to me wants me very much alive."

I follow her out. The ocean roars, and seagulls' cries surround us. Victoriana closes the balcony door. When she turns around, there are tears in her aquamarine eyes.

"Please," she whispers. "You must help me."

7

The frog told her he had been enchanted by a wicked witch.
—"The Frog Prince"

"You want me to help you?"

"*Oui.*"

"Me?"

"*Oui.*"

"Me?"

"Yes, you. You must stop saying zis."

"I'm sorry. It's just . . . you're a princess, and I'm . . . nobody."

She looks down at the shoe I've repaired, turning her foot to study it, her eyes shining. Below, the beachgoers are starting to come out. I've never seen them from so high. Their towels make the beach look like the patchwork quilt on Mom's bed. When I look back, Victoriana's still touching her shoe.

"Your Majesty?" When she doesn't look up, I say, "Princess?"

"Victoriana. I have something important to say, so you must call me my name. And *non*."

"*Non?*"

"No. You are not nobody. You are a hard worker, a good boy. I see you, always working. Zat is why I watch you, to see zat you are ze right boy to help me." She sniffs.

"Of course, I'll help you. But how?" If she wasn't a princess, I'd put my arm around her, do something to comfort her. But I don't. Is it lonely to be so great that no one will touch you?

She answers my unspoken question by grabbing my hand in both of hers and squeezing as if she's falling and I'm her lifeline. Then she sobs, "It is my bruzzer, my dearest, sweetest bruzzer, he is disappeared. You must find him!"

"Where is he?"

"If I knew zat, I would not need your help."

I feel my face get hot, so hot even my ears start to sweat a little.

Seeing my discomfort, she says, "*Pardonnez-moi.* I know you do not mean to humiliate yourself, but I am desperate. My bruzzer, heir to ze Alorian throne, he is lost."

"Lost?" What does she want me to do about it? I mean, not that I wouldn't walk across coals for the girl, but what can I do that a staff of security guards can't?

"*Oui*. He disappeared after being placed under a witch's curse."

Oh. Of course. The hot ones are always crazy. Nice house, too bad no one's home.

"You have . . . witches in your country?"

She rolls her eyes in a very un-princess-like way. "Ze witches, zey are everywhere. It is only zat most people, zey do not see."

I nod, like it makes sense, but I must not do it convincingly enough because she says, "Ze waitress downstairs who has all ze biggest-tipping customers, ze bellman who seems to get ze lightest suitcases. Zis is what witches do. Zey make zere lives easier. I am sure you can think of other examples, something closer to you, perhaps."

I try to think who she could mean. Then I remember: There are no witches. I nod.

"But ze witches in Zalkenbourg, zey are not so harmless. And my poor bruzzer, he is too foolish to know zat ze village girl he liked was really Sieglinde, ze powerful Zalkenbourgian witch in disguise. He went in her cottage—and poof!"

"Poof?"

"She turns him into a frog."

I scratch my ear. "Did you say a frog?"

"*Oui*."

43

I look at her a long time, with her fake frown and her fake tears, and I think she's not as pretty as I thought she was. She obviously thinks I'm a big jerk. I bow, so she can't say I was disrespectful, and say, "Your Highness, I thank you for bringing me your repair. I hope it's met with your approval. I need to get back to work now."

"You do not believe me?"

"I think you're making fun of me. I know I'm just a peasant. Maybe you got bored with clubs." I turn away, but it's difficult.

"*Non.* No. I do not make fun of you. Please. You must see."

She reaches for a French romance novel, resting on the table beside her. From its pages, she pulls a stack of photographs and papers. "Look."

I glance at the photo. It's a guy about my age, handsome with bright red hair and some kind of big mole over his right eye. He wears a military uniform, and he's smiling.

"Zat is Philippe, before ze spell." Victoriana points to the mole. "Zis is ze famous Alorian birthmark. It is shared by many great kings."

She hands me the photo, revealing the second, a frog with a red strip on its head. Like the prince, it has a large spot above its eye.

"Zis is him now," she says, and I see the tears, glittering on her eyelashes.

It does look a lot like the prince would look, if he was

a frog. I gaze into Victoriana's moist eyes and abandon the ideas that she's playing a joke on me. Someone's playing with her is what's happening. "Someone probably kidnapped the prince and has him captive somewhere. They must have painted the frog."

"Zat is what we zought may be. So we consulted an Alorian witch, a powerful sorceress who has a magical earpiece. She can communicate with animals—at least, animals who were once human. I talk wiz my bruzzer."

"You talked to a frog?"

"*Oui.* I ask him questions, questions only Philippe would know, about ze secrets we had as children. It is no doubt to me zis frog is him. And look at his eyes."

I glance back at the photo. His eyes are, indeed, the same ocean color as Victoriana's.

Stop! Of course the frog isn't her brother. Her brother is dead, and she's crazy with grief. Poor girl. Just shows even rich people have problems.

"It was Philippe himself who told me ze sad facts of zis spell," Victoriana says. "She turned him into a frog, and he may only break ze spell by ze kiss of one wiz love in her heart."

"Love?" It seems weird, if the spell was placed by an enemy, that the cure would be love. But then, what about this isn't totally weird? Clearly, these people are taking advantage of Victoriana's innocence or maybe—let's face it—stupidity.

The princess shrugs. "All ze spells say zat, I suppose. We—my parents and I—zought ze problem would be solved easily. My bruzzer is handsome, heir to ze throne, and a play-boy. Every girl loves him and would be happy to kiss him, even as a frog."

"So why not do that?" That would have shown it was a joke and ended it.

She sighs. "Before we could, he disappeared, like I tell you. Poof!" She waves her hands. "My fazzer hunted down ze one who cast ze spell, Sieglinde. She told him my bruzzer was in ze hold of a cargo ship, bound for Miami. We would never find him, and he would never be king. But ze witch promised to reverse ze spell on one condition."

She stares at her shoes.

"What condition?"

"Zat I would agree to marry ze heir of ze Zalkenbourgian throne." From between the photographs, she removes a news-paper clipping. The article is in French, but there's a picture of a blond man, his mouth twisted into a cruel smile, hold-ing what looks like a bayonet over a cowering boy. "Prince Wolfgang is evil to ze core. He visited when I was a small girl, pulling fezzers from my canary and sticking pins in my cat. It is zeir aim for us to marry so zat our countries may unite under Zalkenbourgian rule, but zat is only if I am ze heir. Sieglinde said zey would return Philippe if I agree to marry Wolfgang and Philippe will give up ze throne forever." She grabs my hand and squeezes it so hard it hurts. "You must find Philippe!"

I listen to the waves make their way to the shore, over and over. The seagulls have stopped crying, maybe chased away by beachgoers. Let me get this straight: There's a frog loose somewhere in Miami, and I'm supposed to find it. A beautiful woman wants to pull me into her overflowing bowl of crazy. How do I get out of it? Forget the shoes. I just don't want her to complain to Farnesworth about me.

"Um, you sure you want me? Me?"

"*Oui.*" She shows me another photograph, this time of a cargo ship. "Philippe was in zis ship, which arrived at ze port last week. Chevalier, my hound, found his scent in ze hold. My guards questioned ze crew. At first, zey had no memory of a frog. But when my guards pressed furzer, zey remembered zere had been one on a container bound for what you call ze Keys."

I bet. They got scared of those behemoth guards and said whatever they wanted to get rid of them. The Florida Keys are a string of small islands south—far south—of the mainland, connected by the Overseas Highway. But since I wouldn't be visiting them anytime soon, I played along. "Why not just let your guards look for him in the Keys then?"

Victoriana rises from her seat. I rise too, but she pushes past me and creeps into the hotel room. She opens the door a crack, checking for intruders. Satisfied, she closes it. Then, she returns to the balcony, shutting the French door behind her. She leans in toward me, whispering, "Ze guards, we believe zere is a spy among zem. We need to find someone no one will suspect is helping us, someone ordinary."

"That's where I come in."

"*Oui.* If you agree, I will tell ze guards zat we have been engaged in a flirtation, a . . . making out. Zey will believe me for zey believe me to be—'ow you say—loose. My father will tell zem we have given up our search for Philippe. I will cry. Ze subjects, zey believe zat Philippe is on a top-secret military mission. And you . . ."

"You want me to look for a frog."

"A frog *prince*."

A thought hits me. Even if there's no prince, hanging out in the Keys sounds a lot more exciting than repairing shoes all summer. But I shake my head. "I'm sorry, Princess, but I have to work. My family needs the money. I can't just leave."

The princess laughs. "Oh, if zat is ze only trouble, it is solve. I will pay you—all your expenses and enough money to hire a replacement. And also . . ." She hesitates.

"Yes." I can't do this. I can't. But I want to know what "also" is.

"If you find my bruzzer and bring him back to me, zere will be a reward."

"Reward?" Money. Money to pay bills. Money for college. "What reward?"

The princess fixes me with a long stare from her ocean eyes. One eyelash is still tipped with a tiny tear, but on Victoriana, it looks more like a diamond.

"If you find Philippe and return him to me, I will marry you."

8

"Marry me? I'm only seventeen."

Still, she's beautiful, beautiful and—more important—rich. Marrying her would solve a lot of problems, even if she is nuts.

Victoriana makes a little shooing gesture with her hand, as if my objection is of no importance. "I am a princess. Aloria is a paradise which makes zis place look like ze garbage dump. My husband would never have to worry about ordinary man's troubles. He would know pleasures zat most men only dream of." She reaches into her dress, and I think she's going to show me some of the "pleasures" she's talking about. But, instead, she pulls out a large wad of bills. Hundreds. "For the quest. You can have more if you need."

"I couldn't . . ." I stare at the money, then look at her. The money. Her. I *could*. "Why would you want to marry me?"

"You seem nice. Besides, I maybe should marry *someone*. If I am married, Prince Wolfgang will leave me alone."

Not very flattering. Still, I say, "I need to ask my mother." The standard line I used to give as a kid, when I didn't want to do something. Blame Mom.

She nods. "I knew you were a good boy. You need time to consider whezzer to help a poor girl to reunite her family and save her from ze clutches of an evil prince. So I will give you one day. Zen we will meet."

"Meet? How?"

She produces a fire engine red Jimmy Choo sandal from under her chair cushion. While I'm watching, she pulls on the strap hard enough to snap it. She gazes at it, despondent.

"My favorite shoe—it is broken." She sighs. "When you are ready to speak to me again, you will deliver it to my guard to let me know you are up to ze quest."

"What if I say no?"

She ignores that. "When you do, I will open ze door to my suite on zat night at two o'clock. Bruno will be sleeping, and you may come in to me and get ze magical objects."

Magical objects? "Magical objects? You mean, like a

wand? Or a cursed necklace I can give to my enemies?"

She laughs. "You do not believe me. You think me a stupid, silly girl."

Yes. "No! You're totally sane. I mean, smart . . . I mean . . ."

"I see you, you know, working every night in your leetle shop, and I see you also, always looking around, looking for something exciting, anything, to get your life out of your mind. Zat is why you work so late, to see me."

"To see you? No. I work late because I have shoes to repair, lots of shoes."

"Zat many shoes? I think no. I think business is not so good."

I realize she's smarter than I gave her credit for, even if she is crazy.

I sigh. "I'll think about it."

"While you are thinking, think also of zis." She stands and pulls me hard toward her. Then, she kisses me, running her hands through my hair, reaching down to rumple Ryan's Hollister shirt. Below us, the ocean is pounding like my heart, and my heart is pounding like the drums in a hip-hop song. The gulls are screaming. Finally, she pulls away. "Be my hero, Johnny."

Her lipstick is smudged. I bet it's all over my face too. I realize she wanted it to be, to make her guards believe we're engaged in a make-out session, not discussing my help on a crazy Zalkenbourgian curse. She's using me. And I like it.

When I can finally speak again, I say, "Uh . . . I'll think about it."

"Don't forget zis." She holds up the money, then shoves it into my pocket. I shiver at her hand on my leg.

"What if I don't do it?" I say, though I can feel her kiss on my mouth, the wad of bills in my pocket, her touch, still sending reverberations through my body. She's right. I want to do it, no matter how crazy she is. It would solve everything, all my problems. If only there were really a frog prince.

Which there isn't.

"You will do it," she says. "But you may keep ze money in either case, for your secrecy."

Then, she pulls me in for another kiss, longer than the first. I feel her hands on me, on my chest, my shoulders.

Then, other hands.

Big hands.

"Enough! How dare you touch ze princess?"

Bruno. He rips me away from Victoriana and shoves me to the other side of the balcony.

Victoriana lets out an indignant cry, then recovers with a laugh. "Oh, Bruno, you must allow me my fun. I am a princess, am I not?"

He says something in French, and an angry conversation ensues. Bruno turns toward me and gestures to the door. "Shoo, shoe boy!"

"Not until I say," Victoriana says. She pulls me toward her for what I figure will be another passionate kiss, a dangerous kiss, with Bruno watching. But, instead of my lips, she finds my ear. She whispers, "I know you will help me, please."

Bruno manhandles me out the door of the suite, then to the elevator. He presses the button, shoves me in, and waits until the door closes. All the way down, I feel the shoe in one hand, the bills in my pocket.

When I reach the lobby, I duck into the men's room stall to count the money.

I almost hurt myself when I total it up.

Ten thousand dollars.

9

I make sure Ryan sees my lipsticked face when I return his shirt.

"Liar," he says. "You put it on yourself."

"Zis is her color," I say, laughing.

I spend the rest of the afternoon in a daze, not really listening to the sad tale of some guy's busted loafer because I'm too busy thinking about how I have ten grand in my pocket and I just kissed one of *People* magazine's most beautiful people. After work, I rush home, despite the heat, and show Mom the money.

Once she examines the bills under the light and uses

her counterfeit-detecting pen on them, she says, "Did you steal it?"

"Of course not."

"Of course not. I know you don't steal. But where . . . ?"

I explain the whole story, concluding that I've decided not to do it.

When I finish, she doesn't respond for a long time, fanning herself with a magazine. I'm about to tell her to forget about it. We'll talk later. But then, she says, "I think you should."

"What?" I was sure she'd agree with me that I couldn't take advantage of Victoriana like that. Like me, she has scruples. Why is it that only people with no money have scruples? Do we have no money *because* we have scruples? "You actually think I should take the money when I know I'm not going to find the prince?"

Victoriana's shoe is in my backpack, still on my shoulders, and I feel its heel digging into my back.

"No," Mom says. "I think you should take the money and look for the prince."

"There's a difference? She thinks her brother's been turned into a frog. She's nuts."

"Maybe she's not that nuts. Maybe she has faith. Maybe she must believe in something even when all hope is gone."

So I know what this is about: Dad. Mom really thinks he'll come back someday.

"The girl has her hopes." Mom glances at the wedding photo on the table. "Who says there's no magic?"

"Who says? Again, we're talking frog princes, like the fairy tale." But even as I argue, the fact is I want to do it, not only for the money—though ten grand would solve a lot of problems. With ten grand, I'd be sitting in air-conditioned comfort right now. We could get a lot of creditors off our back and maybe even agree on a payment plan with the others. But more, there's the adventure, the getting out of the bowels of the hotel for once and doing something fun. I want to be one of those crazy people who believes in ghosts or the Loch Ness Monster. They have more fun than sane people. Once, I repaired some hiking shoes for a guy who claimed he was looking for a Sasquatch loose in Florida. Sounds more fun than my summer. And Victoriana said I could keep the money even if I don't find the prince.

But what if I get in trouble for it? I don't know much about Aloria, other than that they have a really hot princess. What if they still believe in torture there? I remember reading once about some kid who visited a foreign country and got publicly beaten with a stick for some minor crime. Maybe they'd behead you for stealing from the princess.

My neck aches a little, just thinking about it.

"I'll think about it," I say, standing up. I know I won't, though. I got to talk to the princess. That will have to be enough.

"Where are you going?" Mom says.

"Back. To repair shoes, like always."

10

"So Ryan says you came back with a face full of lipstick."

Meg throws the word "lipstick" like it's a stink bomb, one I know Ryan enjoyed hurling at her. She's disgusted with me. She thinks I'm another sap under Victoriana's spell. Maybe I am.

"So is she going to make you her boy toy or something?" Meg's voice is like when I sliced my finger with a big sewing needle.

"I was just messing with Ryan about the lipstick," I say, trying to sound cooler than I feel. "It was Marisol's. I borrowed some."

A lie can travel halfway 'round the world while the truth is still putting on its shoes. That's been attributed to Mark Twain, but no one's sure if he actually said it.

Meg looks pleased with my lie, in any case. We have a joint interest in keeping Ryan's manatee-size ego in check. "So is she going to wear the shoes?"

I cradle my hand in my chin like I'm thinking, but really, I'm checking for residual lipstick. Part of me wants to tell Meg everything that happened with Victoriana. I know she'd laugh at the idea of a frog prince. She'd say Victoriana's obviously taken too many drugs. But I promised the princess I'd keep her secret. Besides, another part of me knows Meg wouldn't approve of the kiss.

So I say, "What do you think? I didn't even get to talk to her. She was still passed out."

"Typical." I can tell Meg's sort of happy about being right. Still, she says, "Don't worry. You'll find some other way to make it. You've got talent."

"Yeah, talent for fixing shoes."

"I'd wear your designs in a heartbeat." She reaches over and begins massaging my neck. Her fingers feel strong, and it's nice to have someone rub my neck, even if it's just Meg.

"That feels good. My neck gets really sore, leaning over the counter all day."

"Yeah, mine gets the same way." She starts using both hands, rubbing my shoulders too. She smells like coffee and a little like the ocean. For a second, I close my eyes. "Ever think things happen for a reason?" she asks.

"Like what?"

"Oh, I don't know. You don't know it at the time, but there's some bigger purpose. Like maybe it didn't work out with Victoriana because something else is going to happen." She leans closer.

"I guess."

"It's not so awful being here, is it?"

Yes. Yes, it's awful. But I say, "No, it's just, she's so beautiful."

Meg stops rubbing my shoulders.

"Hey, why'd you stop?"

She walks away, not looking at me. "I have work to do. So do you."

She goes back to her shop and starts rearranging the sandwiches—which already looked perfect—in their glass case. She gets so into what she's doing that I can't catch her eye for the rest of the afternoon. A couple of times, I think I see her glancing at me, but she looks right back down, and I wonder if she's mad at me for saying Victoriana's beautiful. It's hardly news, though.

Oh, well. I'll make it up to her. I have time now.

I start working on Victoriana's shoe, even though I don't want to because delivering it means telling her no, telling her I can't do what she wants. The broken strap is delicate yet strong, and as I repair it, I anticipate seeing her again, slipping it on to her foot.

If only it wasn't going to be the last time I see her.

11

It is a wishing cloak. With it, you will find yourself any place you wish to be.

—"The Salad"

When I finish repairing the shoe, I call the princess's room and ask if I can bring it up.

As expected, his answer is a curt, *"Non.* I will come for it."

He's downstairs almost as soon as I put down the phone. I recognize Bruno, the guard Victoriana said was her most trusted, the one who practically sprained a face muscle glaring at us. I hand him the shoe, then stand there, not knowing what to say next.

Bruno breaks the silence. "If you think she has a message

for you, she does not. Boys like you are only playthings to Her Highness." His English is surprisingly good, with much less of an accent than Victoriana's. "Your dalliance means nothing. Ze princess is already betrothed."

"Really? She doesn't think she is." I regret the words the second they're out of my mouth. Why argue with him?

He scowls. "Ze princess, she is not so smart. Her head is in all kinds of places. She must be protected."

I hear the unspoken words, *from you.*

I shrug. "I just wanted to give her the shoe. Now I have."

It's clear he wants to mess with me some more, but he must decide against it because he leaves. An hour later, one of the chambermaids drops a key card on my counter. I know without asking it's the key to Penthouse B.

At 1:55 in the morning, I cross the lobby, hearing each squeak of my sneakers on the marble floor. It's the perfect time. The late-night partiers have mostly come back, and the room service order cards have been picked up, but the *USA Today*s aren't yet being delivered. The lobby parrot cage is covered, and the swans are asleep. The night clerk is playing an online game, and the morning maids haven't started vacuuming. I am alone, unnoticed. The elevator rushes to the top. I feel my organs clenching against my chest. Wonder if I'll have to knock on her door. Will the guard be waiting outside? Will he chase me off?

When the bell rings, I jump as if attacked by a cat. The elevator door begins to close before I recover, but when I push against it, it opens.

Victoriana is waiting for me when I enter. Dressed in one of the hotel's white terry-cloth robes, her blond hair in braids that almost reach her waist, she looks like an angel from a Christmas card. She presses finger to lips and, with her other hand, takes me by the wrist. Her skin is cold, and I can tell she's afraid, which makes me afraid too. She pulls me inside the suite. It's pitch-dark except for one shattered sliver of moon on the oriental rug, revealing the worn, black shoes of her sleeping guard. I stay close, fearing tripping, fearing any sound, fearing everything. My breath seems loud. If they catch me, will they think I snuck in here to hurt the princess? Will they execute me?

Finally, she pulls me through the bathroom door. I stumble a bit and hear her whisper, "Fool!" under her breath. Then, she pulls the door swiftly, but quietly, shut.

The bathroom is bigger than our apartment, with a Roman tub, a bar, and three sinks. There's even a sofa. The toilet is in a small room of its own. I feel a hand on my shoulder. Victoriana!

"You will help me, yes?" She's smiling.

I blink and forget being called a fool. She's beautiful. To talk to her is bliss like no bliss I've ever felt. I need to tell her no, but I can't. I can't! If I say no, the adventure will end, and I don't want it to. "Uhhhh . . ." I gesture toward the door.

"We won't get caught?"

She shakes her head. "Do not worry. I take care of him." She mimes swallowing a pill.

"You drugged the guard?" It's hot that she's so ruthless.

"Only one sleeping pill, crushed in his mashed turnips." At my questioning look, she says, "Mashed turnips, zey are ze national dish of Aloria, very good for hiding. I once put a caterpillar in my governess's when I was small. And ze pill, it is perfectly safe. I take zem myself, for it is hard to sleep since my bruzzer . . ." She looks down, sad. "But soon, you will find him, and I will sleep soundly once again. We shall sleep soundly togezzer."

She smiles, and it's like standing out on the beach, feeling the sun on my face.

The clouds roll in. I can't help her.

I clear my throat. "Listen, I need to . . ."

"Wait!" She holds up her hand and starts across the floor. She opens the door to the toilet, then reaches behind it and takes out something like earbuds for an iPod. "Zis is ze magical earpiece I told you about, ze one which ze Alorian witch created. It will let you talk wiz ze animals—only ze animals zat once were human."

"Are there many of those?" I ask in spite of myself. She's so pretty that it's easy to forget she's crazy. I wouldn't mind being part of her world, with talking animals and enchanted frogs. It sounds pretty there.

"More zan you would believe. Zey will help you find my bruzzer."

Like Snow White!

"About that. I have to tell you—"

"When you reach ze Keys, you will find ze right animals."

"How?" I shouldn't ask. I'm not doing this. I'm not. I'm not.

"If I knew more, I would already have found him!" She crosses the room again, her shoulders a hard line, and I wonder if I'm supposed to follow her. But she goes behind the bar. I figure she wants a drink, but instead, she pulls out a piece of green cloth. She walks back and hands it to me.

"What's this?" It's velvet, so heavy I feel myself start to sink under its weight.

"A cloak."

I've read enough books to know that a cloak is sort of a big cape, but needless to say, they're not popular in Miami. "Why a cloak?"

"Zis is a special cloak zat will transport you anywhere you want. You must only wish it."

"Wow." She's nuts, and she wants to marry me. What does that say about me?

She nods. "It is an heirloom which has been many years in my family. It belonged to my great-grandmuzzer, who was a witch. She bewitched my great-grandfazzer to marry her, and zat is how she became queen from a commoner. From zen on, she did not need ze cloak, for she had means to go where she wished. But as a girl, I played wiz it, so I know it works."

I examine the cloth. It smells of outdoors, like a place you've been before but don't remember. I wonder if Victoriana used it to get away.

It's just a piece of cloth.

"Wherever you wish, it will go," she says. "I only caution: Do not let others use it."

"Why would I do that?"

She shrugs. "Smarter men zan you have been tricked."

I decide to play along. "Okay, how does it work?"

"You wrap it around you, and zen—"

There's a knock on the door. I jump about a foot and come down on the marble floor in a skid. I hear the dull clunk as my head rams into the Roman tub. "Ow!"

"Princess!"

"*Merde!*" Victoriana's waving her arms at me, gesturing toward the tub, whispering, "He is awake! Hide!" She answers the guard sweetly in French, but the pounding continues.

"Princess!" A string of French words.

I climb inside the tub. It's as deep as a pond, and I lie at the bottom, pulling the cloak around me as if that will keep me from being seen. Victoriana closes the shower curtain. *"Un moment, s'il vous plaît."*

I lie there, hearing Victoriana's breathing and my own.

She flushes the toilet, and then I hear her footsteps toward the door. My heartbeat. I'm a dead man. The door opens.

Victoriana laughs and says something in French.

The guard replies and steps inside. I hear him, walking toward me.

I wish I was home. Oh God, I wish I was home.

And then, I am in darkness.

12

Six swans came flying through the air.

—"The Six Swans"

Everything's black. Cave black. I feel walls around me like I'm in a box. Or a coffin. Is that it? Am I dead? Did the guard kill me? No. Death would be drier. There's something cold and clammy under my hip.

And there's dripping, water dripping on my head. Drip, drip, drip. Am I in a tomb or a catacomb? It feels like something from an Indiana Jones movie. I listen. The voices, Victoriana's and the guard's, are gone.

I sneak my hand down to the cold, clammy thing. It's not moss or some small, dead creature. It's cloth. A washcloth. I feel hard porcelain beneath me, like a bathtub. But something's different. It's small, like a regular bathtub. I smell Irish Spring soap.

We use Irish Spring.

Am I home?

No. Not possible. I was at the hotel, seconds ago, listening to Victoriana with the guard, clutching the cloak around me, trying to hide, wishing I was home.

No.

I pull off the cloak, look up. It's dark, but I see the outlines of familiar shapes. The indisputable truth of it hits me.

I wished to be home, and now I am.

I pull the cloak away and sit up, barely missing the leaky faucet, which pays me back by shooting water into my eye. I peek out from behind the shower curtain.

I'm home. The cloak worked.

The faucet's dripping on my forehead. The washcloth's soaking my jeans. The bathtub is tiny and hard. I wish I was out of this bathtub.

And then, I'm dumped onto the bathroom floor.

Cool!

I wish I was in the kitchen.

I am!

I wish I was back in the bedroom.

This is so bizarre.

But it's happening. It's magic. There's magic here, magic in this cloak. Maybe there's magic in all of it, in the world— the frog, the spell, the witches!

68

Maybe there's magic enough, even for me, for me to find the frog and be with Victoriana, to live like a king instead of a shoe repair guy.

But that's crazy. There's no magic. I blacked out. The guard caught me and hit me in the face. I'm working too hard, not sleeping enough, stressed out. Maybe it's all a dream.

I feel the cloak around me, soft and warm like nothing I own. I didn't dream this. I touch my jeans pocket. The earpiece Victoriana gave me is there too. It's real. I put it into my ear, but of course, there's nothing to test it on.

Still, I hold the cloak tighter around me.

"I wish I was at the hotel."

And then, I am. I blink. It's blinding in the silent lobby. The night clerk is asleep at the desk, his hand still on the mouse, and the screen open to a site the management wouldn't much like. The fountain is off, and the swans are in their house.

I sneak over to the parrot's covered cage and remove the canvas covering. If the cloak works, then maybe . . .

"Hello?" I whisper.

It takes a few tries to wake the bird, but finally, it repeats, "Hello?"

"Um . . ." I'm at a loss for words. "Whatcha been up to, ah, boy?"

Nothing.

"Hello?" I say.

"Hello?" the parrot repeats.

No answer. I fiddle with my earpiece, then try again.

"Hey, if you don't want me bothering you, I won't. Just let me know you understand."

"Would you look at that?" a voice says somewhere in the room. "Boy's trying to talk to that dumb-cluck bird."

I jump back, embarrassed at being caught. "Hey, I was just . . ." I look around. No one's there. I glance at the parrot again.

"AWK!" it squawks.

No. Not him. But if not him, then who? The desk clerk? Still snoring. There's no one else here. Unless . . .

I pull the cover back over the cage, then start toward the fountain where the voice came from. A swan is standing there, dipping a webbed foot into the water. When I get close enough, I look around again before whispering, "Were you talking to me?"

The swan raises his foot close enough to his chest that I can imagine it saying, "Me?" At least, I could if I was crazy. Which maybe I am.

"Yeah, you. See anyone else around here?"

"You seem to prefer speaking to that azure-colored goofball," it says, then turns away.

It works. It works! At least, I think it does. I've never heard a swan say anything before, and now I've got one mad at me.

"I'm sorry," I tell the swan's retreating back, "but everyone knows parrots are the ones that can talk. I mean, usually."

The bird turns back. "Parrots merely mimic, repeat what

they have heard a thousand times. The only animals who can truly speak are those who were once human."

"So you were once human?" Just like Victoriana said.

"Obviously."

"And you were . . . someone turned you into a swan?"

The bird raises the feathers above his beady, black eyes.

"Okay, you were. But I've never heard you talk before, and I've been at this hotel my whole life."

"Maybe," the bird says, "you didn't listen properly."

This is incredible. "So there are others like you, others who can talk?"

"More than you'd think."

"And do you talk to one another?" An idea's dawning on me. "Could you help me? Do you know other talking animals? Would you know where to find more of them, like a network?"

The bird says nothing, walks away, and returns a moment later, followed by five other swans. "My siblings," he says, "Harry, Truman, Jimmy, Mallory, and Margarita."

The swans ignore me, talking among themselves.

"Is it true?" one says.

"Can he really hear us?" says another.

"Yeah, right," says a third. "Ernest's always messing with us."

"Ask him," says the swan I was talking to, who I guess is Ernest.

Finally, another swan turns to me. "I know you can't understand, but I'm Mallory."

"Hi." I start to hold out my hand, then realize they don't have hands. "I'm Johnny."

The swan flips its wings, shocked, then runs over to the others. They all start whispering at the same time, but so softly I can't understand them. Finally, Ernest says, "They want to know what you want."

"What I want? I guess . . . I want to see if you could find out about another, um, transformation. See, there's this guy, a prince, who's been turned into a frog. Have you heard about him? I think he's down in the Keys."

At the word "Keys" they all start whispering again, which I think is a little rude, actually. Finally, I say, "So, do they know anything?"

Ernest turns back to me. "No."

"Oh."

"I mean, no, we haven't heard of this particular frog. But it's possible we might find out about him. There's a great deal of connectivity between transformed beings. I'm told there's even an e-group, though my siblings and I haven't been able to participate due to an unfortunate combination of lack of fingers and the fact that the desk clerk is online all night." He gives the sleeping clerk a reproachful look. "So we may be able to help you. We're from the Keys ourselves. But we'd want something in return."

"Like what?"

"Our sister. You need to find her."

"Is she a swan? There's a swan missing?" I look around, surprised I haven't heard about it before. Mr. Farnesworth loves those swans.

"No, no, not those sisters. One who is still down in Key West, a human. She's the only one with the power to save us, but she doesn't know we exist."

"Why not?"

"We were sent away before she was born." The swan glances around and, seeing no one watching, jumps onto the sofa. When he has made himself comfortable, he begins again.

"Our father was the king of Key West," he says.

"Um, Key West doesn't have a king."

"He was. It's true." He looks at Margarita for validation, and she nods.

"It's true," she says.

"He was the king of Key West," Ernest continues, "and our mother died. Daddy married a mean woman who was really a witch in disguise. She banished us to Plantation Key and turned us into swans. When she found out our father visited us anyway, she sent us to this . . . this petting zoo of a hotel. The only way for the enchantment to be broken is . . ." He begins to cough and spit.

"Are you okay?" I ask.

"I'm sorry. I guess"—cough—"I'm just not used to talking anymore. Margarita, can you tell him?"

Margarita says, "For the enchantment to be broken, our sister must find us and make shirts out of flowers."

Shirts out of flowers? But I let it go. "And you'll help me find the frog if I—?"

"If you promise to look for our sister, Caroline, while you're in the Keys."

"But I don't know anything about her."

"It should be easy to find her. Her name's Caroline, and her father was the king of Key West."

"There's no . . . ," I start, then think better of it. "Okay, I'll look. I promise."

Margarita nods her long neck. "Then we'll help you." She waddles over to the group and says, "Harry! Truman!" When two swans look up, she says, "This young man is looking for a frog who used to be a prince." She turns to me. "What does he look like?"

I take out the photo I've been carrying around and explain that the frog is named Philippe and is the crown prince of Aloria.

Harry, or maybe it's Truman, shakes his head. "Ah, yes, it's hard being a prince. I was once a prince too, Prince Harry of Key West."

With his beak, he plucks the photograph from my fingers, then brings it to the other swans. They examine it, then Harry tucks it under his wing. He turns to me.

"My siblings and I will do everything we can to help. We want to help transformed creatures. But, of course, you must remember your promise to us."

"I will."

The two swans raise their wings as if in salute. Then, looking left and right to make sure no one sees them, they push through the revolving door and down the street.

I watch them leave. Farnesworth is going to flip.

"They'll come back if they find something?" I say to Ernest and Margarita.

"As soon as we hear something, I'll tell you," Margarita says.

I'm still wearing the cloak, so I wish myself back home.

As soon as I do, I'm there in the kitchen. My mother sort of starts when I appear. She stammers, unable to speak.

"It's real," I tell her, "all of it."

13

It being real changes everything. It means I'm not taking Princess Victoriana's money for a free trip bumming around the Keys. I'm taking it for a quest, a discovery—like Christopher Columbus discovering America, only for real. And if I find the frog, I get the princess. Mind-blowing. I woke up this morning an ordinary slob who didn't know there was such a thing as curses and spells and swan people, and now . . .

Whoa.

So I'm going on a quest. For real. First, I send a bill up to

Victoriana's room with the words "Paid in full for services to be rendered" written on it. Then, I need to talk to Meg.

As soon as she comes in, I corner her. "Hey, got a minute?"

"I have to put the coffee on. Have a seat."

I sit, figuring it will be a long wait while she cleans out the old coffee, then starts new. But she walks across the shining white floor, flips a switch, then returns. "'Sup?"

"I have to go away for a while."

"Away?" She looks surprised. She knows I never go anywhere or do anything. I knew there'd be questions, so I'd worked on my lie.

"It's about my father," I say. "We have some news about him."

"Your father?" More surprise. I never talk about my father, mostly because I don't know anything about him. "Wow, that's great, Johnny. But didn't you think he was—?"

"Dead? Yeah, he's been as good as. I haven't seen him in forever. But my mom heard from his sister, my aunt Patty. She says he showed up, and he got some money. He, um, won the lottery."

"Really? The Florida lottery?"

I think fast. She'd be able to find out if he won the Florida lottery, so I say, "Ah, no. The Alabama lottery. That's where he lives, Alabama. So I'm going up to see him. In Alabama." Alabama is a ten-hour drive. "The money would really help now."

"Your mom's sending you?" Meg glances at the coffee-maker to see if the light's on. "Wouldn't it be better to hire a lawyer?"

"That's our backup plan, but it would take a long time. She figures maybe if I showed up, he'd just write a check. Besides, I wouldn't mind seeing him. He's my father."

Her dark eyes meet mine. She looks disappointed, some-how, and for a second, I'm sure she knows I'm lying.

"Yeah, I guess you're really excited about meeting him. Where in Alabama?"

"Montgomery," I say, remembering the name from when we learned state capitals in fifth grade. If I thought hard enough, I could probably come up with the state flower too. "The Yellowhammer State."

Meg nods. "Well, that sure is exciting, him winning the Alabama lottery and all." Again, there's something in her voice like she knows I'm lying. But she can't. All I've ever told her about my father is that he's gone.

"Yeah, anyway, I was hoping you could, um, keep an eye on Mom while I'm gone?"

"In Alabama?"

"Yeah, that's what I said. I worry about her."

"Yeah. She'll worry about you too. I hope you're not doing anything dangerous."

I guess I didn't think out the story well enough, but it's not like I could tell Meg the truth. She'd never believe me. I mean, I didn't believe all the stuff about enchanted frogs, at least not until I met the nice talking swan. Besides, I told Victoriana I'd keep her secret. And Meg doesn't approve of Victoriana. She'd have major problems with me marrying her.

Still, it feels crummy lying to Meg. She's my best friend.

"Don't worry." She touches my hand and looks all sympathetic, which makes me feel worse. "You know what Maya Angelou said."

"What?"

"'All God's children need traveling shoes.' Oh." She points at a one-shoed businessman at my counter. "Looks like you've got an emergency."

It's hours before I talk to Meg again. Every time I try to look at her, she becomes very involved in sweeping crumbs or straightening croissants. So I'm surprised when, at three o'clock, she shows up at my counter.

"I wanted you to have this." She holds out a small, blue drawstring bag. "For luck."

I pull the bag's silken strings and find inside a man's gold ring with a flat white stone. When I look closer, I see every color I can imagine, gleaming like the scales of a reef fish.

"It's an opal," Meg says. "Been in my family for generations."

"You want to give it to me?"

"It's a loan. My grandmother Maeve gave it to me. You can give it back when you return."

"But what if—?"

"Opals are fragile, so don't wear it all the time. But if you're ever in trouble, put it on, and it will bring you luck. Luck o' the Irish, you know."

"Luck. Good. I'll need it.

Meg smirks. "At least, that's what my grandmother says. Superstitious. I'm not sure I believe in luck, but I've worn it for big tests, and I've always done well."

"Could be because you studied?"

And yet, it doesn't sound as dumb as I thought it would. I believe in magic now, so why not good old Irish luck. I return the ring to its bag and pocket it. "Thanks, Meg."

"Only put it on if you're in trouble. But if you're ever having a hard time in Alabama, it may work."

"I will."

"What's going on with the shoes?"

I shrug. "Still breaking."

"No, silly, your designs. The ones you were going to ask Princess Perfect to wear."

"I guess I'll finish them when I get back."

"Do you have the designs you drew?"

"Under the counter."

"Why don't you leave them with me while you're gone?" Meg asks.

"Why?"

"Oh, I don't know. If your mom hires someone to help, they might snoop through them."

I start to point out that I could just leave them at home, but I stop myself. Why not let Meg hold on to them while I'm gone? I trust her. I know she'd never lie to me the way I'm lying to her. So I hand them over.

"When are you going?" she asks.

"I'm not sure. Soon as my mom gets everything together."

Nothing happens the next day or the day after. But on the third morning, when I go to open the shop, I see something jammed in the lock.

It's a white feather.

14

In a hotel, the important stuff happens at night. I don't mean the sleeping. I mean all the stuff that makes the news—the drunks, the affairs, the first kisses on the beach, not to mention my meetings with Victoriana.

So, at one a.m., I head out to the swan house, not knowing what might happen at night.

The swans are all there, waiting. When they see me, they put their heads together and begin to warble. Even though I have on my earbuds, I can't understand, so they must have their own swan language. When I get closer, one of them speaks.

"We have the information you need."

"You know where the frog is?"

"Not exactly." The swan looks down. "But we found someone who knows someone who may know the amphibian's whereabouts."

Oh, well, that sounds hopeful.

"You must come with me to meet him, at the port."

"The Port of Miami?"

"No, the Port of Naples. Of course the Port of Miami."

"It's just . . ." I picture myself walking down the street, all the way to the Port of Miami, with a swan.

But with the cloak, I could be there in seconds. I consider telling the swan I'll take him too. Then I remember Victoriana's warning against letting anyone else use the cloak. "Sure, um, I'm going to take a cab, though. Maybe you could fly, and I'll meet you there. Swans can fly, right?"

The swan gives me a look like, *duh*, and says, "I'm Harry, by the way, the swan you spoke to that first night. I'll go with you. Meet me at the front entrance, and I'll take you to the rendezvous point."

Rendezvous point. Sounds like something from a spy movie.

"Sure," I say. "I just have to go get something."

"Not thinking of chickening out, are you?" He laughs. "Bird joke."

"No. Not chicken. Just need money for the cab. I'll be right there." I look at Harry, who is slim, with black eyes close together. They all look pretty much alike. "Why don't you get started, though. The cab will probably go faster than you can fly."

The swan laughs. "I doubt it."

"Why don't we see?" I need to get the swans out of the way. "I'll race you."

Harry nods his head. "I accept your challenge." And, with that, he's waddling toward the door.

I start for my shop but glance through the front windows. I see Harry flapping his wings. Slowly, he rises above the cars, above the hotel, his white wings forming a heart against the black night.

I head back to the shoe shop and take out the cloak. I wrap it around me and wish to be on Biscayne Boulevard, a block north of the port so the swan won't see me materialize.

And then, I'm there.

The port at night is scary. By day, there's a steady traffic of cruise ship passengers and container trucks carrying cargo shipments. But when the sky darkens, they turn it over to the night. A few feet from me, a woman walks down Biscayne Boulevard. She doesn't even notice my sudden appearance. Then a car pulls over and someone rolls down the window. She climbs in, and they roar away.

I start to walk, hearing the dull *thunk* of my sneakers against pavement. To my left is Biscayne Boulevard. To my right, nothing but dark water. Something moves, and I stop.

Only the moon, glinting off the bay. A cloud rolls across it, and the night is dark. From a block away, I can see the light of a single flashlight inside the port. Drug dealers? What am I doing here?

Stupid. Drug dealers don't carry flashlights. Probably a security guard. That doesn't make me feel any better, though, because a security guard won't let me in. Still, I trudge toward the entrance.

The cloak has landed me on the opposite side of the road from the port. So I fold it into my backpack and wait for a single car to pass. When the coast is clear, I begin to cross.

Out of the darkness, a roar. Then, a whoosh of exhaust and hot Miami air. I jump back onto the median just in time. A motorcycle. Its lights are off, and it almost hits me as it roars through the intersection, then makes a hard left into the port entrance. I can't see the driver's face, but I get a fleeting impression of Arnold Schwarzenegger, when he played a robot in *The Terminator*, a tall, square man, clad in black leather, with short hair on his helmetless head.

I stand on the median, hearing his waning motor. My breath. My heartbeat. I shiver in the nighttime summer heat. I almost died. No, I didn't. I got out of the way. It's okay.

Across the street, the flashlight ray is gone. All dark. I listen for a long time before running across.

When I finally reach the other side, I see a white cross in the sky. A cloud? No, it's Harry. He lands closer to the entrance than I am and inclines his neck as if to say, *Told you,*

85

then gestures for me to follow him.

We just walk through. I'd worried about that, about whether there would be a guard or a gate. But we get through unseen, and for a second, I think it's too easy. Someone should have stopped us. Why didn't they, unless it's a setup?

Crazy.

The cruise ship terminals are dark and locked for the night. But I can hear banging from the Seaboard Marine terminal, where guys are loading containers of cargo. I think that's where we're going, but we pass it, heading to the farthest pitch-black cruise ship terminal. As we get farther from the work noise, I can hear things scurrying on the pavement below. No, not things. Rats. What do they say about rats on a ship? Rats leaving a sinking ship? Finally, we enter an alleyway so small that my shoulders touch walls on both sides.

"Are we hiding from someone?" I ask the swan's white outline, suddenly remembering the motorcycle guy. But the swan only hisses in reply. Then, he lets out a whistle.

Suddenly, the alley is alive with the noises of hundreds of scurrying feet. I feel something against my ankle. A tail. I shudder. From the ground, I hear a small voice, like someone talking, but I can't understand. And yet, I know it's words, not random squeaking.

"What?" I say.

Harry bats me with his wing until I understand that I'm supposed to lean down. I do, taking care not to let my hand brush what I know is a rodent and am met with a pair of gleaming black eyes in the darkness.

"You the guy looking for the frog?" a small voice says.

I nod, then realize no one can see me, so I say, "Yes."

"He was here," the voice says. "Two weeks ago. I seen him hoppin' around like a idiot."

"You saw him?" My stomach jumps like there's a frog inside. "How do you know it was him, and not just some other frog?"

Silence for a moment.

"I known he was a prince on account-a he was goin' around tellin' everyone he was a prince. He was sayin' things like, 'I'm unaccustomed to consorting with vermin.' Vermin! Can you believe dat?"

He pauses long enough for me to realize the question wasn't rhetorical. I say, "No. You, vermin? Of course not! How could he say that?"

"Thank you. Anyway, he was not what you'd call well liked, so no one was too upset when he got shipped out."

"Shipped out?" The alley is hot with no breeze. It smells like palmetto bugs, and I begin to feel dizzy.

"Yeah, they stuck him on a container truck from Seaboard, heading for the Keys."

I know all this from Victoriana, but maybe the rat knows more. "And?"

"Like I said, he wasn't missed." The rat's voice is tiny, and I lean farther down to hear it. "Good ribbons to bad rubbish and all that. So I di'n think anything more about it 'til last week, when some folks started snoopin' around."

I know this too. "Big guys? With a bloodhound?"

"Nah, not them goofballs. Ah, they was here for like ten minutes, sniffing. That dog didn't even try and talk to the other animals here. Real snotty, like. If they'd really been lookin', he woulda talked to us. That's what bloodhounds is famous for."

"Talking to animals? I thought they just sniffed."

"Ah, that's what people think on account-a bloodhounds have them goofy noses. But in actuality, they're experts on interrogation. That's how they find their man."

Who knew? "But this one didn't do that?"

"Didn't even try. It was like they didn't tink da frog was here. Or maybe they didn't *want* to find him. But a few days later, some other guys showed up, guys with accents. *Dogs* with accents, German shepherds. They talked to everyone, and that's when I got interested."

Accents. I remember Victoriana's voice. And her guards. She must have sent someone different the second time, and he did a better job.

"So what happened after you got interested?"

"After I got interested, I was interested. Interested enough to do some investigating myself about where that container went."

"And where did it go?"

"Key Largo, full of goods for the Underwater Hotel, which is good news for you."

"Good news? Why's that good news?" Key Largo is the closest key, but it's also one of the longest and most populated. The frog could be anywhere.

"Good news 'cause right next to the Underwater Hotel is a bar called Sally's, rough place, rough crowd. The animals what hangs there is rough too, probably on account of some of the rough garbage theys eats. They'd probably eat that snooty-pants prince in frog skin alive too."

"Oh." Well, that doesn't sound good.

"But there's this fox there. He's a good guy, and he sorta runs things down there. He's one of us used-to-bes."

"Used-to-bes?"

"That's what we call ourselves, 'used-to-be humans.' Anyway, this fox was a fisherman down on the MacArthur Causeway until one day, he disappeared."

"Disappeared?"

"That's the story with all us used-to-bes. We're the mysterious disappearances, the unsolved mysteries. Cold cases. Everyone assumes we're down in the river with cement overshoes or else ran off. But the truth's way weirder."

Used-to-bes. I think about it, imagining all the animals I once thought were just animals, who had actually been human until, one day, they disappeared without a trace. Probably their families stopped looking for them. God, it made you not want to take a shower in front of the cat! "Can all used-to-bes get transformed back?" My thighs hurt from leaning down so long.

"Yeah, but it's harder for some than others. Some of us have pretty much given up. Anyway, the fox's name is Todd, and he's friendly. If you talk to 'im nice, he'll pro'lly help you out. Tell him Cornelius sent you."

"Cornelius?"

"Fancy name for a rat, right? I used to be a senator. Just be careful not to talk to the fox in front of anyone else. I don't know who those guys were that was looking for the frog, but they looked scary."

Suddenly there's a sound close by. Footsteps. A night watchman, maybe. I try to squeeze closer in between the two walls, but there's nowhere to go. The rat scurries off, and I lean, frozen, feeling the ache in my thighs but unable to take a single step. I'm hot and pained and dead. Deaddeaddeaddead. The footsteps come closer, closer.

I wait a minute, then two, to see if they come back.

Finally Harry whispers, "I think he's gone." The first words he's said since we got here.

"Yeah," I whisper back. "That was close. We should go." I have the information I need, even though it sounds impossible. Sally's. A fox named Todd. Cornelius sent me.

Since Harry's behind me, he moves out first, and I follow. But as I get close enough to see the lights from Seaboard Marine, I hear a familiar roar. A motorcycle! I feel a whoosh of air, then hear a boom and see a flash of white light. A gunshot! Harry's on the ground behind me.

"Harry!" I can't stop myself from screaming his name. I

dive to the ground beside him.

"Got him!" a voice says.

Then, a second voice. A woman. "*Nein*. There is some-one with him."

Oh no. I know what I have to do. I unzip my backpack and pull out the cloak. "Stay with me, Harry," I whisper.

"No," the swan whispers. "It is time for my swan song. Save yourself. Run!"

The motorcycle's wheels shriek in a circle. I fumble with the cloak, finally wrapping it around both of us. "Hang in there, boy! Don't start singing yet!" I clutch at the swan, feeling the smoothness of its white feathers, the warm stickiness of blood. I hear the motorcycle roar again, coming toward me in the same whoosh of air.

I wish I was back at the hotel, I think.

And then, there's a flash.

15

I recognize sounds first. Car horns. People yelling. Crashing waves from the beach. The crackle of neon. I'm on South Beach. In a cloak. Holding a bleeding once-human swan.

I lift my head to see if anyone's watching us, but no. It's the usual South Beach oblivion, people zombified by lights and the liquor. Still, I unwrap the bloody cloak and hide it inside my backpack, then look down at Harry.

He blinks at me. "How . . . how are we here?"

"Shh." I glance at the stain spreading across his snow-white breast. "We're here. I'll get someone to help."

"But . . ." He moves his beak, but no sound comes out.

"Hold that thought," I say. "Don't die on me."

Zipping my backpack as I go, I run into the empty lobby. I can't handle the idea that this guy might die as a swan. I'm even more worried that he might turn human after death.

The night clerk is gone, and I glance first left, then right, seeing no one.

"Help!" I yell. "Outside! Someone's shot a swan!"

I run back toward my shop, meaning to use the phone, to call 911, and tell them . . . I don't know what. I expect to see no one, but instead, I find Meg. She takes in my panting face and bloodied shirt. "What is it?"

"Outside on Collins. Someone's shot a swan!" I can't explain to her that it's not a swan, but a man. "Call nine-one-one."

I start back to the lobby, confident she'll do it. But Meg stops me with a hand on my arm. "You call. I'll go to him . . . it. I'm calmer." She pushes me aside and darts past me.

I'm alone, alone and faced with the impossible knowledge that someone shot at me. Someone knew I was at the port and why. Someone wants to stop me from finding Prince Philippe, maybe enough to kill over it.

When I return to the lobby, the swans are awake, staring out the windows. They see me and swarm around, all speaking at once. I push through them and out the door. Meg cradles Harry in her arms, and for an instant, I'm sure he's dead. But then, he raises his head and stares at me. Meg is applying pressure with a dish towel, though red still pools on the street. I hear a siren. It winds to a stop. Then, running steps.

"Where's the victim?" It's a paramedic.

I gesture toward Harry. The guy looks at Meg. "You hurt, miss?"

"Not her," I say. "The bird."

"A swan? I don't resuscitate birds. I'm a trained professional. You need to call those Miami Animal Rescue guys on TV maybe."

"But he's dying!"

"Actually, he's doing fine." Meg removes the towel from the swan's breast, and I see that the bloody spot on his white feathers seems smaller, barely a scrape. "Just a flesh wound."

"But . . . it was huge." I gape at it, then at Meg.

"I applied pressure." To the paramedic, Meg says, "Look, it's still bleeding. Do you think you could give me a bandage or something so I can put it in a cab to the animal hospital? The manager really does like these swans, and people will freak if they see blood."

"But . . ." I gesture at the puddle on the ground. "He was bleeding to death."

"He was probably just in shock," the paramedic says.

I think, not for the first time, that Meg is like the type of shoe we never repair, a Bass Weejun or Birkenstock sandal, the sort of shoe that's comfortable and lasts forever.

The paramedic finally gives Meg some bandages, and that's when the police show up.

"There was a shooting here?" The officer looks around.

"Yeah," I tell her. "This guy on a motorcycle. He shot a swan."

"This is about a swan?"

"Yeah, a swan."

"A swan?"

"That's illegal, isn't it? Can you go hunting on Collins Avenue that I don't know about?"

The officer looks at her partner, who has just shown up. The partner shakes his head. "Most of the squad's at the port. Someone heard gunshots."

"Did they see the guy who did it?"

"Some of the dock workers saw a blond guy with black clothes."

"That's the guy who shot the swan! He would have shot me if the swan hadn't been in front of me."

I look at Harry. It's true. I could be. Someone was aiming at me. The paramedic has bandaged Harry's wound, and apparently, Meg has sweet-talked him into carrying the swan to a cab on a stretcher. I don't even know why Meg's here so early, but I'm glad she is.

"I could give you a description," I say. "It might be related."

I know it is, and the guy may still be after me.

* * *

After the cops leave, I return to the shop. The cloak is there, all bloody. It saved my life. I wash the blood off, then put the cloak on. I wish myself home.

At home, I pack a backpack with a few changes of clothing, a small tent, and a sleeping bag. Then, I find Mom at the shoe repair. "I have to leave right away," I tell her.

I don't tell her about the shooting. I have to get down to the Keys, the fox, before anyone else does. "Tell Meg I'm sorry I didn't get to say good-bye."

"Wait!" Mom stops me, grabbing my wrist. "The night manager says someone shot a swan in the lobby. Do you know something?"

I lie. "No. Really?" I know she'll find out the truth, but by the time she does, I'll be gone without even a place to charge my cell phone.

"What if it's dangerous?" she asks.

I lie again. "There's no danger. Probably some psycho bird-hater."

And then I leave, taking Meg's opal ring, the cloak, and what I can carry on my back.

I thought my life was boring. It isn't anymore.

16

The Fox said, "Do not shoot me, for I will give you good counsel."

—"The Golden Bird"

Mom and I spend most of our vacations camping in Key Largo because that's as far as we can afford to go. We always drive south on U.S. 1 with its endless fast-food joints, strip malls, and gas stations. After an hour, we reach the road with blue water on both sides.

This time, though, before anyone can talk me out of it, I throw the cloak over my shoulders. "I wish I was at the Underwater Hotel."

And then, I'm there.

Or I'm someplace.

Someplace dark.

I was expecting a lobby. Or a restaurant. Even a room. Instead, it's pitch-dark, darker than the Everglades at night. At least there, there are stars. I pull at the cloak to make sure it's not over my head, then look up. No stars. The place is eerie, silent. My head feels full of pounding pressure, like being on the Mission Space ride at Disney World. Hands before me, I stumble forward. A wall, as smooth as glass. A window. I run my hand along it, feeling cold smoothness. I reach a wall. An inch farther, I feel a light switch.

I flip it on.

Sharp teeth gleam in the sudden light. A shark. A shark! I jump backward, then fall to the floor before realizing I'm not wet. The shark is. I turn, realizing it must be in some sort of tank. The shark proves this by swimming on, not noticing what he can't smell. Am I in an aquarium? I peer through the window. No light above, no end.

I glance around the room. It's furnished like a regular living room. In another window, the same shark swims by.

Underwater Hotel. Could I actually be underwater?

The pressure in my ears tells me I am. I stumble to the sofa, try to get my bearings. The silence is like nothing I've ever heard before.

Then, from another room is a sound. "Ha ha! We made it. How cool is this?"

Someone's here!

A woman giggles. I hear wet footsteps approaching, the

unmistakable sound of flippers meeting floor. "Someone left the light on in this room."

I clutch the cloak around me. "I wish I was above-ground."

"What was that?" I hear a voice say.

A Hummer is barreling toward me. It skids to a stop; the driver, leaning on its horn, is screaming something unintelligible. I jump out of his way, only to land in the path of a Smart car. At least they're getting smaller.

"Crazy!" The driver honks as he swerves around me.

"I wish I was at Sally's," I say, running.

Then, I'm on a barstool in a smoke-filled room that's dark even at eight in the morning. Elvis blares from a jukebox, half drowned out by drunken laughter and the cackling of a bedraggled-looking yellow bird. Two drunks stop talking when they see me.

"Hey, how'd you get here?" a guy with a neck beard says.

"He's a little young for this place," says his friend, who's missing his right hand. The rest of him looks like he must have lost it in a bar fight.

"Pretty too." The first guy fingers my cloak. "What's up with the dress?"

I pull the fabric back, close my eyes, and make what I hope is my last wish. "I wish I was outside, behind this building, not in the street, not underwater, hidden so I can't be seen."

An instant later, I'm in a garbage Dumpster. The cloak has a sick sense of humor, but no one will see me. I'm covered in French fries, and when I stand, a half-empty beer bottle falls, spilling its contents over me. I peer out.

I blink in the sunlight. No one there.

No one except a red fox who's eating what looks like a plate of fish and chips. Disturbed by my movement, he peers up at me, two white-green eyes over a shiny black nose. Still holding a slab of fish between two black paws, he curls his lip and growls.

"Excuse me," I say.

Nothing.

"Mr. Fox, I need to talk to you."

The fox lifts the fish into his white-rimmed mouth and runs.

"Hey, wait! No! Mr. Fox!" I see his fluffy tail disappearing between some bushes, so I try to climb out of the Dumpster. But the sides are slippery with grease and beer and whatever else people throw in bar Dumpsters. What was the fox's name?

"Todd!"

Nothing. The fox left his plate of fish. It looks warm and golden brown with tartar sauce on one side, ketchup on the other. Someone left it for the fox. He'll be back. I settle into the Dumpster. It couldn't smell any nastier than I do. While I wait, I decide to review what I've learned today.

When traveling by magic cloak, specificity is key. You

tell it where you want to go and:

Not underwater

Not anyplace crowded

No place dangerous

Not the middle of the street

Not a biker bar with dudes who want to kill you or date you

I start to close my eyes. It's been a rough day.

A voice jolts me awake. "Excuse me?"

"Huh?" I shift, causing three beer bottles to fall on me. Don't these people recycle?

"Did you call for Todd?"

The fox. I stare. I've never been so close to a wild animal, a *talking* wild animal. Could he have rabies? No. No foam at the mouth. He's cute, actually, with white fluff on his chest. "Are you him?" I adjust the earbuds, which are still in my ears.

"Depends who's asking."

"I'm Johnny. Cornelius sent me." At his puzzled expression, I add, "The rat."

And though it doesn't seem possible, the fox grins slowly, showing sharp white teeth.

"Then I'm Todd."

17

I stay put to tell my story. It's safer, particularly considering I'm sitting here, having a conversation with a woodland creature. I may never get used to that.

I show the fox the photo of the frog and tell him he was last seen on his way to the Underwater Hotel. "Have you seen him?"

The fox nods.

"You have?"

"And I know where he went too."

I wait, expecting him to continue. But he only stares at me, his small intelligent eyes searching my face. When the silence has stretched to a minute, I say, "So are you going to tell me?"

The fox starts like he's heard a thunderclap. But finally, he says, "I was just trying to decide."

"Decide what?"

"Whether to tell you."

"Why wouldn't you?"

"The life of a used-to-be is hard. We were born human, but as animals, our existence is perilous. Anytime, we may be shot at by poachers, hit by cars, attacked by dogs, or hunted for sport. We have to decide who to trust."

"Everyone trusts me."

"Who's everyone?"

I think. Meg trusts me, but that's not a good example, because I lied to her. Mom trusts me, but she's my mother.

Finally, I say, "Well, there's the princess."

"Princess?" The fox frowns as much as a fox can frown. "This is America, kid. I may be a fox, but I'm not stupid. I know there are no princesses here."

"She's not from America. She's from Aloria, and she's . . ." I stop, picturing Victoriana's incredible hotness. She's the answer to all my problems, I want to say, but instead, I say, "She's in trouble. She needs someone to help her, and out of all the people she could have asked, she chose me. She thought I was . . ." Okay, this is embarrassing to say. ". . . a good boy."

"And why would she think that?"

"Because I work really hard to help support my mom

and me. We have a shoe repair shop."

"Shoe repair?" The fox twitches his tail.

"Yeah, I know it sounds lame, but that's what my family does, what I probably *will* do the rest of my life. See, my father walked out on us when I was a kid."

"That's tough." The fox's whiskers move up and down. "I've met many fatherless foxes. Usually, both parents care for the kits, but sometimes, the father is killed, and it's hard for the kits to learn to hunt."

I nod sympathetically. "Yeah, it's been hard for me too. Not the hunting part, but other stuff. But the princess says if I can help her find the frog, she'll marry me."

The fox looks up at me. "Do you want to marry the princess, Johnny?"

"Sure. Who wouldn't? I want money, money to go to school and start my own business and take care of Mom. If I have to marry the princess, I'll marry the princess. Besides . . ."

"Besides, what?"

"She's beautiful."

The fox nods. "Yes, beauty always helps. I had a beautiful wife myself." He's silent a moment. I let him think. Finally, he says, "All right. I'll give you a chance."

"You'll help me?"

"I said I'd give you a chance. But before I can help you, you must pass a test."

"What kind of test?"

"You have to prove you're worthy. The first thing you have to do is go to the inn behind this Dumpster and spend the night."

I remember the bar with the scary-looking dudes who wanted to make me their woman. I don't know if I'd be welcomed back, especially covered in garbage. But I don't have a choice. "Sure."

"But don't think you can fool me. There are two hotels near here. One is a nice bed-and-breakfast, clean and comfortable. The other is the motel you've seen. You must spend the whole night in the less-welcoming motel to succeed."

"Got it."

"Then come back tomorrow, and I'll give you the information you need."

"Okay." I wait for him to tell me something else. He just sits there. Finally, he says, "Go."

"Oh." I gather my cloak and leave.

I walk around the side of the building until I see the door. It's ten and the sun is high in the sky, making the motel look even shabbier than it did earlier. There are motorcycles outside and a few junker cars, one of which has someone asleep in the passenger seat. Sleep. I wouldn't mind some of that myself. Maybe I could check in early. My eyes are already blurry with the thought of it after my long night.

In the distance, I see the other inn. It's a bed-and-breakfast, like Todd said, the type of big, tin-roofed, Key West–style house Mom always wanted to stay in. Emily's

Butterfly House, it's called, and butterflies flutter around red and purple flowers.

But the fox said I had to stay at the rough hotel. I'll obey. I'm turning away when I see something else moving in the flowers.

It's a frog.

It's just a frog. Any old frog, not my frog.

But why not my frog? I take a step toward it, then another. The frog stays still. I keep my eye on it, afraid that if I stop looking, it will disappear.

"Philippe!" I call.

He doesn't look. I take another step, bending forward, and as I come closer, I see it.

A red stripe on the frog's head.

I'm in. I won. I don't need the fox or the inn or anything. I'm not going to get shot at. I just have to catch the frog, something any little boy can do. For once in my life, something is easy!

The best way to catch an animal is to use a towel or blanket. Without taking my eyes off the frog, I reach into my backpack and draw out the cloak.

The frog doesn't twitch.

I take a step forward, then another, never allowing my eyes to leave him. I can see the wart, the red spot. This is my frog. I want to run toward it, but I control myself. The frog isn't moving. He trusts me. I can't scare him away.

Finally, I'm almost close enough to throw the fabric.

One last step.

The frog hops onto the front stairs of the inn.

No. No! Don't hop away. Still, I remain calm. It's just one step. There are three. I try not to think about the crawl space under the house. If he goes through the stairs, I'll have to grub underneath for him.

I move forward. Calm. Calm.

The frog hops onto the second stair.

No!

Calm. Calm.

I take another, larger step. It brings back memories of playing Mother May I on the beach with Meg, sneaking forward, hoping not to be noticed. I hold the cloak out farther, ready to throw.

The frog hops onto the porch.

The inn's door opens, and the frog hops inside.

"No!" I can't stop the shout. The old lady who opened the door stares at me, perplexed. I try to smile, and she lets the door close behind her.

It's okay. The frog's inside now. Trapped. I can get him. Calm.

Maybe they'll even chase him out.

I try to imagine the prince, getting hit with a broom. Better get moving.

I stuff the cloak in my backpack, then start up the stairs.

Inside, it's all blue flowers and white wicker, but there's

no frog anywhere, only a group of tourists, balancing plates in their laps, eating muffins. They stare at me, and I imagine how I must look, seventeen, backpack on back, dirty, and stinking of garbage. I look homeless.

It's okay. I'm not staying. I'll just take my frog and leave.

"May I help you?"

A middle-aged woman with a leather tan, Birkenstock sandals, and a pot of coffee approaches me. She's trying to look friendly, like nothing's wrong.

"No," I say. "I mean, sorry. I mean, I'm trying to catch a frog."

"Frog?" She wrinkles her nose.

"The one that hopped in here when that last guest left." I look around. I don't see it, nor do I see the grossed-out faces of guests whose breakfast has been invaded by a frog. No. They look calm. I bend over and start looking under the tables (all of which have tablecloths) and chairs (all of which have people on them).

"Young man, there was no—"

"There was." I pull the cloak from my backpack. Something—garbage, food, falls off of it, and I get a whiff of the smell, like beer and B.O. The breakfast eaters wrinkle their noses while still trying to pretend they don't see me. They're very accepting here in the Keys.

Still, the coffeepot lady swats at my cloak. "Please put that away."

"I'm sorry. It'll just be a minute." I can't get thrown out of here, not without my frog. I get on hands and knees and start crawling around, through the Clarks and Easy Spirits, brands you'd never see at the Coral Reef. There's a big, wicker sofa with three people on it. Bet he's under there. My knees ache, but I crawl toward it.

"Young man! Young man, please!"

The guests squirm and look at the coffee lady. They move their legs aside.

"I'm sorry," I say, "but do you *want* a frog loose in your place?"

"Frog?" A shriek from one of the sofa ladies.

"There's no frog," the coffee lady says. I crawl through a forest of legs, looking from side to side, Topsider to Mephisto.

I reach the sofa. "Excuse me. Would you mind if I look under that cushion?"

A lady in Jimmy Buffett's Margaritaville sandals jumps up.

There's no frog under the sofa or tables. There's no frog under the buffet or television. There is no frog anywhere.

"Maybe it went back out," says the coffee lady. "Why don't you go look?"

I realize I should. With one final glance around, I start toward the door.

But when I try to leave, the door won't open. I tug at it, then harder. I pull the knob back and forth. Nothing.

"It's stuck," I tell the coffee lady.

"Oh, for Pete's sake." She puts down her pot, laughing through gritted teeth. "Of course it's not." She opens it easily and gestures me out.

"Thanks." I brush past her and step onto the porch.

When I do, my stomach is seized with a knifing pain. I double over, then stagger back into the room, clutching my gut.

"Are you okay?" I see the coffee lady's Birkenstocks, her clenched toes.

"Fine." The pain has subsided. I pull myself up and try to step outside again.

Again, the pain pierces through me. But now, it's in my head as well. I stumble back. "I'm going. I'm fine." I take another step forward. My field of vision narrows so it seems like I'm looking through a toy telescope. My stomach and guts roll inside each other. My head has a heartbeat. I have to go. Have. To. I can barely feel my leg. But still, I take a step.

That's when my legs buckle under me.

18

I'm surrounded by shoes. Ugly shoes. Someone puts something clammy on my head.

"Are you okay?" the coffee lady says. "I'll call the paramedics."

"No, don't," I say, because in that second, I understand. It's the magic. Something, or someone, is keeping me from leaving the inn, maybe to stop me from following the fox's orders about spending the night in the dive motel. Did they lure me here in the first place? Was the frog a mirage?

I know if I step out that door, the pain will come back.

"I don't need the paramedics." The clammy thing on my head is a washcloth. It drips down my face. "But I think I need a place to stay."

"Oh no." The toes clench again. "This is a hotel, not a shelter."

I get it. I've reached the limits of Key Largo casualness. "I have money." I grope for my backpack. Someone's put it in a corner, and I gesture toward it. Finally, a lady in orange-and-white Mephisto Allrounders hands it to me.

"Thanks," I say. "Nice shoes."

She looks down. "Thank you. They're very comfortable."

"Well, you know what George Bernard Shaw said, don't you?" When she shakes her head, I say, "'If a woman rebels against high-heeled shoes, she should take care to do it in a very smart hat.'" I gesture at her visor, which is covered in pom-poms. "You did."

The woman laughs. "I didn't know young people knew about Shaw."

I riffle through my backpack until I find money. Even though it kills me to do it, I show the coffee lady three hundred dollars. "Will this be enough to stay tonight?"

It must be more than enough, because she says, "You have clean clothes?"

"Yeah." I must really stink.

"Good. Then once you feel up to walking, go to the bathroom and change. Your room will be ready soon. You can have a muffin while you wait . . . after you change."

"Of course." I look from Birkenstock to Mephisto. "Actually, I think I'm ready to change now." I need to make another attempt to leave. I just thought of something.

"Wonderful." She gestures me toward the bathroom.

Once there, I wrap the cloak around my shoulders. "I wish I was outside. Right outside. No tricks."

Nothing.

"I wish I was at the other inn, where I belong."

Nothing.

"Everything all right in there?" Someone taps on the door.

"Fine."

Is the coffee lady a witch? Did she trap me here? One memory of her disapproving face says no. She didn't want me to stay. But someone does. Someone cast a spell on me. And on the cloak, so it won't work.

I change, wash as well as I can, and shake the food and garbage off the cloak. Then I head outside and devour three muffins.

An hour later, I'm in a third-floor room, looking down on the fox and the motel I'm supposed to be at. The fox meets my eyes, then looks away. The frog is nowhere in sight, and I haven't heard screams from the lobby to indicate he's there either. Every hour or so, I go downstairs and try to walk outside. Every time, I'm seized with staggering pain. I even try to climb out the window, but I can't.

Finally, I wash my dirty clothes in the bathroom sink, then settle into the four-poster bed and go to sleep. I hope I'll be able to leave tomorrow.

I sleep all day, not even bothering with meals. It's a bed-and-breakfast, so I don't expect lunch. I'm not hungry anyway, only tired, so tired I barely dream.

When I wake, it's dark and the digital clock says eight. I stumble downstairs and try the door. No dice. I go back to bed, but now, I wake hourly. I'm trapped. God, I'm trapped. Am I ever getting out of here? I don't try the door again until midnight. It's the next day. Maybe I can still go to the motel. But no. I can't pass.

I'm too frightened to go back to bed. What if I'm stuck in this alternative universe forever and never see my family. Sooner or later, I won't be able to pay the bill, and they'll get the police to evict me.

At sunrise, I shower, dress, then head downstairs.

"You look refreshed." The coffee lady is setting out trays of Danish. "Ready for breakfast? We have fresh clotted cream."

My stomach aches, a cold, raw hunger that rises from my gut like a bad smell.

I nod. "Definitely. But first, I need to check the . . . ah . . . weather."

She smiles. "It's a hot one, all right."

"I'll bet." I walk to the door. As I suspected, it opens easily now, and when I step out, I feel only hunger pangs, not the stabbing pain I felt yesterday. I take a second, then a third step, then feel a familiar feeling, the same one I used to get at work. Someone's watching me. I look across the street. It's the fox. He's glaring at me. His eyes meet mine. Then, he scurries into the bushes.

I climb the steps. The coffee lady's still there, and I say, "Actually, I lost some time, what with being sick and all. Could I maybe get some muffins to go?"

"Certainly." The coffee lady looks relieved to get rid of me. It's probably the cloak in my backpack. Even though I washed my clothes, I only spot-cleaned the cloak so as not to affect its magic—if it even has any magic left. So it smells. "Let me get you a bag."

When she leaves, I head for the buffet table, grab three muffins, stuff two into my backpack for the fox. For bribes. When the coffee lady returns with a bag, I grab as much food as I reasonably can, thank her, and leave.

Now, to find the fox.

19

Do not take the golden cage. If you do, great misfortune will follow.

> —"The Firebird and the Grey Wolf"

I don't have to look very hard. As soon as I cross the street, the fox comes out from behind the Dumpster. He's been waiting for me.

"Hey," I say.

"I've got nothing to say to you," he says.

"Look, I messed up."

"You think?" The fox turns tail and walks away.

"But I saw the frog."

He turns back, sneering with his little black fox lips.

"The frog? Oh yeah, I'm sure it was the frog. Stupid! It was a mirage. I can't work with someone who falls for tricks like that." He draws back on his haunches, ready to spring into the Dumpster. "Now, if you'll excuse me, I need to find breakfast."

"Wait!" I remember the muffins. "Would you like something that isn't garbage?"

The fox has already jumped, but he turns in midair and manages to land on his feet. Once straightened out, he slits his eyes at me. "What are we talking about?"

I step close, then open the bag in front of him. "Muffins. Scones. Danish. All home baked by the nice lady at the bed-and-breakfast where I've been captive all night."

"Captive!" The fox laughs but reaches a tentative black paw toward a currant scone.

"Not so fast!" I pull the bag away. "Yes, I was trapped, trapped like a prisoner in a jail full of old people. And if you want a scone or a croissant with something called clotted cream, you need to listen to me, or . . ." I shut the bag and make to stuff it into my backpack.

"Or what?" The fox eyes the closed bag.

"Or you can have some leftover bar food that's probably covered in puke." I open the bag and use my hand to waft the scent toward the fox. Even though he's a used-to-be human, he obviously got his new species' keen sense of smell because he sniffs deeply.

"Please," I beg. "I need to find this frog. It's not for

me. It's for my mother."

"Your mother?"

"She worries so much." I hold the bag farther open. "Didn't you have a mother?"

"Oh, all right!" The fox almost sobs. "But only since it's been years since I've had anything sweet. The old lady in the bed-and-breakfast never throws anything away."

"Is that why you didn't want me to stay there, because you hate her?"

"No. The reason I didn't want you to stay there is . . ." He stops and looks around, then jumps on the side of the Dumpster and looks there too.

"What?"

"Shh. I have to make sure no one can hear." The fox jumps down, then runs to the corner of the building and looks around it.

"No one could understand you even if they heard."

"Correction: No people could understand me. But there may be animals. Think about it. When you were on your way over there, did you see anything, a dog, perhaps, or a cat? The innkeeper has some really nosy cats."

I think about it, then shake my head.

"Take one more look. But give me a cran-orange muffin first."

"Okay, but only one." I hand it to him, then take the bag with me. I walk around, as much to reassure myself that no one's watching as to satisfy the fox. I haven't let myself think about it, but now that I'm out, I wonder who trapped me there, who was watching. Will they do it again?

When I've looked under every bush and into every tree, I return to the fox, who has polished off the muffin and is licking his whiskers. "Enjoy it?"

"Yes! More! More!"

"After you help me."

"Well, I shouldn't. You haven't proven yourself very trustworthy."

"But . . ." I take a scone. It's still warm from the oven, and I blow on it.

"Oh, okay." The fox sits back on his haunches, eyes never leaving the scone. "But since you failed the first test, I need you to do something else. Now, instead of just staying in the motel, I want you to steal something for me."

"Steal?"

The fox nods. "In the bar lives a golden bird, the bartender's pride and joy. It sleeps by night in a golden cage, by day in one of wood. The bar is closed for three hours, from four in the morning until seven o'clock. The bar is locked, but the door is unsupervised, so a guest in the hotel could get in—particularly if he had a magic cloak."

"But I don't steal." I think of the swans at the hotel, how Farnesworth loves them. Maybe this bird is like that for the bartender. I also think of the guys who could beat me up or worse. "I can't."

"Fine." The fox turns away.

"Wait! There's nothing else I could do?"

"Nothing. You already failed once. If you want the information to find the frog, I need that bird. I'm trying to help you, you and your poor mother. But no one ever said winning a princess was easy."

The scone in my hand is cold now, and hard. "Are you going to kill the bird?"

"What if I was? Is a bird's life worth a prince's? But no. I won't kill it. I just want to look at it."

I think about that. It must really stink to be turned into a fox and have to eat garbage. Maybe the bird is a used-to-be too. "Is the bird a friend of yours?"

"What difference does it make? Do you want the information?"

I do. It doesn't matter. If that's the only way to get the frog, I'll steal the bird. Sometimes you have to be a little less picky about things to get what you need.

"Okay," I say.

"Atta boy. There's only one thing you have to remember. The bird sleeps in a golden cage. His regular, wooden cage waits beside him for morning. Before you take him, you have to transfer him from one cage to another. If you don't, the bird won't go with you."

"Wooden cage. Got it. But why?"

"It's part of the test."

I nod. I'm trying not to think about the part where I actually have to steal something from those scary bar guys.

"And give me that scone now."

I do. I keep some muffins for myself and give him the rest of the bag. I start to walk away, leaving him feasting on a croissant, when his voice stops me. "Johnny?"

I turn back.

"What is your mother's name?"

The question takes me by surprise, but I say, "Marie."

The fox nods. "Pretty name." He goes back to his scones.

I start toward the motel. It's a long time before nightfall, a very long time. But I don't want anything to mess me up today. The fox might not give me another chance. As I walk up the path to the motel, I see a frog. The frog! It looks right at me before hopping toward the bed-and-breakfast. I start to take a step toward it. It lingers there, staring at me.

No. It's not real, and I need to ignore it. I turn my back and go to the door of the motel. To my relief, it opens. When I look out the door, the frog has vanished.

20

I enter through the side door, a different door than the one that leads to the bar. Hopefully, a safer door. No one's at the desk, so I wait. Nothing. After a few minutes, I ring the bell. I do it softly, so as not to enrage whatever disturbed individual might work in a place like this. Still nothing.

I sit on the floor (because there's no chair) and wait. An hour later, I realize no one's coming. I also realize I'm hungry. I've had nothing but muffins in the past day, and I gave the fox most of those. I hear rough laughter from the bar. My watch says ten a.m. Those guys get an early start. I smell something like food, and I need it bad. I'll ask where the desk clerk is too.

I stand and walk to the bar entrance. It's dark enough to look like night. I linger in the doorway, not wanting to go in. But what are they going to do? Beat me up? I'm a nice, polite person who never gets beat up.

The guys at the bar are the same ones from yesterday, and they're wearing the same clothes. The golden bird, which looks like a canary, hangs over the bar, asleep in his wooden cage. I wait (politely) for the men to finish their conversation before I approach the bartender.

"Excuse me? I wondered if you had any food? I want to check in for the night too."

"I got leftovers from yesterday I could warm up for you." The bartender squints at me. "Hey, didn't I see you out by my Dumpster before?"

"Leftovers will be fine," I say, ignoring the other question, and also ignoring any nagging concern about what leftovers would be like in a place like this.

"Yeah, you was out there, talking to yourself."

"Can you please get me that food?" I hand him a twenty. "Keep the change."

"Ooh, big spender." The bartender laughs but takes the money and turns to look at the refrigerator. "We just got a couple burgers."

"Burgers are fine. Anything."

I hear a noise outside, a motorcycle. It sounds familiar. Too familiar.

No, that's just paranoid. I know nothing about

motorcycles. Probably they all sound alike. Still, I look out the window.

A pair of broad, black-clad shoulders come into view. I turn real quick and duck behind the bar.

"Hey, what the . . ." The bartender stumbles over me.

"Please. I need you to hide me," I whisper. "That guy wants to kill me."

"What guy? What are you talking about? Get outta here."

I hear a door slam, then hard footsteps. I'm a dead man.

I could use the cloak, but then the bartender would be on to me. I reach into my backpack and withdraw one of Victoriana's hundreds. These are going faster than I'd like. I flip it up and show it to the bartender. He reaches for it. I pull it away, mouthing, "Later."

The footsteps come closer, and then a voice says, "Have you seen dis boy?"

He sounds like the robot in the *Terminator* movies. I'm squirming, about to pee my pants.

"He is a stranger here," the accented voice continues. "Skinny. Tall."

"Nah, haven't seen him." That's the bartender.

"Wait a second," another voice says. "Lemme see that."

"You're drunk, Lefty."

I'm flattened against the floor. But still, I can hear my knees rattling. I don't breathe.

"But he looks like that guy—"

"You mean the guy that was here yesterday? That was my cousin, Frank, and he's gone now."

"Your cousin? You treated him like crap and charged him twenty bucks for day-old burgers."

"Didn't say he was my *favorite* cousin. Can we drop it now?" He steps over me and tells the terrorist guy, "I ain't seen him."

"If you do, you vill let me know?" The guy sounds more like Dracula than Schwarzenegger now. "Dere is a reward."

"Reward? What kind of reward?"

A pause. Finally, a voice says, "Five hundred dollars."

I glance up and see the bartender looking at me. I nod. Yes. Yes, I have that.

"I'd tell you if I'd seen him, but I haven't."

A pause. I hear heavy footsteps, pacing. Everything else is silent, even the two drunks. Finally, the guy says, "Very gut. But if he comes here, you vill contact me, day or night?"

And then he leaves. I stay there, not sure what to do, not even breathing. The two guys at the bar could betray me at any second. What's stopping them?

I hear a loud thump, then something rolling, a barstool.

"Lefty's passed out," says the other drunk. "Now would you mind telling me why you lied about the kid behind the bar when the guy offered you five hundred dollars?"

"Code of the bartender, my friend. I protect my customers. Like how I didn't tell your wife about you making time with Lefty's sister last year. Get it?"

"Got it."

I hear a motor, the motor I now know is the motor of the guy who shot at me. I shudder, but I breathe. He's gone now, but he knows I'm in the Keys. I can't let my guard down.

I stand, and the bartender shoves a damp-looking microwaved burger at me. "That'll be five hundred dollars, please."

What about the code of the bartender? "I'll give you six. Three now, three when I check out tomorrow morning, unharmed. Deal?"

The bartender nods. He breaks off a crumb of the bun before handing the burger to me. The crumb, he holds up to the cage over the bar. The bird! "The nice man wants to share with you, baby."

"What kind of bird is that?" I ask. Now that I can look at the bird, and my teeth aren't chattering, I see it's not a canary, like I thought. Rather, it's this freaky-looking thing, sort of a miniature phoenix, more gold than yellow, with long tail feathers and a plume on its head.

"It's my bird. That's what kind."

I take a bite of burger and chew it for a long time while the bartender glares at me. "It's good," I say, though it isn't. "Do you know where the desk clerk is? I want to check in."

"I happen to also be the desk clerk." The bartender turns to his one conscious customer. "Keep an eye on my bird."

He takes me to the front, where I check in using Ryan's

name and no I.D. I pay cash for the room, another two hundred, which it's totally not worth. The bartender hands me the key to room 203. "If you go out, leave the key at the desk."

So the motorcycle guy can get in my room and kill me? But I say, "I'm not going out. And can you send up some food when you start making fresh stuff?" At the look on his face, I add, "Or six o'clock, whichever comes first."

"Will do. Pleasure doing business with you."

I'll bet. He's already gotten $520 from me, with the promise of more, for the simple act of keeping his trap shut. But I head up the creaky, dusty stairs to a room where my key sticks in the rusty lock. I have to wiggle it several times, but finally, it opens. I relock it from the inside, then add the chain. It still doesn't feel safe, so I shove the bed against the door too. Then, sit on it. The room is dim gray, and I am alone with nothing to do. I slept most of the day yesterday. Now I'm wide-awake. I don't dare turn on the television or radio. I want to hear whoever might approach. I take out a notebook and start to sketch a new shoe design, but all I can see is the leather-clad biker, the bartender, the fox, and the bird I'm supposed to steal.

By three, my eyelids start to collapse under their own weight. Three hours before dinner. Guess it won't hurt to sleep, prepare for tonight. I sprawl on the bed, my feet touching the locked door.

I wake to knocking.

"I've got your dinner." It's a woman's voice, Southern accent.

"Can you just leave it there?" I ask.

"Sorry, no. Sam says you have to pay."

Pay. Like the money I've given him isn't enough to cover another bar burger. But my stomach says I need to pay it. "Hold on. I have to get dressed."

"I can vait," she says.

"What?"

"I said I'll wait." Southern accent. I'm cracking up and hearing things.

I take out a Yankees cap someone once left at Meg's shop and cover my hair. Between that and the three-day growth on my cheeks, I look different from usual. "What'd he send me to eat?"

"Uh, I think it's chicken. Chicken, fries, and slaw." Nothing to worry about. I pull the bed away from the door so I can open it.

I take a step back. The girl on the other side could be Victoriana's American sister, a beautiful, slender blonde with startling blue eyes. "Hi," she says in the same soft accent as before. "Can I put this down somewhere?"

I want to grab it from her hand. But now, that seems paranoid, cowardly, ungentlemanly. Besides, I didn't get the money out. I'm going to have to get it, and I can't very well slam the door in her face. I have to let her in.

Something nags me that she totally doesn't look like she

belongs here. But then, I don't belong here either, and here I am.

"Sure." I gesture toward the table. "I'll get my wallet. What do I owe?"

"Twenty bucks." When I glance at the plate, which holds four dry-looking chicken wings, congealed coleslaw, and a pile of fries smaller than my hand, she says, "Sorry. My uncle Sam said I had to charge a room service fee."

"That makes sense." I fumble for my wallet as she walks the plate to the table.

When she gets there, she gasps. "Shoes? You're into shoes?"

That sounds sort of weird, so I say, "Well, not exactly, 'into.'"

"But you were drawin' this one, right?" When I nod, she says, "Sorry, but my folks were in the shoe repair business in South Carolina, and sometimes I just . . ." She turns away, and I hear her throat catch as she says, "I sorta miss it."

A hot girl who knows shoe repair? What are the odds? "Why'd you leave?"

"My family fell on hard times, so they sent me to live with my rich uncle Sam."

Rich Uncle Sam? This guy?

"But I miss my family so much," she says. "Specially my big sister. She's expectin' a baby soon. I wish I could at least visit, but there's no money for bus fare, and I've got no car."

"I'm sorry. I'm away from home too. I know it's tough."

She wipes a tear. "I shouldn't be bothering you with all my stupid problems." Her arm brushes mine. "But would you mind if I look at your drawing? It reminds me of home."

"Sure. It's nothing special. Someday, I want to design really expensive shoes like Ferragamo."

"Oh, we don't have anything like that back home. I come from a small town. I never heard of anyone having shoes that cost more than forty dollars before I got here."

"'Mama always said you can tell a lot about a person by their shoes,'" I say, quoting the movie *Forrest Gump*. "'Where they're going. Where they've been.'"

She laughs. "Where you from?"

I look down at her shoes, flip-flops with no arch support at all. Something tells me to lie, even though she's so beautiful and sweet looking. "Ah, New York. I go to NYU." I think I'm old enough to pass for a college student.

"Woo! College boy! That's why you got on that Yankees cap." She starts to take it off. I shouldn't let her, but I do. She's beautiful. "You're pretty cute."

"You too." It's dawning on me that this girl, this incredibly hot girl, is interested in me. Not like Victoriana, who just wanted me for what I could do for her, but really interested.

"My name's Norina. What's yours?"

"John."

"John, you want to take me out tonight?"

I start to nod, then remember I have to stay the night. The whole night. And I need to steal the bird. Maybe I can go out with her, then come back. No. Last night, I fell into a trap. I can't chance it again. "Sorry. I really can't leave tonight."

She pouts at me, and I add, "It's not that I don't want to. I just need to get up super-early in the morning."

She shrugs. "It's okay. You don't owe me an explanation. I just . . ." She looks at my drawing again. "I felt lonely, and I thought it might be fun to be with someone."

An inspiration strikes me. "How about tomorrow? I can see you then."

With any luck, I'll be gone tomorrow, off in pursuit of the frog. But if I'm still around, it wouldn't be bad to have a good-looking girl to hang out with.

"Sure," she says. "I should get going now."

And then she leaves.

I finish the chicken and fries, leaving the gross-looking slaw. At first, I think I'll wait for Norina to come back for the plate, so I can see her again. But then I realize that would be a terrible idea. I can't resist temptation a second time. So I leave the dish outside the door. Still, I look down the hall to see if she's there. She's not. No one is.

After I eat, I turn out the lights, pull my chair up to the window, and look out. It's barely dark out, but there's not much going on. A few cars in the parking lot, and a motorcycle, but not *the* motorcycle. I see Norina bringing a bag of trash to the Dumpster. She takes out something and leaves it on a paper plate. So she's been the one feeding Todd.

She glances up toward my window, and I think she sees me despite the darkness. I pull the curtain closed over my face. When I look a second later, she's gone. I must've nodded off then, because when I look next, the cars and motorcycles are, except for one that might be Sam's or a lone guest's, all gone. Out of the window is nothing but stars. I glance at the digital clock on the table where I put the shoe drawings. Four a.m. Time to get going.

21

I take everything with me. I won't be back. I realize I cheated Sam out of his three hundred bucks. I think about leaving it, just because I'm ridiculously honest, but decide against it. I'm stealing his bird, after all. I'm going to need to use the cloak and be good and gone by the time he wakes up.

Now I wrap the cloak around me as I step outside into the hallway.

The motel is too quiet, quiet enough that every step creaks and thunders. I use the cloak to get downstairs, but not into the bar, not yet. If I'm wrong, if the fox was mistaken about the bar being empty, I want to make a quick escape. I stand outside the door. The light above it is burned out, but the moon shines bright. I see my shadow, twenty feet high. The darkness is comforting, but scary. Anyone could be out there, including the person who enchanted me yesterday.

I peer inside the bar. No one there, just like the fox said. No one but the bird. I'm either alone or as good as caught, so I flick on my flashlight and shine it on the cage. It gleams, as golden as morning. Even the bird's feathers seem like twenty-four karat. I make sure not to shine the light in the bird's eyes. I don't want to wake it.

I remember the fox's instructions: Move the bird from the golden cage to the wooden one. But why? It would be much easier to transport it in the cage it's in. Still, I remember what happened last time I didn't follow the fox's orders.

I use the cloak to wish myself inside. No tricks. When I get in, I stuff the cloak inside my backpack and shine the flashlight along the floor, searching for the wooden cage. Finally, I see it, along the far wall. It's on its side and latched. I go to open it, but the latch sticks. I pull on it. The door snaps off.

I swear under my breath. How am I going to put the bird in a broken cage? Still, I take it by its carry handle.

The handle falls off too.

How does this guy even keep the bird in this crummy cage? But maybe that's why he doesn't keep it there at night.

He switches it to the stronger cage, then uses the less flashy one by day.

I take the cage by one wooden side only to find my hand full of twigs.

I swear again.

I glance up at the bird. My eyes are used to the darkness now, so I turn off the flashlight. The bird sleeps soundly. I'm going to have to take the golden cage. What difference does it make? If the fox wants the bird out of its cage, he'll have to do it himself.

Still, in the dim half-light, it nags at me. If it's a test of worthiness, I'm unworthy. But with no other choice, I pull a bar stool up to the cage, then balance on it to reach the bird. A touch of moonlight glances off its brilliant bars. With my fingertips, I touch it.

"Squawk!"

I jump. The stool begins to sway. Just in time, I grab the bar for balance. I look up at the bird. Impossibly, he's asleep. I reach for him again.

"Squawk!"

This time, I'm expecting it, so I don't jump. But I do let go. The squawking stops, and again, the bird sleeps.

I reach for the cage a third time. The bird begins again to squawk and scream, but this time, I ignore it, removing the cage from its perch. It's heavy, but not so heavy I can't handle it. If only the dumb bird wasn't sleep-squawking in my ear.

"Shut up!" I tell it. But it doesn't. Then, above me, I hear footsteps, heavy footsteps running. I'm doomed. Norina or Uncle Sam will catch me. They'll call the cops or worse. They'll call that guy who wants to kill me. I drop the cage, just catching it with my body before it crashes to the floor. I set it down. As soon as I release it, the bird again stops squawking and goes back to sleep.

The footsteps are on the stairs now, coming closer. Too close. Whoever's coming for me has no reason to be quiet. I look around for a place to hide, but there's no way I can hide the bird or the broken wooden cage. I'm doomed.

I remember the cloak. I pull it from my backpack and throw it around myself.

I wish I was in the Dumpster with the fox. I make my wish just as a sliver of outside light hits the floor beside me.

I'm safe. Well, as safe as you can be when you're in a Dumpster just outside a place you tried to rob; I tug on the cloak.

Beside me, the fox stirs.

"Do you have it?" he demands.

"Not exactly."

"Exactly? You either have it, or you don't."

"I don't," I admit.

"Why not? Can't you follow simple instructions?" The fox sounds like my mother when I mess up.

"They weren't simple. The bird screamed its head off when I tried to move it." Again, I feel for the cloak, but something's on top of it. It's also wet.

"You tried to move it in its golden cage. Didn't you? That wasn't the bird squawking, but the cage itself. It's under alarm, so it can't be moved. That's why the bird has to be moved in the wooden cage."

"But that one broke."

"Whatever you say." He's silent a moment. I am too. We sit, smelling beer and garbage, hearing the flies around us. The food in Sam's wasn't good fresh. Rotten, it's unbearable.

Finally, the fox says, "Well?"

"Well, what?"

"Are you going to go back and get me that bird?"

"Are you crazy? If I go back, they'll catch me and put me in jail. Or call that serial killer who's stalking me."

"Well, you can't stay here. Get out of my Dumpster."

"I can't leave now."

"You can, and you will."

"Just give me a second." Again, I fumble for the cloak.

Sharp nails pierce my arm. I look, and the fox is baring its teeth at me.

"Please," I say, "I just need—"

"And I need that bird. I may be a once-human, but I am currently a fox, and right now, I'm feeling a bit rabid. Go, and don't come back without that bird."

I make a final reach for the cloak, but the fox lunges at me, and I'm forced to stumble out of the Dumpster, empty-handed.

I hear noises near the hotel entrance. I stumble around the other side, toward the street. If I can just cross it, I can escape.

Then, in the moonlight, I see a gleam of golden feathers.

"Looking for this?" Norina's voice says.

22

"What? No, um . . . I wasn't looking for anything. I was just . . ."

"Pawin' through mah Dumpster for fun?"

"No, I was . . ." *Talking to a fox?* "I guess, actually, I was looking for something. My retainer. That's it. My retainer. I left it on the plate before, when you brought me dinner."

Good. That's good. Glad her uncle wasn't the one who found me. I notice the bird and cage are both completely quiet now. Stupid bird. Still, I smile. "Guess I'll look in the morning. I'm tired." I yawn and start to walk past her. I know

I won't be here in the morning.

"You're lyin'."

"No, I'm not!"

"You weren't wearing any retainer when I brought up your food. I'd of noticed. Besides, your teeth are crooked."

She's got me there. "It's an expander." I quicken my steps. Please don't follow me.

She laughs. "What I think is, you came down to steal this here bird, and then, when you heard me coming, you used that magic cloak of yours to get outta there."

I'm almost inside, but at the words "magic cloak," I stop dead. How could she know? How did she find out?

She points at my startled face, and laughs. "Gotcha, huh?"

I rearrange my expression and manage a laugh that sounds more like a cough. "Oh yeah, you're pretty funny."

"I didn't mean funny. I mean, I figured you out. See, when I saw you the first time—when you came in the bar two days ago—I thought I was imagining things. I mean, how often do you see someone in a magic cloak?"

"Never. Magic cloaks don't exist." But I know I'm caught.

"See, I wasn't drunk like the rest of the folks there, so I saw you. But when you left, I figured that was that. Then, yesterday, you came back. I thought maybe it's fate. And just now, when I saw you pop into the garbage, I was sure."

Why did I have to go to the Dumpster? The cloak could

have taken me back to Miami. To Key West. To the South of France. I need to start planning this stuff out better. But considering I'm going to end up in jail or dead, I guess it's too late now.

"Look, I'm sorry. But you've got your uncle's bird back, so can you let me go?"

"I don't want the bird. I want something else."

"What else?" But I know what she wants. She wants the cloak, and if I have to, I'll give it to her to get free. But first, I'll talk her into giving me the bird too, in exchange.

"I want you to take me someplace with that cloak. If I'm gonna let you get away with bird-napping, I guess I won't have a job here much longer. So I want you to take me home to South Carolina."

"Take you?" She doesn't even want the cloak. She'll give me the bird, and she doesn't want the cloak back? What luck.

Strange, though, that she doesn't seem to think a magic cloak is unusual at all, or want it for herself.

I push the thought back. She's a country girl. She's nice and trusting. She just wants to go home. I can take her and be back in a few minutes to give the bird to the fox.

Victoriana warned me against letting anyone else use the cloak. But what choice do I have? I'm nabbed. Nailed. I have to go along, or I'm done for anyway. "Okay."

"You'll do it?"

"Yes, but I have to get the cloak. That's what's at the

bottom of the Dumpster. And I do need the bird."

"Ah, what the heck? Uncle Sam's been giving me less than minimum wage anyway."

"And I need some privacy," I say, because I can't very well have a conversation with a fox in front of her.

"Privacy?" Her blue eyes narrow. "How do I know you're not gonna ditch me?"

I think a second, then hand her my backpack. It's got everything in it except the clothes on my back, the money, and Meg's ring, which I keep in my pocket. "Hold on to this. It's got my I.D. in it. You could find me."

She looks down, thinking. "All right. But I'm gonna be back in five." She hands me the golden cage with the sleeping bird inside.

"Five minutes."

I have to work fast. Once Norina disappears around the corner, I run to the Dumpster, planning to bang on it to rouse the fox. But he's already out, dragging my cloak in his teeth.

"I'll take that," I say.

"And I"—he gestures his paw toward the bird—"will take that."

I glare at the bird. It's sleeping now, as before. Stupid bird. I'm glad to be rid of it. But I say, "I need some information first, and quick. She's coming back."

"Right. The frog left Key Largo. He knew he was

being pursued, so he got in a trailer that said the 'McDougal Family.'"

"How am I supposed to find that? They could be anywhere."

"It also had 'Big Pine Key National Key Deer Refuge or Bust' written in shoe polish on the windows."

"You're kidding, right?"

"Wish I was. Anyway, that was several days ago, so they should be there by now. The ranger at that park is named Wendell. He might be able to give you some information."

"You're sure? It sounds too easy."

"I don't know how easy it will be to find one frog in a huge nature preserve, but that's the information you needed. Now, give me my bird."

There's nothing to do but put it in front of him. I wonder what he wants with it. To eat it, maybe. But he only opens the cage door with his paw and plucks a single feather from the bird's tail. He closes the door back up. "You can take it back now."

"That's it?" It's hard not to scream. "You needed a feather? Why couldn't I have gotten the feather instead of spending two nights in this place and getting caught stealing?"

The fox shrugs his furry red shoulders. "It's a test of worthiness, for you and for me. If you want a princess, you have to prove yourself. However, there is one final thing you may do to show your gratitude."

"What's that?" I'm not feeling very grateful.

"You could kill me."

I hear a whoosh of a car on U.S. 1, but it passes and there's silence.

"What?" I must have heard him wrong.

But he repeats, "Kill me. I left a knife in the Dumpster. If you cut my throat, it would answer my fondest desires. I've done my best to help you. Now grant my wish to die."

"But why?" My hand's shaking, banging against the birdcage.

"I'm a man, living as a fox. Do you need another reason?"

"But maybe you'll get changed back." It doesn't make sense. Why did he need the bird's feather if he wanted to die? None of it makes sense.

"It's been a long time. I have no hope."

I can't picture myself killing a fox. I don't hunt. No one hunts in South Beach. And even when we had to dissect a virtual cat in biology class, I felt sick to my stomach. This isn't just any fox either. This is a fox who's really a man, so killing him would be like murder. I can't do it. "I'm sorry."

"It's all right." The fox turns his back on me.

"I'm sure things will work out."

"You have what you want. Now leave."

"But I didn't want to—"

"Go!"

So I do. I don't even take the bird with me. Sam will find it himself. I take my cloak and leave.

When I get around the building's side, Norina's waiting there, close enough that she could have heard. But, of course, she couldn't understand the fox. She didn't have the magical earpiece.

"Ready?" I say too cheerfully.

"Am I ever!" She grins and looks at the cloak. "How's this thing work, exactly?"

I remember not to be stupid. "Well, first, you give me my backpack."

She does. I look through it. Everything's there. "Okay, then." I pull the cloak around my shoulders, then hers. As I wrap it around both of us, I say, "What you have to do is wish where you want to go. But you need to be really specific because otherwise—"

And before I can finish my sentence, we're someplace else.

23

Whilst he was sleeping she took the cloak from his shoulders, hung it on her own, and wished herself home again.

—"The Salad"

I've never been to South Carolina before. Maybe that's why I'm having trouble visualizing it. But I kind of thought there'd be light.

There's none. No light, and hardly any air. It feels like the time when I was eight and got locked in the storage closet. Except, that time, there were at least the shoe parts, pieces of leather, something familiar. I feel around me. Nothing to my left. To my right, I feel someone. Norina. She's moved away from me.

"Norina, is that you?"

"Yes."

"Sorry. It's really dark here. Anyway, you didn't let me finish. I was going to tell you that you need to be really specific about where you want to go. Like, you can't just say you want to go to South Carolina or even just the town. That's how you end up underwater or in the middle of the street or wherever we are now. You have to wish exactly where you want to go."

"I understand." Norina's voice sounds different. Older, maybe. But things always sound different in the dark. I wonder where we are. A cave, maybe? My eyes aren't getting used to this darkness. It's darker than dark here.

"Anyway." Try to stay calm. "If you come over here, we can use the cloak again, and go exactly where you want to go. Your parents' house or something."

"That von't be necessary."

Von't? An icy chill prickles across my arms. I gather the cloak closer. That's when I realize I don't have it anymore. Norina must have grabbed it. "Norina, I think you have my . . ."

But I stop. I know there's no Norina, never was. I remember Victoriana's words: Smarter men than you have been tricked. And her description of the witch who dressed up as a village girl to cast a spell on Prince Philippe. I hear a match strike, and I know I'm in the presence of that very same witch. The darkness is because I'm underground.

A circle of light grows around her, revealing the hooked

nose and humped back of a crone. Sieglinde. She's real.

"We're not in South Carolina, are we?"

"Of course not," the crone says. "Ve are in Zalkenbourg. But it is no matter. As soon as Siegfried comes, you vill be novere at all."

"Siegfried?"

"My son, Siegfried. You have seen him, I believe. He rides a motorcycle."

Yeah. I've seen him.

"Of course, I could kill you myself, but Siegfried vishes to do the honors. He vas in grave trouble ven he failed to kill you in Miami, so I promised that I vould vait for him."

Oh. Well, as long as that's what he wants.

"Thank you for the tip about being specific, by the vay." She pulls the cloak around her. "I vish to be aboveground, in the house, in the kitchen."

She takes the candle with her when she goes, so I'm in darkness again.

24

I'm in Zalkenbourg, underground, waiting for some scary dude named Siegfried, with no cloak. I'm a dead man, and I'm not even a man yet. I'm just a kid. I think of every regret I have in the world, not saying good-bye to my mother, lying to Meg, going on this dangerous quest at all.

I hear noises, scratching. Is it Sieglinde or Siegfried? No. It's just rats. And not the helpful, talking kind either. The kind with rabies.

I'm. So. Dead.

The place smells like dirt and rot. I feel the air being

sucked from my lungs, and with the air I have left, I start praying, praying for my mother to be okay, for her to survive without me.

If I die here, no one will ever know what happened to me. I'll be like the used-to-bes, people who vanished without a trace.

I step on something small. Probably a bug. But maybe, just maybe it's the matchbook Sieglinde had.

I fall to my knees, looking for it. Light would be good. I don't find a match, though. I feel in my pocket on the impossible chance I have anything that will help me, but all I find is a ring. Meg's ring. Regret surges through my veins. I'll never give Meg's ring back.

That time I got locked in the storage closet, I panicked. I heard the door click locked behind me, and immediately, I felt my lungs collapsing, like now. I couldn't even scream, so I passed out in sheer terror. My mother found me an hour later. Meg had told her that sometimes, when we played hide-and-seek, I hid in that closet. She'd saved my life.

I'll never see Meg again.

I slide the ring onto my finger, remembering her giving it to me, for luck. I could use some luck now. I continue feeling around the room. Maybe there's a trapdoor I'm not seeing. Or maybe I'm not really underground, and there are windows. Maybe.

"Hey, where am I?"

I freeze at the voice. She's back. The witch.

"I don't know where you are." I try to keep my voice even. Maybe Siegfried's not with her. "But if you give me back my cloak, I'll—"

"Johnny?"

"Of course it's Johnny. You know it's—"

"Johnny, where are we? How'd we get here?"

The voice in the darkness doesn't sound like Sieglinde's anymore. Instead, it sounds exactly like the voice I want to hear more than any other. It sounds like Meg.

Which means it's all a lie. Maybe I've passed out again, and my airless brain is playing tricks on me. Or maybe the witch is trying a new voice.

Or maybe I'm dead.

"Johnny?" Meg's voice says.

"Stop it. You can't make me believe it's Meg."

"But it is Meg." The voice in the darkness comes closer. I shove at her, push her away. "Ow! Who else would it be?"

I flail my arms in the air, but she knows not to come close again.

"Johnny?" she says in the distance. "Who do you think it is?"

"Oh, I don't know. Maybe some ugly old crone who's getting her son, Siegfried, to come kill me?"

"What?" She laughs, and it sounds just like Meg's laugh. But Sieglinde has fooled me before. "How'd you get into this mess, Johnny? I knew when I gave you the ring, you'd prob-ably need it. I didn't think it would be so soon."

"What? What ring? How'd you know about the ring?"

"I'm the one who gave it to you, dummy. Oh, I said it was for luck. But really, I knew you'd get in a jam sometime, looking for that frog prince. And then, you'd need my help."

The room, which felt cold before, is hot now, closing in on me in all directions.

"Ha! That proves you're not Meg. Meg didn't know about the frog prince. I told her I was looking for my father."

"Who won the Alabama lottery?"

"Yes, who . . ." I stop. "How'd you know about that?"

"Because I'm Meg. That's what you told me. And I knew you were lying because there's no lottery in Alabama. My aunt lives there, and they vote on it every few years, but it never passes. Some people drive to Florida to buy a ticket, but you said he didn't do that. You said he won the Alabama lottery."

They've been watching me, I realize. Watching me with Meg, watching me talk to my mother. Maybe even with Victoriana. That explains the frog at the bed-and-breakfast. The witch was there too. She created the frog, or the illusion of him.

"Why did you lie?" she says, still using Meg's voice.

And it's Meg's voice that makes me respond, makes me have to respond. "I had to lie. I couldn't tell Meg I was looking for the frog so I could—"

"Flirt with the princess? Why couldn't you tell Meg that, Johnny?"

"Because it . . . I don't need to explain this to you."

"Because it would have hurt her feelings, right? Because she's so ugly you know no one will ever look at her the way you look at Victoriana?"

"No! That's not it. You're pretty. I mean, Meg is. I mean . . ." I don't know what I mean. I'm confused from the tightness, the lack of oxygen to my brain, the walls closing in. "Can you please just leave me? Isn't it enough that you've lured me here, that you're waiting for some guy named Siegfried to come smash my head in, without having to pretend you're Meg, my best friend in the world?"

"I *am* Meg."

"Fine. Prove it. Tell me something only Meg would know."

"Okay." The voice is small in the darkness.

"And it can't be something from the past few weeks, since Victoriana checked in."

"All right." A pause. She's thinking, and for a moment, I let myself hope. What if it is Meg? What if she's here? If she could help me get out? Meg always knows what to do.

"I thought of something," Meg's voice says.

"What?"

"Imelda Marcos was quoted as saying, 'I don't have three thousand pairs of shoes. I had one thousand sixty.'"

Imelda Marcos. She was the wife of Ferdinand Marcos, former dictator of the Philippines, long before I was born. The reason I know about her was she owned more than a thousand pairs of shoes.

Meg found that quote when we first started collecting

153

them. She got it off a website. No one else I know would have a clue who Imelda Marcos is.

"Meg!"

"Yeah, dummy. It's me."

"But how'd you get here?" Even as I say it, relief washes over me.

"The ring I gave you, the opal ring. It's magical."

"Magical?" At one time, this would have surprised me. Not now.

"My grandmother on the Murphy side was a witch. She's the one who gave me the ring. She used to make me carry it when I was little. She told me, 'If you get lost, Meggie girl, just put it on your finger.' Its power is that it makes the person who gave it to you come wherever you are."

"But you don't have any powers? I was hoping maybe you could get me out of here, or at least make some light so I can escape. Some guy named Siegfried's coming to kill me."

"So you said." I hear movement, like she's rummaging in her purse. "I can't get you out with magic, but I do have this." Her face is illuminated by a tiny flashlight, the kind you attach to your keys. "Lucky I was holding my purse when you put on the ring."

"Not so lucky. You're stuck with me because I put on the ring when I was trapped."

She shrugs. "It has some glitches, I guess. But we shouldn't waste time talking about that. We need to find a way out. Where are we anyway?"

"Zalkenbourg. It's in Europe, I guess. A witch tricked me into using my magic cloak to bring her here."

"Sorry I asked." She shines the flashlight. It's barely enough of a glow to illuminate a foot of wall, but it does its job. The floor is dirt, the walls of concrete. Shiny black bugs scurry away. No door. Meg slides the light to the ceiling.

Jackpot.

A trapdoor. I rush over to it, but even when I stand on my toes, it's too high, almost a foot above my head.

"Maybe if you get on my back, you could reach it," I say.

"But how would you get out?"

"You could go get help." Even as I say it, I know I'm lying. We're in a country I can't even spell, much less speak the language. But I know they're not looking for Meg. She wasn't the one who decided to risk her life for this stupid quest. She also wasn't the one who let the witch use her cloak. So she shouldn't get killed by Siegfried for my mistakes.

I crouch low so she can climb on my back. When she's up, I shine the flashlight onto the trapdoor and walk, piggybacking her. She pushes it and, to my surprise, it gives.

"Can you make it?" I ask as something scurries across my foot.

She reaches up. "I think so. But wait a sec."

"What?"

"Give me my ring back."

If that doesn't beat all. She's leaving me here, to die in

Europe, and she wants to make sure I don't take her ring with me. But I say, "Sure. I guess it's an heirloom, right?"

"It does come in handy sometimes."

I tug it off my finger and hand it up to her. "Hurry. You're getting heavy."

She takes it, then straightens herself on my shoulders to reach the door. I try to hold the light steady, though my hand is shaking and my back aches. Finally, Meg pushes up the trapdoor. She looks out, and I feel air. Real outside air, filling my lungs. I breathe in deep.

"Middle of nowhere," Meg says, looking out.

"Can you get up?" I turn off the flashlight, but there's still some light from the full moon, peering out through tall pines.

"I think so." She swings first one, then the other elbow onto the ground above, then pulls herself up. "Dirt. And pine needles. We're outside."

"At least you are."

She steps on my shoulder.

"Ouch!" I say as her foot lands on my cheek.

"Sorry." The foot comes back down onto my shoulder. Meg pushes herself out. "Made it. Now you."

"Huh?"

She reaches down for me. "I'll pull you out."

I draw in a hard breath. I should have known Meg wouldn't ditch me here. But when I reach up so she can pull me out, she starts to backslide into the hole. I let go.

"Get farther back, maybe."

The next time, I slip from her grip and onto the floor. A cockroach or beetle or some kind of Zalkenbourgian bug skitters across my hand. It's huge, and it makes me think of Siegfried, coming here, maybe soon. Sieglinde had the cloak after all. She only had to find him and bring him back. If he gets here and sees Meg, she'll be dead meat too.

I make a decision. "You should go."

"And leave you here? I don't think so."

"I'm the one who got into this mess. You shouldn't pay for it."

"But maybe I could—"

I don't stand up. "Look, I've got a plan. When they get here, they'll have the cloak, a magic cloak that transports you wherever you want to go. Now that I've got your flashlight, I'll be able to see them. I'll sneak up in the dark, turn on the light, and grab the cloak. So I'll wish to be someplace impossible to guess, like the football stadium, and then I'll be there. I'll hide out a while. They'll never find me."

"Oookayy." I can tell she doesn't understand. She doesn't get it about the cloak. "Look, I'll find someone who speaks English, and I'll bring them back for you."

"Okay." I think how unlikely this is, if the witch is working for the king. But I say, "You need to leave now. Please, Meg, don't let me be responsible for you getting hurt."

"I'll find someone."

"You've got a credit card in your purse, right? For

emergencies? You can buy a ticket home. And then, you can tell my mother what happened to me, so she won't wonder like with my dad."

She draws in a breath. "Oh, Johnny."

"I didn't mean it that way. I'll get back somehow."

I think I hear a sniff. "I don't know."

"I do." I make a decision. I look away from Meg's moon-lit face. Before I chicken out, I say, "Go away, Meg. They could be back any second, without warning. Just shut the door behind you so they won't know you were here. I'm not talking anymore."

I walk away, and a minute later, I hear the trapdoor thump closed.

I'm alone again, in the dark, and now it's worse because Meg was here and now she isn't. There's nothing to do but think about dying. You don't usually think about that. I mean, everyone knows they're going to die eventually. But not any time soon. The most enormous bug so far walks across my hand. I don't do anything. What does it matter?

25

We shouldn't have worried about Sieglinde catching us. She takes a long time, long enough for me to sit in the corner in the dark, thinking about all the things I've never done: I've never been on a sports team at school. I've never traveled to another country, not even Canada. I've never been in love.

I think of Meg in some dark, unknown countryside. All I know is, there were pine trees, lots of them. Lots of needles on the ground too, probably. Was she wearing shoes? Amazingly, I didn't even notice. I hope she had on sneakers, but I bet she was wearing flip-flops. Sometimes, shoes can make the difference between life and death.

Why didn't I loan Meg my shoes?

I don't want Meg to die. I want her to tell my mother what happened, so my mother won't spend the rest of her life looking for me.

She will anyway.

Then, I hear voices.

"Is dark in here," a man's voice says. "Did you bring a candle?"

"No." Sieglinde's voice. "He vill not be hard to find, though."

"Ve could go back and get vun."

"No! Do you not ever vant to finish this? I begin to think you lost him on purpose!"

"No, Mama, I did not. He—"

"Enough excuses!"

Their voices are getting closer. I've been standing in the corner, but now, I slide my shoes off and take one silent step closer. I still have Meg's flashlight in my hand.

"Vere is he?" Siegfried's voice is a whisper.

Just then, I feel a piece of fabric against my leg. It's soft, fuzzy, like velvet. The cloak!

Leaning away from the voices, I crouch and try to grab it.

"Here he is!" Sieglinde screams.

I tug at the cloak, but I can't budge it. Someone's holding the other side, or standing on it. Still, I don't let go. It's my only lifeline, my only hope.

An arm slides around my neck. It's strong, and I know it must be Siegfried's, though it's slimmer than I thought it would be. Still, I don't let go of the cloak. I think about what Sieglinde said about Siegfried losing me on purpose. Maybe if I struggle, he'll let me go. I start to squirm, pulling the cloak.

The arm clamps more tightly around my throat.

"I must not let you get away this time!" Siegfried whispers.

I have an idea. I relax, stop fighting, though I still grip the cloak's tail in one hand. With the other, I hold up Meg's flashlight.

When I stop struggling, Siegfried relaxes also.

"Vill you surrender?" he whispers.

"Never!" I shine the light in his eyes. This causes him, blinded, to loose his grip on me. But only for a second. I run at Sieglinde, who's holding the other end of the cloak. I end up on my back with a high-heel on my chest.

"Stop! Ve haf decided ve do not vant to kill you."

"I don't believe you."

"Believe vat you vill. But if you give us vat ve vant, ve vill let you go. If ve kill you, she vill only find some other stupid, lovesick boy to do her bidding. You must tell her that you haf seen the Frog Prince, that ve haf him."

"What? Do you have him?"

"That does not matter. Tell her that he is in grave danger and that she must marry Prince Volfgang if she vants to see her brother ever again. That is vat you must do."

"I can't do that."

I give the cloak a mighty tug. Siegfried's grip is back on my throat. It tightens, and I feel myself passing out, maybe dying.

And then, all of a sudden, I'm bathed in light.

26

I'm dead. That's the only explanation. I'm dead and in heaven. The grass below me is soft and sweet smelling, not pine needles or dirt. The light is a full moon, peering through gently waving tree branches, and reflected off a babbling river. A girl leans over me, stroking my hair.

"Johnny!" She collapses against me, and I feel her tears on my cheek. "Johnny!"

She knows my name. "Are you an angel?" This could work.

"Hardly."

And then, I see the girl's short, not-very-angelic hair, and I realize it's Meg. Meg saved me. I glance around, looking for Sieglinde and Siegfried, but they're not here. I see the shape of a farmhouse and a silo in the distance.

"How'd I get here?"

"The ring, silly."

"The ring?"

"If you give it to someone, and they put it on, it brings you to them. The giving is part of the magic."

I remember my anger when Meg asked for the ring back. But she had known all along she could use it to save me.

"So where are we now?" I ask. My throat still hurts from where Siegfried choked me.

Meg thinks. "I can run a mile in about eight minutes. But I think I was running faster than usual today. So we're probably about a mile and a half from where we were. We should get moving."

I glance down at her feet. Bare. She's holding her flip-flops in her hand. How did she run a mile in bare feet?

"We'd better start walking, but why don't you put my shoes on?" I say, even though I have no idea how we're going to get anywhere. We're in a strange country, no passports, no maps. We don't speak the language.

I begin to stand, but as I do, I feel something tugging.

"But then again," I say, "maybe we don't have to walk."

Because what I feel tugging is the cloak. I must have had a good grip on it when Meg brought me here, to get it away from Sieglinde.

Quickly, I wrap the cloak around Meg and me. Almost as quickly, I hear voices, dogs barking, even horses' hooves. They're closing in. They've found us.

"I wish I was in the National Key Deer Refuge on Big Pine Key."

And then, we are.

"What just happened?" Meg asks.

I blink in the light around me. It's not moonlight anymore. We're not in Zalkenbourg or even Europe. We've traveled halfway around the world like Mark Twain's lie, and judging from the position of the sun in the sky, I'd guess it's high noon in Florida.

"Magic." I pull the cloak off my shoulders. "Victoriana gave me a magic cloak. I wished to be in the National Key Deer Refuge, and now, here we are."

"Did you wish to be *here*?" Meg gestures downward.

Yes, downward. We're up in a tree. A royal poinciana, by the looks of it, which is a good thing because it's a big tree with lots of fluffy orange flowers to hide us, but a bad thing because we're forty feet up. Something buzzes over my head. I look up and see that it's actually a buzzard. It turns and starts to swoop again. I flail my arms. "Hey! We're not dead!"

"Not yet." Meg looks down. "How do we get back to the ground?"

"Wish again." But then I think of something. Norina—Sieglinde—was around the corner when I talked to the fox.

165

At the time, I assumed she couldn't understand his words, so she wouldn't know where I was going. That was before I knew Norina was a witch, though. What if she did understand the fox? "We should make sure we're not being followed first."

"Wait here, you mean? Up here?"

"Just a few minutes. That way, if someone's chasing us, they might not see us up here, but we could see them."

As Meg thinks about this, a swarm of blue butterflies rises up from some red flowers and flies across our noses. "Okay. It's really pretty up here." Her brown eyes scan the horizon of bright sky and emerald wilderness. "Besides, we can talk."

"Talk?" Suddenly, the sun seems too hot for sitting. "Talk about what?"

The buzzard makes another loop. I make a grab for Meg.

"Ohhh, I don't know." Meg shifts closer on the branch we're now sharing. "Maybe you can tell me why you lied about where you were going."

This is what I was afraid of. I search for a good excuse.

Found one. "I couldn't tell you. Princess Victoriana swore me to secrecy." But now that the secret's out, I tell Meg about the Frog Prince, Victoriana looking for her brother, the magic earbuds, the fox, and the golden bird. "She's worried about the press."

"And you thought I, your best friend, would sell you out to *Inside Edition*?"

Okay, not such a good excuse after all.

"Of course not. But I just told her I wouldn't tell anyone. Besides, I knew you wouldn't approve."

"Why wouldn't I approve?"

Because, of course, I didn't tell her the whole story. Meg doesn't know the part about Princess Victoriana saying she'd marry me if I found her brother.

"Because you don't like Victoriana." Which is true also.

Meg shrugs. "Why'd you do it?"

"I don't know. She offered me money. And the adventure, I guess."

"You enjoy being chased by witches?"

"Until last week, I didn't know there were witches, or enchanted foxes or talking swans. You never told me that your grandmother was a witch," I add pointedly. "Today, I was in another country. Okay, I was only there an hour and I was trapped in a dungeon, but still. Every day I work in the hotel, and I see people from all over. Some of them are from boring places, and they travel around selling rope or bowling balls. But at least they've been to those places. I never go anywhere but school, the hotel, and if I'm lucky, the beach."

"I go to those places too."

"Yeah, but you've been to New York at least. I've never been farther than Disney World. So when Victoriana made me this offer, I figured it would be an opportunity to see things I'd never seen before—which is just about everything."

167

A hot breeze ripples across the branches. I decide to look around. Below is a canopy of green with blue stretching out in the distance. I inhale the fishy odor of mangroves. The branches shake, almost like a child shivering. I look down, afraid of falling.

Below, I see a deer, nosing through the underbrush. I've never seen a deer before, except in the zoo. This one is smaller than those deer, about the size of a Labrador. "Look."

Meg nods. "It's a Key deer. They're an endangered species."

The deer raises her head, maybe sensing us, and sniffs the air. Then she turns and, without further dawdling, disappears into the underbrush. I sigh. "At least, I saw that one."

We sit, silent, the comfortable way only good friends can sit. Meg's breathing and mine and the rustling of leaves below us all blend into one song. Other than that, there's silence. I can see the Overseas Highway in the distance, but I can't hear the cars. Only air and birds and Meg, leaning close to rest her arm against mine.

Finally, Meg says, "We could go to New York, you know. We could go wherever you want, Europe, anywhere. We wouldn't even need a passport with that cloak."

I don't know if she's trying to be sympathetic or if she wants to keep me away from my mission of finding the frog, away from Victoriana. Either way, I shake my head. "I should probably get back to work. I don't think Sieglinde and Siegfried are here. Maybe they have to use commercial airlines to get back. That would explain why Sieglinde tricked me into using the cloak to get to Zalkenbourg."

"My witch grandmother couldn't travel magically. She didn't even have a broom."

Good to know. "So maybe I have a day or two before they catch up with me. I'll take you back with the cloak, but then, I need to get started."

Meg's lips twitch. "You want to dump me off at the hotel?"

"Sure. What else? You've got work and stuff."

"I guess." She looks up, squinting in the sunlight. "I was just thinking maybe I could help you. This summer's been pretty boring for me too."

"Help me? How?"

"Well, I already did help you once, didn't I? You'd be dead if I hadn't shown up."

That's true. Suddenly, it seems like a good idea, having Meg along, not being alone.

"It would be cool to have an adventure," Meg says.

"Tell you what," I say, knowing that by saying it, I'm agreeing to take her with me. "Next time we get in trouble, we'll throw the cloak around us and wish like crazy to be in New York."

She grins. "Deal."

"Only we have to wish to be someplace specific. Otherwise, we'll end up in the middle of Fifth Avenue or something."

"We could wish to be in a theater seat."

"An *unoccupied* theater seat," I amend.

"Or, better yet, the top of the Empire State Building."

I picture myself, clutching the spire like King Kong in the movie. "The observation deck of the Empire State Building."

"Agreed," Meg says, "but for now, we should wish to be on the ground, under this tree."

"Exactly under it, no tricks."

So I wrap the cloak around both of us, and we wish.

27

"Ralph Waldo Emerson said, 'Few people know how to take a walk. The qualifications are endurance, plain clothes, old shoes, an eye for nature, good humor, vast curiosity, good speech, good silence, and nothing too much.'" I say this to Meg as we trudge down the path to the ranger station. I'd thought about wishing us there, but if Sieglinde heard me talking to Todd, she might be waiting. Besides, it's a nice day, and I should get the lay of the land, maybe even look for the frog. Of course, in miles of unkempt brush, it will be hard to find him.

"I was wondering when the shoes were going to come

in," Meg says. "I couldn't believe you'd have a quote without shoes."

"All the good quotes have shoes," I assure her. "And Emerson was right. Shoes are important." I glance at the old Nikes I brought for the trip, then at Meg's flip-flops. "Yours aren't so good."

"'I still have my feet on the ground,'" she says. "'I just wear better shoes.' Oprah Winfrey said that." But she grimaces. "I *am* getting a blister. Maybe we can pop back home sometime and get my sneakers."

"Can you manage for now?"

"Yeah. I think I should give you this, though." She holds out the opal ring. "In case we get separated again."

So I take it, and we trudge closer to the ranger station. There's tall grass on all sides of us, and the mangrove odor gets stronger as the path becomes more sand than dirt. The bright heat radiates up, stinging my eyes. I want to fish my sunglasses out of my backpack, but I know Meg has none, so I squint in solidarity. Every few minutes, a large bird blocks the sun, and for an instant, there's relief before the beating heat returns. There are no clouds.

"Can we sit a minute?" Meg asks after a while.

We amble toward a tree stump and squeeze onto opposite sides of it. While Meg examines her blisters, I watch the sky. It's the same bright blue as home, but the birds are different. Here, each bird is at least as big as a cat—spoonbills, ibises, herons of different colors, white, pink, blue, and gray, but with the same angular wings and long necks. They remind me of swans. I promised to help the swans find their sister. Right now, I can't even help myself.

"Do you have a picture of the frog?" Meg asks.

"Sure." I unzip my backpack and shuffle through it, but the first photo I find isn't the frog. It's one of the prince.

"Who's that?" Meg says.

"That's the prince, before he was a frog."

She reaches for the photo. "Wow, he's hot."

"You think? He has that birthmark thing on his fore-head." But I can see he's good-looking, with an athletic build, probably from playing some princely sport like polo.

"I'd kiss him back into princedom anytime," Meg says.

I find the picture of the frog and stick it on top of the prince photo real quick, before Meg can drool anymore. "Yeah, well, this is what you're looking for anyway. A frog. Not a guy."

"Got it." She examines the picture, then switches it with the other one. "Mind if I keep this one in my backpack for a while? He is soooo hot."

I shake my head. "Fine. If you like goofy playboys."

"Guess I do—just like you like rich, drunk princesses." She tucks the photo into her purse. And then the sun is, once again, clouded by a giant shape. I glance up.

A turkey vulture. I point it out.

Then a rare breeze tickles my nose, bringing with it an odor.

"Do you smell that?" I ask Meg.

She nods. "Mangroves. They smell like an open cesspool, but they're pretty."

I shake my head. "Not mangroves. Something's dead, something big."

Something makes me stand up and follow the smell off the path and through the grass, even though it slaps my face and scratches my arms. For long moments, it's lost in the sweeter aroma of the ocean, and I wonder if I'm wrong, if it's mangroves after all. I hope so because the stench I smelled was bigger than a possum or a squirrel could make. What I smelled could have been human.

But just as I'm about to chalk it up to mangroves, I smell it again. I push through the tall grass, holding my breath against the stink. Then I see it.

I exhale in relief. I go back to Meg.

"It's just a deer," I say. Because now that I know what it is, I realize what I'd been worried about. I was afraid it was the prince.

"Who would kill a deer in a deer refuge?" Meg asks. "That's just wrong."

Good point. We decide to tell the ranger—if we ever find him.

Going through the razor-sharp grass has left me with stinging cuts on my arms and legs. Meg reaches for my backpack. "Got anything useful in there, like sunglasses or socks or a first-aid kit?"

I nod sheepishly. "I didn't want to wear the glasses, since you didn't have any."

"How about this?" she says, pulling out the glasses. "I'll wear them, but I'll do something about your cuts."

When Meg says that, I remember the swan. She held it, and he got better. Did Meg heal him, somehow? Does she have witch skills after all? But she pulls out the first-aid kit, swabs the cuts with Neosporin, then covers them with Band-Aids. They feel a little better, but not healed. Okay, I'm just crazy. Meg puts a Band-Aid on her own blister too.

Soon, we see people, hikers and beachgoers. Then, we reach the ranger station.

28

"We're looking for the ranger," I tell the lady at the information desk.

"I can help you." She glances at the door behind her, which says RANGER'S OFFICE. "What do you need? Maps? Guidebooks? Tour information?" She hands me one of each, glancing again at the door. "There you go."

"Um, thanks." I take them from her. "But I really want to speak to the ranger."

"He's not here. Maybe another day. Or next week." She reaches into a drawer and hands me a sticker that says I BRAKE

FOR KEY DEER. "Here. Have a bumper sticker."

This isn't good. I need the ranger now. "Is he on a trail?"

"Margaret?" says a voice from the office. "Have you reached the National Guard yet?"

Margaret turns and cracks open the door, then whispers, "They're not coming."

"Not coming! Why not?"

"Shh." Margaret looks back at me. "They don't believe you. Say it's urban legend."

"The National Guard doesn't believe me?" The voice is even louder. "Let them come over here and look around. See if they think it's an urban legend when they're staring it in the face."

Margaret glances back at me again, then whispers into the door. "Wendell, I've been telling these nice young people how the ranger isn't in today."

Wendell! That's the name the fox gave me.

"Look," I say. "I know that's the ranger. I'm not leaving until I talk to him."

I'm not usually pushy like this, but being trapped underground makes you bold.

"I can call the police," Margaret says.

"And tell them what? That I'm in a national park, expecting to speak to a ranger, but the ranger can't talk to me because he's hiding in his office? Yeah, I'm sure they'll arrest me."

Meg puts her hand on my shoulder. "Let us speak to Wendell. Then we'll leave."

"I'm afraid I can't."

"It's okay, Margaret." The door opens. "They're all going to find out anyway."

The ranger is a short, balding man in a brown uniform with shorts. His scalp is sunburned and peeling. What's left of his hair is unkempt. He looks like he's gotten less sleep than I have. He gestures us into his office.

"All right," he says when we get in. "Where'd you see it?"

"See what?"

"You're here to report a dead Key deer, aren't you?"

"Yes. I mean, no. I mean, we did see a deer, but that's not why we're here."

"So you found another one? Another one?"

He bursts into tears, and not some manlike tears either, where you pretend you're brushing something off your face and, incidentally, wipe a tear. Nope. He starts bawling like a kid who spilled his Slushie, clutching his head. Finally, he sits down and begins rocking back and forth, saying, "Ruined. It's all ruined."

Margaret walks behind him and strokes his back. When he keeps saying, "Ruined," she puts her arms around him.

"There, there." She glares at me. "See what you did?"

"What I did?" I don't understand. What's the big deal? "I just said . . ."

"This is a Key deer refuge."

"I know. So?"

"So someone is killing the Key deer. That's a problem."

"Not some*one*," Wendell says. "Some*thing*. *Things*. Monsters. There are monsters. It's all ruined. No one believes me."

"There, there," Margaret repeats. "It will be all right."

"I'm a good ranger. When I was a kid, I was a science wiz, and my parents thought I should be a doctor. But noooooo. I wanted to save the planet. Now I'll be singlehandedly responsible for the demise of a species."

He starts to sob again, harder, and his words after that are indistinguishable from his sobs. I look at Meg. She shrugs but starts toward him.

"Excuse me," she says. "May I change the subject?"

Wendell lets out a mighty sniff, then drags it in again. "Ch-change the s-subject?"

Meg nods. "Just for a moment."

"You want to change the subject?" Another sniff.

"Yes. If it's not too much trouble."

"No . . . no. I'd love to change the subject." He looks at Meg with red-rimmed eyes and running nose. "What s-subject did you want to discuss?" Another sniff.

Meg gestures at Margaret. "Maybe you could get him a tissue."

Margaret notices the snot dripping from Wendell's nose, sighs, and stands. "All right. But I'll have to go to the supply closet. He used up the last box. Don't you upset him."

"How could he be any more upset?"

"You haven't seen him when he really gets going."

When she leaves, Meg says, "We're looking for a frog."

"A frog."

Meg gestures toward my bag, for me to show the ranger the photo. I already have it out. "This is him. Have you seen him?"

The ranger glances at the photo, and I see recognition in his eyes. He's seen that frog.

But he says, "I don't think so."

"It would have come into the park with a family, a trailer with kids."

"You can't have the frog!" Wendell says.

"So you do have it?" I say.

Wendell thinks a second, then makes a decision. "Yes. And I'm not giving it back. I took it away from those kids who brought it in. It's a nonnative species."

"It's from Aloria."

"Exactly. It's a rare Alorian marine frog, and it has no business being in a national park in the United States. I may go down in history as the ranger who was in charge when the Key deer died off. I'm not also going to be the one who befouled the ecosystem by introducing a European frog."

"What?" I'm completely confused.

But Meg chimes in. "You never did pay attention in science class, Johnny. What he's saying is, when people bring in animals that don't belong here, the animals can escape and damage the environment. Like those little turtles kids get as pets."

"Right!" Ranger Wendell says. "Red-eared sliders. Noxious beasts!"

"People release them in canals," Meg says, "and they reproduce and eat all the food."

"Starving out the native species and destroying the food chain." Wendell nods his head up and down. "Not on my watch!"

"Or the Burmese pythons," Meg adds.

Wendell shudders. "Don't even get me started on pythons. They grow and grow until their owners can't handle them. So they release them."

"And then, it's good-bye house cats," Meg says.

"Exactly."

"So let me understand," I say. "You took the frog away from a family because you wanted to make sure they didn't release it in the park?"

"Yes. It was my duty as a ranger."

"And what did you do with it then?" This is exciting. Maybe he still has it.

He falters. "Well, um, with a nonnative species, the proper response is to euthanize it."

"Euthanize!" Meg and I both exclaim at once. We look at each other. He killed the frog? He killed the prince?

"You . . . euthanized it . . . him?" I say.

"I know it sounds cruel, but our ecosystem is more

important than any one—"

"Where's the frog?" I'm in his face, screaming. "Where's the frog, you murderer?"

"Johnny." Meg's at my shoulder, pulling me away. "Let him answer."

"But he killed the frog. He murdered—"

"I didn't euthanize the frog, okay?" Wendell whispers.

"You didn't kill him?"

He looks around, then whispers, "No, okay? I was supposed to euthanize the frog, but ranger salaries being what they are and all . . ."

"You sold it?" Meg says.

"Not yet. But I've . . ." He looks around again, then walks to the window, glances out, and comes back. "I've listed it for sale with a certain reptile and amphibian collectors' site."

"You took it from kids so you could sell it?"

"It was best for the ecosystem. If I sell it to someone in a colder climate, there will be no risk of its living if it's accidentally released."

"What a jerk," I say.

"This is good news, Johnny. It means he still has the frog."

She's right. "Great. I'll buy it from you for a thousand dollars."

I see Wendell's eyes light up at the number. Then they narrow. "I can't do that. It has to go to a less hospitable climate. I can't sell it to anyone from Florida."

I'm starting to get upset again when Meg says, "Ooooh, we're not from Florida. We're from Minnesota, dontcha know. We'll take it back there."

"How do I know you're not from the Environmental Protection Agency?"

"We're kids!" I need that frog. I can't let him get killed or sent to a "less hospitable climate" to freeze to death. I start looking around. "Is he here?"

"If you're kids, why do you want the frog so much?"

Meg shrugs. "We just like frogs."

"Right. Two high school students have a thousand dollars to spend because they just like frogs. You don't look rich."

I'm getting a headache. The frog is in the park, maybe in this building. He could be in a box, suffocating or something. "Listen, I need that frog."

"No. Get out of here!"

"If you don't give it to me, I'll call the EPA."

"That won't get you your frog. I don't have it anyway."

"Johnny," Meg interrupts. "You should tell him why we really want the frog."

I gape at her. Does she mean tell him the *real* reason? "He'll think we're crazy."

Meg shrugs. "If we're crazy, he'll know we're not from the EPA or the cops. It's a frog. Why would he care if he's selling it to a crazy person?"

She has a point. We have nothing to lose. If he doesn't give me the frog, I'll use the cloak to break in tonight and steal it. But I'd rather not. I don't like stealing. Besides, the last time I stole livestock, I ended up underground in Zalkenbourg.

So I tell him.

29

In the forest lived two giants who had caused great mischief.
—"The Valiant Tailor"

"You expect me to believe that?" Wendell says when I'm finished.

I sigh. "I know it sounds crazy, magic and all that."

"Oh, it's not the magic part I'm having trouble with. I believe in magic."

"You do?"

"Yes. I didn't used to. But I couldn't *not* believe in magic now. I'm being plagued with magical creatures myself."

I think of the dead Key deer. Does he mean they're being killed by magic?

"The part I don't believe is a princess choosing a little wimp like you for her quest."

"Excuse me?"

"Oh, don't act all shocked with me. I went to high school. I know how it is. There are the jock boys, and the rich kids. They're the ones with all the power. And then, at the bottom of the ladder, are people like us. The losers."

Losers. It's what I've always thought, always suspected others were thinking about me. But to have this guy say it is just too much.

"He's not a loser," Meg says. "He's on the wrestling team at school."

"Wrestling?" I think of those guys on *Friday Night Smackdown*. But when Meg gives me a dirty look, I say, "Yeah, wrestling. State champ, hundred-sixty-five-pound division." I have no idea if there's a hundred-sixty-five-pound division. What am I talking about?

"Hundred-sixty-five-pound division, eh?" Wendell says.

"They call him David because he fights guys bigger than him, like David and Goliath in the Bible," Meg says. "Once, he stopped the football team from beating up a freshman."

"The football team?" Wendell looks at me with new respect. "He fought the whole football team, the linebacker and everything?"

"Yup." I'm getting into this now. Teach this guy to call me a loser. I'm a hero—of *biblical* proportions. "One guy weighed over three hundred pounds. I had him begging for mercy."

"So you can fight giants?" Wendell's practically jumping up and down now.

"Giants?" Sure. Whatever. "If there were giants, I could probably fight them. I'm a hero, after all."

"So, can we have the frog now?" Meg says.

"I have money," I add, "so name your price for the frog."

Wendell stares out the window.

"Wendell?" Meg says. "Your price?"

"Yeah." I reach for my backpack. "A grand for a frog is fair."

Nothing.

"Wendell?" Meg waves her hand in front of his face. "Johnny wants to give you *money* for the *frog.*"

"Money? Oh, I don't want money." Back to the window.

What's this guy's problem? But then, I think I know. "We promise not to release him. No siree. This frog's going right back to Aloria. In fact, he's human. Humans can't be a nonnative species, can they?"

"That's not it." Wendell walks away from the window and starts rummaging through his desk. I want that frog. Who knows if he's even feeding him right, if he has enough air. Prince Philippe could be starving to death because he refuses to eat bugs.

Wendell pulls a pair of binoculars from his desk. He

walks back to the window and starts looking through them like he's trying to locate something, Finally, he gestures to me. "Look."

I peer through them. Grass. Tall grass. And sand. In the sand is a big hole. A Key deer sniffs around it, looking for water.

"So? It's a hole?"

"Look around the edges," Wendell says.

Now I see that the hole has an elongated shape, like a foot. And at the end of the foot . . . toes! It's a footprint. A footprint almost as big as a Key deer. Who would have such a big foot?

Wendell reads my thoughts. "We've been beset by giants."

"Um . . . giants?"

"Yes, giants. Plagued by giants, two of them, which is two too many. That's what's eating the deer, and no one— not the EPA, the Monroe County police, the Sierra Club, or the National Guard—believe me."

I glance at the footprint again. Giants. There's no such thing. And then, I remember my mother telling me a legend about a giant in the Florida Keys, like the Abominable Snowman or the Loch Ness Monster. I never believed it, of course. But back then, I didn't believe in witches or talking animals or magic cloaks either.

"You believe me, don't you?" Ranger Wendell says.

I nod.

"And I know you can help me. You can kill them."

"Sure, I can . . . what?" I tear my eyes away from the binoculars and stare at him.

"What?" Meg says at the same time.

"You can kill giants." Wendell's all happy, smiling now. "You're young. You're strong. You were chosen by the princess to accomplish her quest. You have experience defeating the mighty, so I know you can help me with my little, er, giant problem."

"But . . ."

"Kill the giants, and you get the frog. Otherwise, I put him on eBay, and I won't sell him to you."

"That may be against eBay policy," I tell him. "You could get banned."

"Think I care if I get banned from eBay?"

And then he starts to cry again.

Between sobs, he says, "If I don't do something about these giants, all the deer will die, and I'll be responsible."

Meg reaches over and pats his back. I look at her, incredulous. "Have you tried showing photos of the footprints to the EPA?" she asks. "Or photos of the giants?"

He nods. "They all think they're fake, like the Loch Ness photo." He opens his desk and pulls out two photos. They're blurry, and the giants are mostly obscured by trees. They do look fake. "People have been spreading rumors about giants in Florida for years. Skunk apes, they're called. No one believes it. If I push it, I could lose my job."

They say you shouldn't judge a man unless you've walked a mile in his shoes. I glance down at Wendell's shoes, no-name hiking boots so worn down I wouldn't want to walk a step in them. This man has a *giant* problem.

I hear Meg saying, "We need to see the frog if we're even going to think about fighting the giants."

Wendell raises his tear-stained face. "I have him right here." He walks over to a tank that has a bunch of toads and frogs. He reaches in, takes out a wet, croaking frog not nearly as big as the one I saw on Key Largo. "Meet the *Alorius marinus*."

The frog pees on his hand. He doesn't wince.

It has a reddish orange spot and the family birthmark. It's the prince. No doubt about it. But Wendell holds it away from me. If I could just grab it . . . I pull my backpack up and out from my shoulders, intent on getting the cloak. If I can get the cloak and the frog, and . . .

Meg. I need to get Meg too.

In that one second of hesitation, Wendell sees what I'm thinking. "Oh no, you don't." He pulls away the frog. "Trying to take it, were you?"

"He was just trying to get this." Meg holds up the earbuds.

"Headphones?" Wendell clutches the frog so tightly I worry he'll crush him. "Unlikely."

"These are special ones that let me talk to him—if he's the right frog. Try them."

Wendell tries, using only one hand, to get the earbuds in his ears. I don't offer to help. I have the cloak now, Meg poised beside me. If Wendell drops the frog, we grab it.

He doesn't though. He gets the earbuds in, then looks at me. "Now what?"

"Say hello. See if he understands you."

Wendell tilts his head toward the frog. "Hey, little guy. How goes it? Flies good?"

The frog lets out a massive croak that blows back Wendell's hair and causes us all to jump. Wendell pulls out the earbuds.

"What'd he say?" I ask.

"He called me a not very nice name."

"He doesn't like being held captive. You should give him to me."

"He doesn't like the *food* here, and I'll give him to you when you kill those giants."

I hold out my hand. "Let me talk to him."

I hope he'll hand me the frog or, at least, put him down. He only gives me the earbuds. I slip them in, still looking for my opportunity, and lean real close to the frog.

"Victoriana sent me," I whisper.

The frog doesn't respond for a second. When he does, he says, "Victoriana? What do you know of Victoriana?"

"She's staying at the hotel where I work in South Beach. She sent me to—"

"My sister is a heartless party girl who would no sooner

concern herself about family zan wear cloze from ze thrift shop."

"That's not true." I remember Victoriana's anguish.

"No. Zat *ees* true. If you say Victoriana sent you, zen you are a trick. You are send by ze witch to kill me."

"I'm here to save you. Tonight . . ." I stop myself before I say I'm going to come back tonight and steal him. "I'm going to kill some giants. After that, I'll be back."

The frog practically jumps from Wendell's hand. "I spit in your face—*Pfft!*" He lets out a fountain of frog spittle. "I will escape. I will be a free frog!"

"How will you find a girl to kiss you if you run, er, hop away?"

The frog's bulging eyes roll up. "Oh, I haf my ways. Even in zis warty skin, I haf my charms. I haf made ze plan. When a family comes wiz a teenage daughter, I will go wiz zem."

"Whatever. I'll come back for you later. Tomorrow, after I've killed the giants."

"And I will be gone, Zalkenbourgian infidel!" The frog spits again, but this time, I'm able to get out of the way before he hits me.

"Oooookayyy," I say.

"What'd he tell you?" Meg asks.

"He's pretty angry," I say.

Wendell drops the frog back into the tank, where he croaks in protest. Since I still have in the earbuds, I know he's expressing his opinion of us and our mothers in a French accent and, eventually, in French. I remove the earbuds.

"Now what?" Wendell asks.

"I guess we'll camp here. We need supplies." I try and think what I'd need if I was actually going to kill a giant. "Those binoculars, for one thing, and um, some stuff for a trap."

"How will you make a trap for giants?" Wendell wants to know. "Take a box and stick and hope the giants wander in? That would have to be some box."

"It's none of your business how I'm going to do it. You haven't done it."

"Don't belittle him." Meg rubs my shoulders. "He knows what he's doing."

"Just tell me where they are," I say.

Wendell tells us the giants like to hang out in a stand of large trees where they're mostly hidden. Then we leave.

30

When we get a suitable distance away, Meg throws her arms around me. "Oh, Johnny, I'm sorry I got you into that. I had no idea . . ."

"It's okay. I'm not killing any giants."

She laughs. "I sort of figured you had a plan. What is it?"

"We disappear for the day, pretend we're staking it all out, then come back at night and steal the frog."

"Disappear? Where to?"

I think about it. "We should set up the tent, to make it look good. Then maybe we could go back to the hotel and get you some decent shoes, in case we need to make a quick getaway."

She looks down at her flip-flops. "I messed you up, didn't I? You'd have just grabbed the frog and left if it hadn't been for me. Are you sure you want me along?"

"Sure. You already saved my life once. Besides, I like having you around."

"You do?" She looks surprised.

"Of course. You're my best friend."

"Oh." She looks away quickly and starts walking faster. "Oh, of course."

We walk in silence. I wonder if there really could be giants. I have no reason to believe there aren't. But if there are, I want to avoid them. "Let's check this place out."

We reach a tall tree. Meg nudges me. "Maybe we should use the cloak to get up."

"No. This one's not tall enough."

"It's pretty tall. How do you know?"

"A person's foot's about fifteen percent of his height. So a five-foot-tall woman has about a nine-inch foot. Those footprints were about one and a half feet long, judging from the way they looked next to the Key deer. So the giants were roughly ten feet tall. We need a tree twice as tall as that, so they won't see us."

"Wow, that's really smart."

I feel myself flush and look to see if she's joking. No one ever says I'm smart. Usually, the adjectives people come up with are words like "nice," "reliable," or "sweet," words you'd use to describe a yellow Lab or an economy car. Even Victoriana called me a good boy. But Meg doesn't seem to be goofing. Okay, being called smart isn't like being called hot, but it's way better than reliable.

So I say, "Thanks."

We walk until we find a taller tree. Then, we wish ourselves into it. The wind's picked up, and the sun is higher. It burns my eyes, so I shield them, squinting off into the distance. When I do, I see something totally unthinkable.

"Look," I whisper.

"I see it." But when I glance at her, she's facing the opposite direction.

I pull out Wendell's binoculars. A giant. Two giants because what Meg's looking at is the other one. I see them through the viewfinder, hunting through the brush.

"No way I'm spending the night out here," I say.

"Nuh-uh," Meg agrees.

But we decide to pretend we're going to, to satisfy Wendell. So I say, "We'd better pitch the tent before they get closer. You stay here in the tree. If you call, I'll come up with the cloak."

"Shouldn't I help?"

"No."

"Why not?"

"Ummm . . ." I shake my head. I was going to say I didn't want her to put herself in danger. But Meg won't like that. She's not some girly girl like Victoriana, who wants a guy to protect her. So I say, "We need a lookout."

"Okay, but hurry."

I wish myself down and start to pitch the tent. Finally, I finish, and I'm staking it when I hear Meg. "Johnny!"

Her voice is hoarse, like she's been yelling for a while. She gestures frantically to her left. The giant is close enough that I can see the dark hair covering much of his body, his only clothing the hide of an enormous animal tied at the waist. His face is dirty and stained with deer's blood. I think of the line in "Jack and the Beanstalk": "I'll grind your bones to make my bread." He could easily, though he seems like more of a meat eater than a carb guy. He steps toward me. Stay calm. We had a plan. Get the cloak. But when I reach for it, it's not there. I look around and finally spot it a few feet away. Now the other giant's advancing. I know he sees me because there's a gleam in his eye. I think he has only one— the other is gouged out and sealed shut.

No time to think. I grab at the cloak, but it's caught on a branch. The one-eyed giant is walking faster now. I smell a powerful nasty odor, like rotten eggs, skunk spray, and human feces. The stench alone would kill a deer. The ground shakes. I tug at the cloak. It holds fast. Above me, Meg's yelling, "I'm coming down! I'll distract him!"

"No!" The scream rips at me as I pull. Footsteps boom. I tug harder. *Please, please don't come down, Meg.* The giant is so close I can see it has full lips the color and texture of a dog's paw pad, and very sharp teeth. I yank the cloak. It gives way with a rip just as the closer giant reaches toward me. I wrap the tattered fabric around my shoulders. "I wish I was in the tree with Meg."

And then, I'm beside her. She didn't come down.

"You're safe!" she says, and I can see she's been crying. But the giants have seen us. The one-eyed giant has reached the tree. He pushes it, making it swing harder than any wind. The smell is so overpowering that even when I breathe through my mouth, I can taste it. I lose my grip on Meg and grab the branch. The giant butts his head against the tree.

Now the other giant's there too. We're doomed. I try to spread the cloak around both of us, but a gust of wind takes it off Meg's shoulders.

"Just wish yourself away," Meg says. "At least one of us should live."

"Not an option."

The second giant rams the tree. I know any second, they'll start acting together, shaking it back and forth. One might even crawl on the other's back and climb toward us.

But something else happens. The one-eyed giant sees the other giant. He lets out a roar and runs toward him. They both hit the tree, and it sways back and forth. By then, they're on the ground, fighting each other like two kids tussling over the last cookie. They roll away from the tree, and in that second, I'm able to wrap the tiniest scrap of cloak around both our shoulders. Over the giants' roars, I wish to be the first place I can think of.

And then, I'm there.

31

"Where are we?" Meg looks around. "I feel like I've been here, but . . ."

I grab the cloak from around our shoulders and start to fold it before anyone sees it. It smells much better here. "We're in Penn Station."

"Penn Station?"

"New York City? When you went last year, you told me people were all over this place like PETA members at a fur convention, so I figured it might be a place where they wouldn't notice two kids crash-landing dressed as the Phantom of the Opera."

And truly, they don't notice. A professor type in a tan jacket seems to stare right at us, then turns and buries his face in a newspaper. A gangsta-looking guy does a double take, then turns away, saying into his cell phone, "I gotta call you back. I don't feel so good," and rubs his eyes. A guy toting a bass knocks into me. I start to say, "Excuse me," but he yells at me in another language.

I turn to Meg. "Guess I was right. We need to kill some time before tonight. So maybe we should see the sights. Like, go to the Statue of Liberty. My great-grandparents came in through Ellis Island."

Meg accepts this pretty readily. "Should we take the subway or use the cloak?"

In an instant, we're in the statue's torch. It's not open to the public, so it's empty, and we stare down. From the torch, we can see the top of the statue's crown, the bridge of her nose, and down her pretty green size-two-thousand dress to the star of the pedestal.

"Look," I say to Meg. "The book in her hand has a date on it. July, then some Roman numerals . . ." I squint to see them.

"July fourth, seventeen seventy-six," Meg says. "The date of the Declaration of Independence."

A moment later, she points at the bay. "You can see the shadows of the clouds. They look like continents."

I grip the railing and lean down. Meg's right. They do look like continents.

200

"We were in Europe today," I say. "And now we're in New York. How surreal is that?"

"Real surreal," she agrees.

I could be with Victoriana, traveling with her and seeing these things. She's probably seen it all, done it all, been everywhere.

Meg grabs my hand. "This is so exciting, Johnny. Thank you for letting me come."

I feel suddenly dizzy at the height. But I grip Meg's hand, and she squeezes back. I feel better. "I'm glad you're here." And I am.

After we've had our fill, we switch to the pedestal. As in the train station, people see us when we land, but as before, they sort of don't. A kid crashes into us. "Hey, I didn't see you." His mother yells at him to be careful, completely oblivious.

I wonder if people at home would react the same way, if I would. Have I ever seen anything strange and unusual—and magical—but just ignored it because I didn't believe what my eyes were telling me? I've been hearing stories about giants and yeti and Sasquatch all my life, but who believed them? Maybe it's all real—the Loch Ness Monster, UFOs, everything. Maybe the crazy people are the only ones who know the truth. If human beings can transform into swans, what *can't* happen?

"Are you glad you know that magic is real?" Meg says, reading my thoughts.

"I am," I say, "even though people would think I was on drugs if I told them."

She shrugs. "I wouldn't, even if I wasn't here." And I know it's true. She'd believe me because she's my best friend.

After we look up my great-grandparents on the monument at the Ellis Island Museum, we go to the Museum of Natural History and find the dinosaurs. Then, it's off to the Central Park Zoo.

It's there that Meg asks me about the earphones. "I didn't know you had those things. Can you talk to this guy?" She points to the polar bear in his environment.

"No." I hesitate. "I mean, maybe. It only works on animals who used to be human."

"Are there a lot of those?"

"More than you'd think." I tell her about the swans in the lobby, the rat at the Port of Miami, and the fox.

"No way. The swans? Seriously?"

"Totally serious."

She takes the earbuds from me and leans forward. "Hey! Hellooo! Mr. Bear?"

The bear swims slowly around, and Meg adds, "Maybe after this is over, we'll go to the North Pole together. We should see the bears while they're still there."

I nod, even though I know it won't happen. I'll be with Victoriana.

We wander around awhile longer, looking at animals,

trying to talk to them (none talk back), and eating zoo food until finally they announce they're closing.

I look at my watch. Six. "There's still time. I don't want to go back too early."

"I hear New York pizza's good. And then, maybe the top of the Empire State Building."

An hour later, we're there. We don't use the cloak. I wanted to feel what it's like to be in the elevator, zooming up 102 floors. We can see Central Park on one side, all the way to New Jersey on the other.

Meg points at something down below. "Look at that!"

"What?" The street in one place is painted white.

"That's where the Thanksgiving Day Parade is."

"Wow. From up here, it looks even smaller than on TV."

Meg climbs onto one of the telescope things. "It's like being a bird." She spreads her arms and stands straight, the waning sun behind her, wind ruffling her short hair. She looks wild and suddenly beautiful, not like the girl I'm used to. She rotates so she's facing the street.

I grab her hand. "Watch out!"

"For what?" She gestures at the chain-link fence that comes up over the wall, to keep anyone from jumping, I guess. "It's completely safe."

"You could trip."

She laughs. "Only if I was a klutz, or drunk." She holds out her other hand, the one I'm not already holding. "Come on up. You can see better."

I do, and I can, far above the wall. I wobble a bit, and Meg steadies me, her hand on my waist. It reminds me of when we played together as kids, all the times she was more mature, more of a girl. I straighten up, and for a second, we are nose to nose, with only the wind between us. I can feel my heartbeat, or maybe it's Meg's.

"Do you remember," Meg says, "when I asked you to take me to the eighth-grade dance to make Ben Abercrombie jealous?"

I look down. The people and cars below are so small, like toys. "Sure."

"You know, Ben asked me to that dance."

I look at her, and her short hair flutters around her face like brown butterflies. "Huh?"

"He asked me, but I said no because I was going with you."

I laugh. "You never told me that. I'd have understood if you'd canceled on me to go with your dream guy. You were so hot for him."

"No, you don't get it. Ben asked me *before* I asked you. I told him I couldn't go with him because I was going with you."

I shake my head. "Okay, I'm confused. So you used me as an excuse to get out of going with him?"

"No." She drops my hand and moves away. "Never mind. It was stupid."

I remember that dance, three years ago. Meg got her hair done at the hotel salon, and she wore a black lace dress that made her look grown-up and glamorous. Ben Abercrombie glared at us the whole night. I'd congratulated Meg on making him stew. But there was one moment on the dance floor when I was holding her, and I forgot I was there to make Ben jealous. I'd wanted to kiss her.

I look at Meg and understand. I could have. And it would all have changed.

She steps down. "We need to get going."

"No, wait."

The sun is setting, and down below, the lights of Manhattan, which are always up, seem brighter against the gray semidusk. From here, you can only hear the horns and the people on the ground if you really concentrate, and I don't. I don't want to think about anything but where I am, who I'm with. I don't know whether it's that I don't want to leave, or that I want to stay, but I grab Meg's elbow, pull her toward me, and help her up. She leans against me, head against my shoulders, and in that second, I know, against the lights and the bright and the heat and the gray, I really want to kiss her.

No, I don't. Me? Kiss Meg? I can't. I want lots of things. Money. Adventure. Victoriana—a princess, for God's sake. I want more than I've always had.

Don't I?

And yet, Meg's in my arms, like she was that night at

the dance, and for more than an instant, I think *this* is what I want.

I lean closer. "I wish we could stay here."

"Why can't we?" Meg leans closer too.

"Excuse me? Are you using that?" Below us, a man and a little girl gaze up at us. "My kid wants to see. Can you find someplace else to make out?"

"Oh, sure." I don't even correct him about the making-out part. But, in that second, I'm glad for the interruption. Kissing Meg would have been a big mistake. It would change everything, things I don't want to change.

I step down and hold out my hand to her. "You're right. We should go."

All the way down two elevators, Meg doesn't look at me. Is she mad at me because I almost kissed her? Or is she mad at me because I didn't? In any case, I violated some boundary between us, so now I have to earn back her trust.

So when we reach the bottom, I say, "Sorry."

"For what?" She still doesn't look at me.

"For ki . . . your friendship means a lot to me, Meg. More than almost anything. I wouldn't want to do anything to mess us up."

She looks down at the marble floor, tracing the alternating marble squares with her toe.

Finally, she sighs. "No, me neither."

"Do you want to go now?" I don't want to leave yet, not with her mad at me. And also, I want today, this day, to last longer. Victoriana's beautiful, and rich, and I promised her I'd find her brother, that I'd marry her. But once I do, it will never be the same, being with Meg again like this, being a kid. Am I making a huge mistake? I wanted my life to change, but now that I'm on the verge of it, I'm frightened.

As long as I stay here, I don't have to decide.

So when Meg says, "Let's walk a little," I'm happy to.

We walk toward Times Square because that's where the lights and horns and taxis and people are all converging. Darkness has fallen now, but it's hard to tell because it's so bright with red and pink and green and gold, all combining to make the sky look still blue, or maybe it's because the buildings are so high you can't see the sky anyway. We nudge past a crowd looking at a mostly naked guy in a cowboy hat playing a guitar. Horns honk. Traffic whooshes.

Above us are lit-up signs and letters scrolling a news headline.

And suddenly, they say something I can't ignore.

PLAYGIRL PRINCESS TO MARRY ZALKENBOURGIAN HEIR

Victoriana! She's marrying Wolfgang! The cat torturer.

She's marrying him. But why? I did all this work, stayed in the bed-and-breakfast, got sick, stole a bird, all so she wouldn't marry him.

"She said she was marrying me," I say before I remember Meg's there.

"What?"

"Nothing. We need to go."

Then she sees the scrolling news too, and I see her face registering that she understood what I said. "Marry you?"

"We've got to go." Before she can protest, I wrap the cloak around us. Compared to the Naked Cowboy, we might as well be invisible.

And then, in a second, we're back at the park in Florida.

32

I land outside in case Ranger Wendell is still there. But everything's dark, still. It's almost too perfect. I hear voices, people singing campfire songs far away. And crickets.

And Meg's voice.

"You were going to *marry* Victoriana?" She pulls away. Against the night, I can see her silhouette. Even in the darkness, her shoulders look angry.

"I can explain."

"Oh, can you?" The shadow's hands move to her hips. "Go ahead."

"Can we talk later, maybe? After I get the frog?" *After I think of an excuse.*

"Were you planning on telling me?"

I don't have an answer. "I wish I was in the ranger station."

And then, I am.

It's even darker in here, but more silent, which is good. I find Wendell's office. The door's locked, but I wish myself onto the other side, then walk to the desk where the tank was. I leave the light out but crack open the curtain to allow in a sliver of moonlight. I don't look out, don't want to see Meg, still waiting there, angry. The tank gleams like a hidden diamond. I run my hand along its smooth, glass side, up to the top. I remove the cover and stick my hand in.

Sharp pain sears through my finger, then my whole hand. Something bit me. Hard. Frogs don't have teeth, do they? I pull out my hand and flip on the light switch. No one's here. When my eyes adjust, I peer into the tank.

Scorpions. The whole tank is crawling with them. I've been bitten by a scorpion. And, not only that, but the frog isn't even here.

My hand is burning like it's cut in two. I glance back into the tank. He must be there, hidden behind something. He couldn't have run away.

Then I see a sheet of memo paper. I squint at the writing, but a scorpion's on it.

My hand throbs, pounds. I wish I could cut it off. It feels

like it's twice its usual size, and now the pain spreads to my arm, my torso, my head. My tongue feels like it's swelling in my mouth. My legs hurt so, they can't support me. My field of vision narrows to one red dot. My knees buckle. I'm on the floor.

In my last conscious act, I use my left hand to pull out Meg's ring. Bring Meg to me. Then, with my thumb and middle fingers, I barely push it onto my left pinky. The red dot gets smaller. Then the pain overwhelms me.

33

It's dark, and I hear rain, very close rain. My hand doesn't hurt anymore. I hold up my arm, wondering if the hand is missing. I wiggle the fingers. Am I dead? Do I feel better because I'm feeling no pain? No. At least, I don't think so.

"You're awake." The voice in the darkness startles me. Then, a circle of light, a flashlight. My eyes readjust, and I see I'm in a tent. With Meg. Meg!

She holds up a sheet of paper. "Wendell knew you'd try to steal the frog."

I take the paper in my hand (which feels totally fine). It says:

The frog stays with me until you kill the giants. No tricks.

"But how'd you get the note?" I examine my hand.

"I took it out of the tank, of course."

"But the scorpions—"

"No big. Not all scorpions are poisonous. And if you're friendly with them and don't just stick your hand in and disturb them, they don't bite."

I turn my hand. A dime-size, red, C-shaped scar is the only sign of trauma. Is it possible a nonpoisonous scorpion bit me? Then, why did it hurt so much?

But I feel fine now.

"Well, that's that," Meg says. "You can't kill the giants, so I guess it's over."

She turns her face away as she says it, and I suspect she's smiling. She can't stand Victoriana, and she's furious at me for . . .

It's all coming back to me. She knows I agreed to marry the princess. She hates me.

Still, I say, "Guess you're right."

But when I think of it, all of it, Victoriana marrying Prince Wolfgang, me and Mom, losing the business, me maybe having to work as a shoe-shop boy the rest of my life, I can't handle it. I turn away, trying to keep my face out of the circle of flashlight.

Outside is silent. Even the campfire singing has ended, and I wonder how much time has passed. Not even a cricket or cicada chirps.

Meg breaks it. "What is it, Johnny?"

"It's over."

"Your quest? Your adventure? Yeah, I think so."

"It wasn't just an adventure. It's . . . everything."

"What do you mean?"

I don't want to talk to her. I want to curl up in a ball and sleep for all the days I haven't slept, sleep until the giants come back and stomp on me, and I won't even notice because I'm sleeping so soundly. I want to sleep like a little kid who falls asleep in front of the television and wakes the next morning, in bed, not even knowing or caring how he got there. I want to forget. But I have no time. I tell Meg about Mom and me and our debt.

"Marrying Victoriana was a way out. I can't afford college. We might not even be able to keep the business open much longer."

"So you want to marry her for the money?"

I hesitate before saying, "Yeah."

But my face must betray that it wouldn't exactly be torture because Meg says, "Oh, it's because she's hot."

"It's mostly the money. It just doesn't hurt that she's hot. And she's nicer than people think. But I'm seventeen, so I wouldn't want to marry anyone if it wasn't for the money. The money would fix everything."

I examine my hand. It's fixed too, amazingly fixed. Before, I'd have sworn it was the size of a bowling ball. Even the small bite mark seems almost gone. I'm still wearing Meg's ring, the ring that brought her to my rescue.

Now I hand it back to her.

"I have to find the frog," I tell her. "I made a promise. I can't let Victoriana marry Prince Wolfgang. He'll kill her, and it would be on my head. And I can't let Mom lose her business either, not without trying everything."

"You've already been trapped in a dungeon and bitten by a scorpion. Now you want to be eaten by giants?"

"That's a chance I'll have to take." I start to stand. It's surprisingly easy. I look around for the cloak. Except it's not there. It's missing. I look at Meg. "Give it back."

"Give what back?"

"You know."

Meg purses her lips, thinking.

"Come on, Meg. You're not being fair. I've made my decision."

Meg's silent a moment longer before saying, "You're right. I can't stop you. But I can make you wait. If we're going to fight giants, we should get a full night's sleep."

"We? Did you say we? You're staying?"

"I can't let you get killed. Your mother would be miserable. I'll take the cloak and get in the tree. If I see one coming, I'll put on the ring and bring you to me."

"And what will I be doing while you're in the tree?"

She stares directly into my eyes, then places her hand on my forehead and strokes it lightly. Her hands are cool, and my eyes start to shut.

"Sleep," she whispers. "Sleep."

34

Just you wait here. I will finish off the giants by myself.
—"The Valiant Tailor"

I wake to the angry beeping of my cell phone, which is out of batteries. I switch it off. There's no reception here anyway, and Meg called her mother from New York City.

It's eight in the morning, and I wonder if Meg's been in the tree all night. I look out the tent and see the cloak. Meg must have thrown it down. I wish myself into the tree, next to her, even though I still don't know why she's staying with me. She's leaning against a branch, resting her head in her hand, staring at the tent. "Oh!"

"Did I frighten you?" I ask.

At first, she looks like she's not going to answer me, and I remember she's angry. But then, she gestures downward. "It's a pretty scary scene, isn't it?"

From the tree, I survey the damage on the ground below. The giants were here, if not last night, then during the day. Everything is ransacked. A Styrofoam cooler I bought is crushed like a peanut in the hands of an impatient kid. Shoes, clothes are everywhere. The food is gone, wrappers strewn like seaweed across the dirt, hanging from the weeds.

Nearby, the grass and pine needles are mottled down in what is unmistakably the shape of four giant legs and two giant rear ends. Maybe they thought we'd come back, so they could eat us.

Meg peers through Wendell's binoculars.

"Any sign of them?" I ask.

She shakes her head and hands them to me.

I look and see nothing, even far off in the distance. "Maybe we should go down," I say.

"Are you sure you want to do this?"

I don't want to answer her, so I pretend I don't hear her. I wish.

I land in a leg print more than three times the size of one of my own legs. I could lie down comfortably in each of the giant rear end prints (not that I'd want to).

"Only a giant could kill something this big," I say.

Meg's examining a handprint the size of a puddle, but when I say that, she stops. "You know, you're right." She grins, happy I'm giving up, I guess.

"Don't gloat."

"Gloat? Who's gloating? I have an idea."

An hour later, we return from Winn-Dixie, toting five whole turkeys, some rope, and a bag of rocks. We gathered the rocks on the walk there, but we used the cloak to get back. Turkeys are heavy. Now we're prepared.

"'Between saying and doing,'" I say, "'many a pair of shoes is worn out.'"

"Who said that?" Meg asks.

"I'm not sure."

Meg sits lookout in the tree while I arrange everything. I know the traps I discussed with Wendell won't work, but this one just might. I take the turkeys and place them inside the tent. I open the wrappers to give the giants the scent. When it's all ready, I take the bag of rocks and go high into the tree, where Meg's scanning the horizon.

"Nothing so far?" I ask.

Meg shakes her head. "They'll be here, though. They're looking for food. They know we're camping here, and based on experience, they know you're slower and easier to catch than a Key deer."

"Gee, thanks. Nothing yet?"

She shakes her head. I imagine what it would be like to be a deer or a mouse, something chased and preyed upon all the time. These past few days, I've felt like that. After a while, you must get good at hiding. Either that or you get dead.

It makes my life seem pretty easy.

Meg lowers her binoculars. "Have you ever thought of how it would be, being married to Victoriana? Like, what would you do all day?"

I say, "I guess I'll have no problems. I'll hang with Victoriana."

"And what? Make out all day? Sounds like a good life—if you're Ryan. But I always thought you wanted to accomplish something."

"I can't accomplish anything now. If I was married to Victoriana, I could still design shoes. I just wouldn't have to repair them. I wouldn't have to scrounge for materials either. I could be one of those celebrities who has a hobby like writing children's books or releasing albums of my songs." But I see her point. I remember Victoriana, led around by body-guards, having to hide in bathrooms to get a moment alone, to put on a façade so the press doesn't know what she's really like. It could be hard to have things that easy.

And I'd miss Meg.

"Maybe you could come visit sometime," I say.

She sniffs. "I don't think I'll have time."

Neither of us speaks for a while after that, Meg scanning the treetops with the binoculars, me doing the same with my bare eyes. Gradually, the sun turns the sky red and orange, pink and gold, as if one of the giants has used a paintbrush on it.

"Ho-hum," I say. "Should have brought a deck of cards."

"We could play Four Truths and a Lie."

"What's that?" I shift in the tree.

"It's where you say five things about yourself, and the other person has to guess which one is false."

"But that would be too easy. We've been friends forever."

Meg's shadow moves in, staring at me. "Sometimes, people have secrets, even from their closest friends, things you'd have thought they'd tell you, since you're such a good friend."

I get it. I didn't tell her how bad our finances were, and I didn't tell her about Victoriana either. I say, "Okay. Why not? I'll go first."

I try to think of something tricky, but it's hard. Finally, I say, "My first kiss was with Jennifer Garcia in seventh grade."

"Jennifer? Eww." Meg holds her nose.

"She's pretty."

"Pretty mean. I hope that's the lie."

It isn't. I go on. "I haven't seen or heard from my father since I was two. One day, he just disappeared. Three: I sent a secret admirer valentine to Hailey Feinberg in eighth grade."

"That was you?"

"Yep . . . I mean, maybe. I mean . . . four: I got an A on my trig final. Five: I stole a bag of chips out of your backpack yesterday."

"I knew that was what happened to them." Meg slaps my shoulder.

"See? There's no way to fool you."

"I bet I can fool you."

"Okay, so which one was the lie?"

"I'm hoping it was Jennifer, but I'm pretty sure it was the trig final. No way you aced that. I only got a B, and I'm smarter than you."

"Are not . . . okay, you got me. Now you go."

She thinks a minute, then says, "All right. One: I do one hundred percent of the cleaning in my family's business."

That's true. Her mother is old, and her brothers are complete bums.

"Two: I have a box of ashes from when I burned the letters Andrew gave me."

Andrew. Her ex. Total jerk. He dumped her for another girl, and I can totally see Meg doing that. "You should toss them. He's so not worth it."

"Three: My family buys some of the pastries we sell as homemade."

"You do?"

"Yeah."

"Four: I can't whistle."

I know she can't. I've heard her try. I'm about to say this, but then, she says, dramatically, "And five: I am secretly, madly in love with you."

"Aha! That's obviously the lie. You made it too easy."

She chuckles. "Yeah, I guess we can't fool each other."

And then, in the distance, I see something moving.

Something big. I tap Meg on the shoulder and point.

"Do you see them?"

I point again to the moving spot, then up at her binoculars. She twists her body, shoulders making contact with mine, and looks. Then she hands the binoculars to me.

It's a giant, barely visible among the slash pines. He's heading toward us. But just one? That will be a problem.

Then, behind him, I spy the second. I exhale and realize I've been holding my breath. The two giants walk like hunters, slow and surprisingly silent. Sunset is the time when most wildlife comes out. It's also the time when I bet they're most hungry, most in need of a kill. I remember the deer carcasses and hope we don't end up like that. I tighten the cloak around us. We may need it for a quick escape.

Finally, they're close enough that I can hear footsteps. The front one—the one with the missing eye—emerges from the trees. He gazes first to one side, then the other. He looks hungry.

A step closer. Then another. The second giant, the one who chased me, emerges from the brush too. He crouches, as if he's listening to the ground. I sit, frozen, the binoculars clutched in my hand. My fingers ache from holding them up so long. Yet, I don't dare change position. They're too close.

The front giant stops walking then, sniffs the air. I don't know if what he's smelling is the turkeys, or us. He glances back at the other giant, then speeds his own step. *Boom. Boom.* I understand by the fact that he doesn't signal to the other giant, that he doesn't want to share. This is what Meg suspected when we saw them fighting before, what we counted on. The two-eyed giant sees his companion running and speeds up too. I hold my breath, not daring to look at Meg, but I can tell from the stillness in the air that she's holding her breath too.

The two-eyed giant gives a mighty sniff, then a roar. It takes me an instant to realize that the roar is his massive stomach growling.

And then, he pounces. In a swift movement for someone so large, he's lifted the tent and obliterated it. He seizes one turkey and holds it up. It's a big turkey, almost as big as his head, too large to swallow whole. He has some trouble with the wrapper, but finally, he undoes it and rips apart the cavity. He removes the organs and swallows them, bag and all. A huge drumstick is next. He rips the meat off with his teeth like Ryan eating a Buffalo chicken wing, then spits out the bone.

Meanwhile, One-Eye has arrived. He seizes a turkey. Two-Eye tries to push him away, but One-Eye pushes back and starts to eat. Two-Eye must decide it's easier to share because he goes back to his turkey. The wings are next, then the breast. He displays the wishbone like a child at Thanksgiving, then drops it.

It takes no more than two minutes. When he's finished, he seizes a second turkey and starts to annihilate that one. One-Eye does too. All we can hear is crunching bones and the tearing of flesh.

Finally, Two-Eye finishes the second turkey. He reaches for the last only to find something in his way. One-Eye. One-Eye still has bones and flesh hanging from his mouth, but he's not about to give up the last turkey. He pulls but only rips off a drumstick. Two-Eye laughs in triumph. One-Eye growls in rage. He crouches and launches himself at his companion. The other falls, striking his head on the tree we're in. It shakes and bends, and we grab on. I see Meg beside me, mouth frozen mid-shriek. We don't want them to see us and decide we're bigger food. My hand comes down on hers, and we hang on.

Two-Eye seizes a huge coral rock. Holding it in both hands, he runs at his companion. One-Eye screams right before he gets bashed on the head. He's knocked to the ground, bleeding. Two-Eye clobbers him again, and I can tell he's down for good.

Two-Eye, now alone, grabs the turkey from the giant's limp fingers. He does a dance of triumph until he trips on a giant outstretched leg. With a mighty crash, he rockets to the ground, his head hitting the same rock that felled his companion.

He moves no more.

35

Meg and I stare down at the giants. Neither stirs. I mouth, "Dead?"

"Check," Meg mouths.

We use the cloak to move to the ground. I tiptoe, eyes low to avoid slipping on any innards. I feel light breathing, like an industrial fan on high. Not dead, just out cold. The boulder they used lies nearby. I could finish them off with two good bashes, but I can't. They're human beings, really big, smelly ones. I can't kill anyone.

And who knows? Maybe they're under a curse themselves.

Maybe they're guys with families like Cornelius.

It had been Meg's idea to have the giants take each other out. Our plan had been to throw pebbles from the tree as they slept off their turkey dinner, until, each thinking it was the other, they'd get into a fight. I didn't think it would work, but I went along because I had no better ideas. I'd been the one who thought of buying an odd number of turkeys, though.

"I'm going to tie them up," I whisper. "Wendell can decide what to do with them. I'll take you up the tree. Then I'll go back with the cloak."

Meg thinks about it, then says, "I'll help you with them."

"No. This is my quest, my danger. Besides, you're the brains of this operation, and I'm the brawn."

Meg smirks. "Some brawn." But I wish us back into the tree, take the cloak, and go before she can argue more.

When I get back down, I decide to start with the legs. That way, if the giants wake, they won't be able to run. I wind the rope around four legs the size of a cord of wood, around and around, over and under. I use every knot I ever learned in Boy Scouts. It's hard to concentrate with the smell.

I do the same with the arms, then walk around tugging the rope to make sure it's tight. When I'm completely satisfied, I get Meg, and we take a picture with her cell phone.

"Let's go tell Wendell," I say.

When we reach his office, he says, "I know you tried to

steal the frog. Be glad the scorpion didn't bite you."

He gestures toward the tank and the sign on it that reads:

Androctonus australis: Yellow fat-tailed scorpion
Warning: Deadly to humans

I look at Meg. "But it bit me. How could—"

"Must not have been much of a bite." She gestures toward Wendell. "Something you want to tell him?"

Other than thanks for siccing a poisonous scorpion on me? Not really. But I say, "The giants are all tied up in the woods. I'll take my frog now."

The ranger starts a little. "Tied up? You were supposed to kill them."

I prepared for this. "Look, if I'd killed those giants, it would have been murder. You'd have solicited murder, which last time I looked, was a crime. It would be pretty hard to hide bodies that big. I knocked them out and tied them up." I leave out the part about how the giants did it themselves. "You can call the police or the EPA, and they'll believe you. You can give them to the Barnum and Bailey Circus if you want."

Wendell thinks about it, then says, "But that wasn't our deal. Our deal was to kill them, so I don't see why I should give you the frog." He rises from his chair and opens the door. "It's been a pleasure doing business with you."

I cannot believe this. After all I did, this jerk won't give me the frog? I feel my hands itching and know that's what it feels like when you really want to hit someone. But I'm no tough guy, like Meg says, so I take a bunch of deep breaths. Doesn't help.

Meg's voice interrupts my thoughts. "Okay, Johnny, so let's just untie them, and we'll leave."

Wendell stops. "Untie them?"

"Well, yeah. You didn't want them tied up. This way, you can find someone else to kill them. Come on, Johnny. They should be close to waking now. Dusk is when they feed."

I laugh. "Okay. Let's go. You have the scissors?"

"Right in my backpack." We start toward the door.

"Wait!" Wendell runs around and blocks our way. "You can't untie them."

"Watch me." I start to shoulder past him.

"Okay, okay. Maybe I was a little hasty. You can have the frog. Just show me the giants in person."

"Gladly." But when we start toward the door, I see something that makes me stop.

It's the tank on Margaret's information desk. It says, *Alorian Marine Frog.*

The top of the tank is open.

The tank is empty.

I grab Meg's arm and point. She looks from my face to the tank. Back at my face. She starts toward Wendell. "Excuse me? Ranger?"

"What?"

"Did you put the frog someplace special for safekeeping?"

Wendell turns. "Yes, it's right over on Margaret's . . ." His face freezes, and I know. The frog was supposed to be in that tank. If he's not, it's because he's dodging traffic, hopping down the Overseas Highway or worse, kidnapped by the Zalkenbourgians.

Wendell's talking or, at least, moving his lips. But I can't hear him above the sound of my own voice in my head, saying, *It's over. It's over.* I'm floundering through blackness, and I grab the only thing I can touch. Wendell.

"What have you done with him? Where is he?" My head may explode.

"I d-don't . . ." Wendell's stammering. "I can't . . . he was here. I took him home, but I brought him back this morning." He's looking at the floor, the shelves, under Margaret's desk. Nothing.

"He's not here, you idiot!"

I feel Meg's hand on my arm, trying to calm me.

"Did you see anyone?" she's asking Margaret. "A woman, very beautiful, with long, blond hair, or a man, six-five at least." She eases me away from Wendell, and I cling to her instead.

Margaret, who has her hand on the phone about to call the police, says, "No one like that."

"How about . . ." Now, I remember the prince's words,

Ze first family wiz a teenage girl. "Any young girls, young women?"

Margaret looks at Wendell. He nods. "Well, there was one family from Ohio."

Hope slowly flutters one eyelid, not completely dead yet.

"They had a sixteen-year-old daughter. She was looking at the frog, thought he was cute."

"Are they still in the park?" At this point, I would have absolutely no problem with attacking a sixteen-year-old Ohio girl and wrestling the frog from her hands.

But Margaret shakes her head. "Nope. They were leaving. Just stopped by to get souvenirs and sign the guest register."

I run over to the guest register. It's summer, crowded, and there's almost a page of entries for today. But only one from Ohio.

Debi and Rob Stephen, Tessa, and Rob, Jr.,
  Columbus, OH.

Under comments, it says

A great place to stop on the way to Key West!

Key West! They're on their way to Key West. Now all I have to do is go to Key West and . . . oh, boy.

I have to check every hotel in Key West.

And while I'm there, I also promised to look for the swans' sister.

Hope lies down, saying it feels too tired to move on.

"Were they camping?" Meg asks.

230

Good question. There are fewer campgrounds than hotels.

But Margaret shakes her head. "No, but they had a mini-van. White, I think."

Well, that narrows it right down. Every third car is a mini-van, and half are white.

Meg tries to pump her for more information, but the only thing she remembers is, "Red hair. The girl had lovely, long red hair."

"Well, then, I guess we should go to Key West and look for a girl with long red hair." Meg holds out her hand and leads me to the door.

Once outside, I say, "It's no use. How can we find one frog in all of Key West?"

"Guess we just start south and head north."

So we wish ourselves to the Southernmost Point.

36

That which you have promised, must you perform.
　　　　　　　　　　　　—"The Frog Prince"

"Ever play Frogger?" I ask Meg. "It's this old game Mom used to play when she was a kid, and last year, she bought it for me."

"Yeah, what about it?"

"It looks sort of easy, but it isn't. You have to guide your frog across the highway, and there are cars and trucks coming from every direction. Bicycles too. And just when you think you made it, you have to guide your frog across a pond on logs, and he drowns."

"So you're saying our frog is like that?"

"I'm saying *I'm* like that. I've dodged traffic. I've gone underwater, and I'm still dodging stuff. I can't believe you're still here with me. *Why* are you still here with me?"

She shrugs. "I've never been to Key West before."

The Southernmost Point is nothing but a big, striped cylinder that looks like a black beer can against the blue waves behind it, where everyone crowds around to take pictures. On it is writing that says, "Conch Republic: 90 Miles to Cuba." We stand, watching the water as it laps hungrily at the cement-covered land and thinking about what to do.

"'Wynken, Blynken, and Nod, one night, sailed off in a wooden shoe,'" Meg recites. But I shake my head. I'm not in the mood to think of shoe quotes. We start down Duval Street.

Jimmy Buffett's song about changes in latitude, changes in attitude streams from the doorway of a shop completely devoted to chickens. I keep my eyes out for red-haired girls or white minivans, but almost everyone's on foot. Meg makes me stop to put a quarter in a donation can that says, "Save the Chickens."

The first motel we see is called Eros and advertises a clothing-optional Jacuzzi. "We can probably skip that one," Meg says. "Doesn't sound like a family establishment."

"You never know," I say, sort of wanting to look in. "Some people are free spirits."

We compromise by checking the parking lot.

"Wastin' away again in Margaritaville," sings Jimmy

Buffett as we walk toward the house where Ernest Hemingway, the famous writer, lived. That reminds me of the swans Jimmy, Ernest, and Margarita, all named after Key West things. I promised the swans I'd look for their sister, Caroline, here. But no time now.

We're about to pass the house when I see a girl about my age with copper-colored hair. She's inside the gates, so I yell, "Tessa? Are you Tessa from Ohio?"

She stares like I might be a stalker, but I say, "Are you?"

"Nope. I'm Hailey from South Carolina." Her accent is unmistakable.

I scan every crowd, every tour bus and ask at the desk of each hotel. We crisscross the streets that intersect Duval. Nothing. When we pass Harry Truman's winter home, I feel another pang, thinking of Harry the swan and his brother, Truman. We pass bars crowded with tourists wearing nothing more than string bikinis and walk by T-shirt shops and nudist hotels. I approach every redhead and almost get beat up twice. I keep my backpack unzipped so I can whip out the cloak. It's almost sunset when we reach the other end of Duval Street.

"We should go there." Meg points to the sign that says MALLORY SQUARE. "Everyone comes here because it's the best place to watch the sunset. Maybe you'll find your redhead."

I nod, even though I suspect Meg just wants to watch the sunset. Girls love stuff like that. Still, Meg's right. It's crowded. There's a good chance our Ohio tourists are here.

Mallory. That was the last swan.

The square is mobbed. A man with nipple rings eats fire on a small stage, and another man does flips on stilts. Vendors sell your-name-on-a-grain-of-rice necklaces. There are at least ten redheads in sight. I start toward one.

"Let me." Meg approaches the girl. "Tessa?"

She turns, and I feel a sudden leap of hope. But then, I see she's at least thirty.

"Sorry," Meg says. "Thought you were someone else."

Over and over, Meg repeats this process, and each time, it's the wrong girl. I say, "We should leave."

"No." Meg's voice is patient, but her eyes are steely. "I've camped with you, gone without food, unwrapped slimy turkeys, watched giants wrestle, pulled you out when you got bitten by a scorpion, and spent several hours I'll never get back listening to you talk about Princess Perfect. But sometimes, Johnny, you have to stop and watch the sunset. If you really think those fifteen minutes are going to make a big difference, go on without me. Here. Take the ring." She hands it to me. "If you need me, you have it. Otherwise, see you later."

And then, she turns toward the sun-reddened ocean, and I know she's not going to move.

For about a second, I think about leaving, but I know she's right. It won't matter. We've been to thirty hotels. We can go to more later, and hopefully, the Stephen family will stay more than one night. I say, "Sure. Let's watch the sunset."

I've seen many sunsets on South Beach, and they're beautiful. But the one at Mallory Square is different. Maybe it's the latitude or something about the atmosphere. Or maybe, like Jimmy Buffett says, it's the attitude, taking the time out to watch it, but the sun seems redder here. It streaks the sky not just orange and pink, but purple and gold too. Meg reaches for my hand, and I take it. The crowd around has grown silent. There's little movement except the triangles of sailboats bobbing up and down against the blue. Light streams off the water, turning the world into a painting instead of a corny vacation postcard.

"Here's a story I heard once," Meg says. "Madame Pompadour, she was this lady in the court of Louis the Fifteenth."

"Everyone knows that." Even though I didn't.

"Anyway, she loved fashion, and one day, a shoemaker delivered the most gorgeous pair of silk shoes. Of course, she was delighted. But on the first day, she took only a few steps, and they fell to pieces. Furious, she sent for the shoemaker. When he saw the wreck of his beautiful shoes, he spread out his hands and said, 'But Madame, you must have walked in them.'"

"Ha! That's a good one. What made you think of it?"

"Oh, I don't know. Seems like a lot of people want shoes they can't walk in."

I know she's not talking about real shoes. She's talking about me and Victoriana. But when I look at her, she won't

meet my eyes. Behind us, a guy with a guitar begins singing "Brown-Eyed Girl." I think of the Empire State Building
yesterday, when I almost kissed Meg. She's been my best
friend my whole life. We do homework together. She models
my shoes and listens when I ramble about my dreams. Isn't
that love? The sky is a strange shade of lavender, and I lean
toward Meg.

And then, out of the corner of my eye, I see her.
Sieglinde. She's pretty again, like she was when she was
Norina, but a little different. Still, I know it's her, and she's
scanning the crowds, looking for something. Does she know
about the redhead? No. Her eyes are downcast, like she's
looking for the frog. She knows he's here. If she sees me, it
will be a disaster. She might take me hostage again, so she
can pump me for information. She might take Meg. I won't
let her take Meg.

I tug on the cloak in my backpack, then wrap it
around us.

Meg looks startled. "What are you . . . ?"

I don't have time to explain. I whisper the first place I
can think of. "I wish I was in the Key West cemetery."

An instant later, I'm sitting on a crypt that says:

I TOLD YOU I WAS SICK

B. P. ROBERTS

MAY 17, 1929–JUNE 18, 1979

Meg looks at it and laughs. "Always an adventure." She squeezes my hand under the cloak. "Why are we here, exactly?"

"I saw her."

"Tessa. I thought you wanted—"

"Not Tessa. *Her.* Sieglinde. I saw her at Mallory Square. She knows the frog is here. I had to get us away."

Meg glances around. The cemetery is almost empty, probably because everyone's at Mallory Square. Crumbling tombstones, some more than a hundred years old, surround us. In one corner are mausoleums, those sort of big, above-ground houses for the dead. It reminds me of the Haunted Mansion at Disney World. "But why here?" Meg asks.

"First place I thought of. Mom and I were here once. We took a ghost tour."

Meg doesn't look so sure. She glances around again, and despite the summer heat, I feel her shiver under the cloak. So I'm not surprised when she says, "It creeps me out. Why don't we go see if there are any hotels around here?"

"Okay." I ball the cloak up in my backpack, but I leave the zipper open. I start toward the main entrance. Even though Meg's icked out by the place—or maybe because she is—I say, "Did you know there was a grave robbery here once?"

Meg tries to ignore me, but I repeat it. "Did you know—?"

"Yuck. Don't tell me."

"This old guy, he was a count or something, was in love with this girl who died. She was in one of the mausoleums, so one night—"

"Not listening! Not listening!"

". . . he broke in and stole her body. He dressed her in a wedding dress and kept her."

"Stop! Didn't she smell?"

I shrug. "I guess. He replaced a lot of her skin with wax."

"I hate you." Meg's step quickens, but she can't run away because there are lots of tiny headstones, the kind you see a lot in old cemeteries, the kind for babies.

"Come on," I say, "it's a love story. In fact . . ." I stop.

"What?" Meg stops right next to a mausoleum. The sun is almost down now. I walk faster to catch up, pointing at the mausoleum.

"In fact what?" Meg says.

"In fact, she was buried right . . . here!" I grab Meg's arm, hard. She shrieks and pulls away, then runs as fast as she can, out of the dusky graveyard. Some other tourists turn to tsk at us for spoiling the solemn mood. I laugh and run after her.

When we reach the gate, I see something that makes me gasp and stop.

It's a house, a bed-and-breakfast, actually. The name on the sign is CAROLINE'S. It's an old, tin-roofed building in a shade of purple so garish I can see it even in the near dark.

None of that is really what I notice. What I notice is the sign, a banner hanging from a tree. It says:

HOME OF THE KING OF KEY WEST

And, below, in smaller letters:

FANTASY FEST, 1980

"Meg! Wait! Look!"

"I'm not looking. I'm not waiting either. I don't like graveyards."

"Not the graveyard. There. It's the house. The King of Key West. We have to go there. I promised the swans."

37

The king went so often to see his dear children that the queen
was offended by his absence.

—"The Six Swans"

"Excuse me," I say to the woman who opens the door. "Are
you Caroline?"

She's about my mother's age, tall and slim with an unusu-
ally long neck. Could she really be the swans' sister?

"Sure am." She smiles. People are friendly in Key West.
"Who's looking?"

"Johnny." I gesture toward Meg. "And Meg. We're from
Miami. We know some friends of yours, but you'd better sit
down."

She laughs. "You think I need to sit down, hon? You think

you can tell me anything that would give me a shock?"

It's clear she thinks my answer will be no. But she doesn't know I'm about to tell her she has six siblings who've been transmogrified into swans. So I say, "Um, maybe. See. I saw your sign. It says someone here is the King of Key West."

She sighs. "Oh, that was my crazy dad. I just keep it here for local color. My father is one of those weird Key West legends—that just happens to be true."

"Okay, well—"

"Why don't you have a seat?" She gestures toward a wrought-iron table. "And I'll tell you the story."

And before I can say that we're in a hurry, she's off getting a pitcher of lemonade for us and a beer for herself. Meg and I exchange looks and sit at the table. In the distance, I can hear people laughing, a band playing "Freebird." I look toward the cemetery.

Finally, Caroline sits and tells her story. "My father called himself the King of Key West because one year, at Fantasy Fest, he rode a float that showed the Conchs seceding from the United States and being ruled over by him."

"Conchs?" Meg asks.

"A conch is a shellfish. They also call people from Key West Conchs, and call Key West the Conch Republic. Some people joke about Conch secession, but to my father, it was no joke. He was convinced that if Key West seceded, he'd be their king."

I think I see something fluttering in the darkened

cemetery, but when I look again, it's only a leaf. Caroline continues her story, which I'm guessing she tells anyone who'll listen.

"My father was a little crazy in other ways. He said when he was young, he went to the Ocala National Forest in the center of the state. He got lost there. It was close to dark, and he was afraid. Just as he was about to lie down for the night, he saw an old woman. She said she'd help him find his way out if he agreed to marry her daughter. Otherwise, he'd be doomed to wander forever.

"He agreed, figuring he'd escape later. But it turned out the daughter was beautiful. They got married and had me.

"My mom was beautiful, but it turns out that wasn't enough. My parents hated each other. He said she was a witch. She said he was a fool. I know the second was true. He also said there was a curse on him. He did other weird stuff too."

"Weird stuff?" I say, looking for an opening.

"Like one day, I saw my father wake early in the morning. He got in his truck, not realizing that I'd secretly hidden in the truck bed. He drove until he reached a beautiful park. At the park, there was a pond, and in that pond, there were six swans. Dad fed the swans, talked and sang to them. When he finally left, I saw him wipe a tear from his eye."

A group enters the cemetery, maybe a ghost tour. The sky is dark except for the light of the full moon and their flashlights. I scan their faces. None is familiar.

"Turns out, he did this every day," Caroline continues. "Once, my mother seemed mad that he'd gone, and I said, 'Don't worry. He's only gone to feed the swans.'

"My mother turned away, but not before I saw her face turn pink. I knew I'd said the wrong thing. I told her not to be upset. When she turned, her anger had melted away, and she said, 'I merely think he should spend time with you, not the swans.'

"The next day, I followed my father again. He drove quickly, and I was excited about seeing the swans. When we reached the pond, I wanted to shout with glee. I didn't, though, because I knew it would alert my father to my presence. I shouldn't have worried, though." She stops speaking and stares ahead, remembering.

I know what's coming, but I say, "What happened?"

She looks at me as though she's forgotten I was there and says, "They were gone, the beautiful swans. My father called the names he'd given them as if they were children, but they didn't come. I was crying then, and my father found me. I helped him look for the swans until finally, we couldn't look anymore because the sun had set, and there was no moon. We went back every day for a month, but the swans were never there again."

Caroline wipes a tear from her eye. "He made me promise that I'd look for them all my life, even if he was gone. He told me that once I was eighteen, I could break the curse."

"Did he tell you what the curse was?" Meg asks.

Caroline shakes her head. "He died a year later. He was never the same after the swans left."

"And your mother?" I remember Harry talking about the witch who'd turned them all into swans. I don't have a good track record with witches.

But Caroline says, "She disappeared. The neighbors raised me, and when I was of age, I moved back here." She gestures toward the King of Key West sign. "Guess I'm part of Conch lore."

I glance at Meg and say, "What if I told you I could find those swans?"

"I'd say you were crazy. I'm way more than eighteen. Swans don't live that long."

"But people do. And that's what these swans were—your brothers and sisters."

"I think you need to leave now." Caroline points at the street.

"I know it sounds crazy," Meg says, "but he's talked to those swans. They live in the fountain at the hotel where we work."

"Right."

"They were turned into birds by their wicked step . . ." I stop, remembering I'm talking about Caroline's mother.

"Go," she says. "You may think I'm this crazy Conch, but I'm not that nuts." She grasps my shoulder to lead me away.

"Please," I say. "I told your brother Harry I'd find you."

She stops walking. "My brother, who?"

"Harry. They're all named after Key West things. There's Harry and Truman, Ernest, Mallory, Margarita, and—"

"Johnny!" Meg's voice cuts me off. She grabs my arm and points to the gray cemetery. "Look!"

I look. At first, I see nothing but moldering tombstones, but as my eyes adjust, I spot what Meg's so excited about.

A frog.

I pull away from Caroline. "Okay, I'm going."

"Wait!" she calls after me.

But I can't wait. The frog hops closer to a group of tourists. I reach for Meg's hand. "Come on!"

38

By some silent agreement, we don't run. We don't want to scare him. When we reach the cemetery, the tourists have moved on. All is silent. A chill ripples across my arms. All the while, I keep my eyes on the gray grass and gray dirt.

What was that? Something moving between two crumbling baby tombstones. I drop the backpack and take a step forward. Another. No movement. I stop, listening. Nothing but faraway music and an engine sputtering. Then, the engine stops, and there's Meg's breathing.

I hold my own breath, hearing what I've been listening

for, the rustling of a small creature moving. I crouch low, still holding my breath, until I hear it again. I rise and touch Meg's hand. She's heard it too. With our eyes, we agree that I'll go ahead.

I move my foot above a bare spot of grass. I stop. Silence. I slide sideways, my hand brushing the smooth coolness of granite. I lean over, scanning the grass for my prey. Meg has taken a side path around. Now she crouches low. In the shadows, she could be a panther, stalking a jackrabbit. For an instant, our eyes meet, and I silently thank God for Meg. Then there's a rustling, and a bit of movement in a bunch of grave flowers. I lunge, feel the frog's coolness beneath me. I close my hands around it, but catch only dead, dried petals. I look to Meg. She'll get it. I know she'll get it. But I gasp and stop. The catlike figure in the shadows isn't Meg. The crouching figure rises, and it is tall, broad shouldered. Siegfried!

There's movement. I drop the flowers. The frog hops farther away.

"Get it, you idiot!" A shrill voice behind a crypt. I look toward it and see Sieglinde, Sieglinde and Meg. They're locked in some sort of combat, Sieglinde holding Meg at bay as if under some sort of spell.

"Get it, Johnny!" Meg says. "You can do it! It has to be you!"

That's all I need. I lunge for the frog. Siegfried lunges at the same time. The frog hops away. We both miss catching it and are locked, arm in arm, for an instant. I see his face.

He's a kid. A *big* kid, but a boy younger than I am. Maybe fourteen. Definitely not old enough to drive legally. I can take this kid.

Except, oh yeah. He's got magical powers.

But maybe not. When I saw him at the port, he shot me with a gun.

Yeah, a gun is *way* less threatening than magical powers.

I see the frog again, hopping away past a tombstone that says BELOVED WIFE. For an instant, Siegfried seems to freeze. I run at the frog. I lunge. Siegfried recovers and dives through the air. The frog makes to jump again.

"You have to trust me, Philippe!" I say to him. "I'm here for your family. These guys want to kill you! One of us will get you, and you want it to be me."

The frog stops midspring, and I tackle him, just as Siegfried finally reaches me.

I summon all my strength, more strength than I knew I possessed, and kick him in the stomach. He yells in pain. I wrap the frog in my shirt. At the same moment, Meg breaks free from Sieglinde's spell-lock and rushes toward me. "The cloak!" she yells and pulls it from my still-open backpack.

Sieglinde's right behind her, screaming, "You fool! Idiot!" at Siegfried, but he's down for the count. She runs and lunges for the cloak just as Meg gets it wrapped around both of us.

"You have the frog?" she says.

"Yes." I feel its cold frog heart beating against my stomach. It doesn't struggle. "Yes!"

"I wish I was in my bedroom!" Meg whispers.

I feel the cloak being ripped away from me.

39

"Where are we?" Meg asks me.

Not her house, that's for sure. The room is dark, lit only by moonlight, and strange objects surround us. And yet, as my eyes become more used to the darkness, I make out the mast of a pirate ship, a giant parrot, stuff I've never seen before.

"Ribbit!" In my hand, the frog croaks his indignation. I push myself up on my elbow and look out the window.

Tombstones. The cemetery. Sieglinde!

I hear a woman's voice, shrieking. She's out there. Right

outside screaming at Siegfried for letting me get away. I realize the shapes around me are old Fantasy Fest floats. A jester's mouth grins wide at me from a corner. The cloak took us to *a* bedroom, but not Meg's.

"We're at Caroline's house," I whisper to Meg. "But why . . . ?"

I tug at the cloak and look at it. It's been ripped in half. Sieglinde must have the rest.

"I think we lost our transportation," I say. "I guess it couldn't take us that far."

"But we have the frog," Meg says.

"For how long, though? She's right out there."

A shadow crosses the moon.

"If only we could make him back into a prince," Meg says. "It would be easier to keep track of him."

"Good luck," I say. "We need to find someone who loves him. And he's a jerk."

"Ribbit! Ribbit!" The frog hops and croaks in protest.

"There, there, little frog." Meg pats him, and he calms down. "It would help if you could be nicer to him. What did the spell say *exactly*?"

I try to remember Victoriana's words. "The spell can be broken . . ." I picture Victoriana's balcony, the ocean, her blond hair streaming in the breeze. It was a week ago, but it seems like forever. ". . . by the kiss of one with love in her heart."

"Love in her heart," Meg repeats. She reaches over and

puts her hand out for the frog. "Come here, little guy. You're a cute little froggie."

"What are you—?"

"Well, he *was* hot, and it's not like I have a boyfriend or anything. Plus, he's a prince." The frog hops onto her hand. She places it in one of the few bare spots on the floor.

She kneels and leans toward him. "Let's just see if it works."

"Wait!" I grab her arm. "What are you doing?"

"This." In the moonlight, I watch as she holds the frog down, stretches out her neck, and before I can speak again, she plants a kiss on his warty green head.

40

He was no frog but a king's son with beautiful eyes.

—"The Frog Prince"

"*Mon dieu!* Where am I?" The man—because that's what he is now—is in my lap, flailing his arms, and speaking with a French accent. "Who are you? And where . . ." He turns, squashing my knee as he does. ". . . where is ze fair maiden who has saved me?"

Meg laughs. "I'm afraid that's me."

"You?" Even in the darkness, I see surprise contort the Prince's handsome face. He looks at Meg, wrinkles his nose, then looks back at me. "She?"

"Yeah, her. Would you mind shoving over, buddy? You're

254

sort of on my leg." I'm trying to stay calm even though, in that one instant before Meg kissed the prince, I realized the truth, the wonderful truth that filled me with joy, the awful truth that struck me down with despair.

I love Meg. Not Victoriana. Definitely not Victoriana. Meg. Meg, who tried on my shoes and encouraged me. Meg, who showed me the parade route from the top of the Empire State Building, Meg, who saved me from Sieglinde. When I picture myself being with someone, maybe for the rest of my life, it's not a glamorous blonde in thousand-dollar shoes. It's a skinny, dark-haired girl in an apron. All those times, in New York, in the tree, at Mallory Square, I should have kissed her.

I realize I thought Meg loved me. And yet, she kissed the frog, and he became a prince. She did say he was hot when she saw his photo. Is that love? My only hope is that he won't like her back. Then I'll help her get over it.

But the prince stands and offers his hand to Meg. "Ah, *oui*. I did not recognize. I was so dazzled by ze beauty before me zat I did not see . . ."

And Meg, who never giggles or act girly, stares up at him. "Wow, you're so . . . tall."

"And I have an excellent physique. I lift weights on every morning, except in ze past few weeks, when I have been a frog. But now, I start again to please my beloved."

Meg giggles. Giggles! "Aw, that is soooooo sweet."

"No sweeter zan you, fair lady. You have saved my life

and broken ze spell. Now you will haf your reward. I will take you back to Aloria to become a princess. A queen, even. You are a lucky girl."

Lucky girl? Ha! I wait for Meg to tell this clown where to get off. But she doesn't. She just sits, mouth slightly open, and stares.

And, I realize, he's hot. It's exactly like me with Victoriana. Meg's seen this guy on the cover of magazines they sell in the lobby. He's inches taller than me with a build you don't get from repairing shoes. Meg might be immune to the hotness of a guy like Ryan, but Ryan's not a prince. A handsome prince—isn't that what every girl wants?

"Close your mouth, Meg," I tell her.

"What?" Her eyes never leave the prince's face. "Oh, sorry. I was just thinking about how lucky we are. Now we can both go to Aloria, me with my sweet prince, you with your princess."

My princess. I think of Victoriana. Can I be happy with her? Do I have a choice?

"We should leave," I tell Meg, who's still drooling over Prince Philippe. I have to repeat it because she doesn't hear me the first time. Or the second.

Finally, though, she says, "But how? I don't think the cloak works."

I wrap what's left of the cloak around me and quickly wish I was home. I do wish that. I wish I was anywhere but here. But she's right. It doesn't work. Taking us a few yards away from the cemetery was the cloak's last-gasp act. Now, we're stuck here with no transportation, and this miserable prince, easy prey for Sieglinde.

"Hey! Who the heck is in here?" Someone else is in the room. "Meg, look out!" I pull Meg away from the prince, in front of me, and we start to run.

"I have a gun, and I'm not afraid to use it," the voice continues. Caroline!

"Caroline, it's us!" I start to stand, but she turns on the light, and I dive behind a papier-mâché SpongeBob so no one can see through the window.

"You coulda knocked on the door," she says.

"I'm sorry. We'll get out of here right now." Though I have no idea how.

"Wait! Wait! I was looking for you anyway. You have to tell me about the swans!"

I look at her. She's holding something strange in her hand, like fat Hawaiian shirts. She's out of breath, but in between pants, she says, "I have to see the swans! I believe you now."

I start to hatch a plan. "What changed your mind?"

"The names. That was what he called them. Harry, Truman, Ernest, Jimmy, Mallory, and Margarita. Those were their names. Key West names, like my name, Caroline."

"Who is zis fool?" the prince asks. Meg takes his hand.

Caroline ignores him. "That's what he was calling the day I saw him at the pond. My father was devastated when they left. He made me promise something."

Beside me, Philippe and Meg hold hands. He murmurs something that sounds like "my dear leetle mongoose." I wish he'd turn back into a frog and hop away. But I don't want Sieglinde to stick me back in that hole, so I say, "Could we go in the other room, maybe? I'm a little worried about being seen through the window."

"Sure. Absolutely."

Once we get to the living room, and Caroline has closed the curtains, she shows me what she's been holding.

Shirts made out of flowers.

That's what Margarita said. Their sister had to find them and make shirts out of flowers! She did it. She knew.

"After the swans left," Caroline says, "my father went on a long journey. He took me with him. I knew he was looking for the swans, but he never found them, and he returned home in despair. That summer, he sat me down. I was only a little kid, but he told me I had to remember what he said."

"Which was?" But I know.

"That someday I must find the swans again. Before I did, I was to make six shirts of flowers to give to them. When I did these things, the curse would break. He never told me what the curse was.

"He died soon after. I didn't make the shirts until I was grown-up. By then, I knew my dad was nuts, that I'd never see a swan in Key West again. But I still felt like I had to make them, as a sort of tribute to him."

"He wasn't crazy." I examine the shirts. They're made of bougainvillea and hibiscus. The flowers still have a lot of color, and I remember my mother, drying flowers and hanging them upside down. "The shirts were the way to turn them human again. But they had to come from you."

"If you believe in witches and magic," Caroline says.

"Oh, zere are witches, milady," Philippe interrupts, and we all turn to look at him. "Witches are where you last expect them. I, like you, did not believe, and I have been a frog zese three months, until my leetle grackle . . ." He turns to look at Meg. "My leetle crow made me human again."

Please let me slap this guy. Please. Just once. But I think I've figured out a way home, and I can keep my promise too. That's good, at least. "If you drive us back to Miami, I'll show you where the swans are."

Caroline looks at the prince, then at me, and shrugs. "I guess it can't hurt, but . . ." She looks the prince up and down. I look too. He must have been riding when he got enchanted. Either that, or he's a pretentious jerk because he has on jodhpurs and a red riding jacket and carries a crop. "Is he going to wear that, though?"

41

The swan skins flew off, and her siblings stood before her, alive and well.

—"The Six Swans"

Two hours later, we're in the car. The prince has, with great protest, been talked into a pair of old jeans, a T-shirt that says "I'm a drinker, not a fighter," and some flip-flops. He's very confused by the flip-flops. He and Meg are crammed into the backseat of Caroline's ancient Toyota Tercel, kissing. I sit in front with Caroline, holding some of the flower shirts that wouldn't fit in the trunk.

"Don't move around too much," Caroline says. "Those are delicate."

At least, if I don't move, I can't turn and see Meg and

Philippe. She actually *likes* this guy? Between kisses, he calls her "my dear leetle turtle," "my tiny newt," and "my dainty komodo dragon." I notice he doesn't choose any cute animals, but maybe he's developed a thing for reptiles and amphibians during his stint as a frog. Meg giggles every few minutes in very un-Meg-like fashion. I ask Caroline if I can turn on the radio, to drown it out, but every time a romantic song comes on, Meg pronounces it "our song" until I switch to rap. It's like she's doing it on purpose to torture me. Except she doesn't know she's torturing me because she doesn't know I love her.

And it's a four-hour drive to South Beach!

We approach the Seven Mile Bridge, which is, as its name suggests, a seven-mile-long bridge that connects the lower Keys to the upper. It's only two lanes wide, which makes it scary. By day, it's a beautiful view, suspended between sky and water. Now, it's a black hole, an abyss, like going through Space Mountain at Disney World without a lap bar.

"We will move to my castle in Aloria, of course," Philippe says to Meg over the rap, "and be married right away."

Four! Hours!

"You mean, after I finish college, right?" Meg says.

"College?" Philippe says the word like he's never heard it before, even though the rest of his English is good. "But why, my leetle lizard? No wife of mine will have need of college. You will not have to work, after all."

Hoo-boy. Meg's not going to like that one. But she says

nothing, probably giving Philippe more rope so he can hang himself.

And he does. "Education in a young woman is unnecessary. It only encourages zem to ask . . . unattractive questions and form negative opinions. A princess must be charming."

Here's a quote—Steve Martin in the movie *Roxanne*: "As much as I really admire your shoes . . . I really wouldn't want to be *in* your shoes at this particular time and place."

I wouldn't want to be in the prince's flip-flops at this moment, when he's telling Meg not to act too smart.

I wait for Meg to rip him a new one, but she says, "So, what would I be doing every day if I'm not working or going to college. Your laundry?"

"Laundry?" The prince laughs. "You make me laugh, my leetle hyena. We will have servants to do zat."

"And me?" Meg's voice is still calm. "What will I do?"

Philippe pauses, like he's thinking, which is obviously a difficult process for him. I watch the black, churning water hundreds of feet below us. Finally, he says, "You will do what my muzzer does, and my grandmuzzer before her. You will shop, socialize, have babies, work on your appearance . . ."

"My . . . appearance?"

Danger! Danger! I chuckle to myself, which makes the flower shirts rustle so Caroline glares at me. "Sorry."

"*Oui*," Philippe says. "A princess must always look her best, and it is a full-time job too—nails, hair, makeup, ze workout. Of course, *ma mère* and sister, zey are natural beauties, but zere are also excellent surgeons in Europe."

"Oh!" Meg's shriek is so loud it startles Caroline, and the car jerks to the left, almost into the path of an oncoming car. She overcorrects, and I see my life flash before my eyes.

"Are you mad, woman?" Philippe yells.

"Excuse me?" Caroline turns to glare at him, which causes the car to lurch again.

"He's sorry," Meg says, "but can you please look at the road?"

"I am not sorry," Philippe says. "Zis is why women should not drive."

"Of course," Meg says. "That's really very sensible." In the rearview, I see her edge closer to Philippe. "So do you want to tell me more about the plastic surgeons? I always wanted a smaller nose."

"Ze nose is not a problem. You have a lovely nose."

"Well, thank you."

"It is your chin which is too small."

"You know," Meg says, "you are really hot. Maybe we should just make out instead of talk."

They kiss, and I wonder what it would be like if we fell off the bridge.

I try to sleep, though it's difficult because Caroline scolds me every time I move. I wake long enough to give Caroline directions when we reach the mainland. Then I sleep some more.

It's almost five in the morning when we pull into the valet at the Coral Reef. Home. I think about all the things that have happened in the past few days, and I wish I could go back in time to when I knew about bills, knew about hard work, but didn't know about talking animals or witches or giants, a time when Meg was my best friend and wasn't going to be queen of Aloria.

I wonder how many people think their lives are difficult, when really, they could be a lot worse. I wonder how many people don't know how good they have it.

"I can't believe this is happening," Caroline says beside me.

"Yeah, me neither."

But then, I realize, she's talking about the swans, being reunited with her brothers and sisters. I guess some good did come from this. It just didn't come to me.

"Yeah, it's great," I say. "Let's go."

The lobby is silent, empty. The night guy is staring at his computer screen. Caroline looks around, dazzled, as we enter, carrying the shirts. "Wow. They live here?"

"It is rather substandard, it not?" the prince says, and before I can stop myself, I tell him to shut up.

"What? What did zis peasant say to me?"

"Hey, loser, I spent a lot of time looking for you. I did it for your sister 'cause she's worried sick and, unlike you, she's nice. The least you can do is shut your cakehole for two minutes."

"You cannot speak to me like zis! I am a prince!"

"Without me, you'd still be a frog. A dead one."

Meg presses her finger to Philippe's lips. "Don't let him bother you, darling. He's just jealous of our love."

I swear, she smiles when she says it.

Philippe says, "Ah, you are so right, my leetle sea urchin."

Meanwhile, Caroline has spotted the fountain, the swan house. "Oh my God! Are these them?" She runs toward them, flower shirts flapping.

Her shrieks are loud enough to pull the night guy from his monitor. "May I help you?"

Ignore us. Ignore us, as usual. "Oh, it's okay. She's with me."

"Tell her she's not allowed to pet the swans."

I look at Caroline, and that's exactly what she's doing. Touching them, talking to them, even though she's not wearing the magic earpiece. They surround her, craning their necks in every direction and making happy swan sounds.

"Tell her," the night guy says. He's gathering his stuff, keys, magazines. I glance at my watch and realize why he looked up. It's because he's leaving. Which can only mean . . .

Farnesworth!

I start toward Caroline, just as she brings out the first flower shirt. "Wait!" I say. "You may need to wait until . . ."

The swans are flying around Caroline, their long necks surrounding her like snakes. The door revolves, and Farnesworth steps in.

"What are you doing to my—?"

But it's too late. The flower shirt is over the first swan's head. His wings sink down under its weight. His neck folds in two, and for an instant, it's like he's disappeared.

Then, he rises, one foot. Two, until he's a man, a grown man with longish hair, wearing worn jeans, a Hawaiian print shirt, and sandals.

"Hey, sis," the swan-turned-man says. "I'm Jimmy." He takes a shirt from Caroline and lifts it over one of his siblings' heads. I can tell this one is Harry because he has a small healing wound under his wing. This swan, too, folds under, then rises as a small man with gray hair and glasses. Caroline lifts another shirt onto the third swan, and an identical man appears.

"Of course!" I laugh. "Harry and Truman! Twins!"

"No! What are you people doing? Where are my swans?" Farnesworth runs toward Caroline and tries to pull the shirts away from her, but the remaining three swans chase him away, pecking at him with their black beaks until he retreats. The lobby is swimming with feathers and flowers. Then, the three swan-turned-men each seize another shirt and drape them over the remaining swans' heads. Soon, a man with a thick beard appears, then a girl with flaming red hair, as red as the sunset at Mallory Square, and another girl with black hair with a flower in it. Ernest! Mallory! Margarita!

Margarita walks over to Farnesworth. Her stride is graceful, like a dancer in one of those old black-and-white movies. She says, "I'm sorry, Farnie, but do you know what it's like, eating nothing but birdseed for thirty years?"

"But where are they? What have you done to them?"

He buries his face in his hands, and I can see real tears dripping down his cheeks.

I try to explain. "They're human now. They were always human. They were under a curse. Maybe you could get some real swans and—"

"Out!" he screams at me. "Out of my lobby! Out of my hotel!"

Is he serious? This is so not my fault. Well, I guess, technically, it is because I brought Caroline in. But it's not my fault the swans were really people.

Farnesworth advances toward me, his face the color of a lobster in the tank at the hotel restaurant. One of the swans, the bearded one, Ernest, gets between us and tries to help. "Mr. Farnesworth. Frank. Be reasonable. The boy was merely trying to help."

"Frank? I don't even know who you are."

"I'm Ernest, your favorite swan. You spent hours talking to me, confiding in me your dreams of writing a novel someday."

"Confiding what? I did no such thing. Where are my swans?"

"And now, we can write together. We can drive to my father's home in Key West for Hemingway Days, the festival of my namesake, Ernest Hemingway."

Harry or Truman intercedes. "We can be friends, Frank, real human friends. We like you."

"I'm calling the police. I don't want friends. I want my birds. And I want you OUT!"

Meg takes my arm and pulls me toward the shoe shop. "I'll make sure he leaves, Mr. F. He just has to clear out his stuff."

"Good!" Farnesworth is still shaking with anger, but he backs off. As I leave, the swans are still trying to convince him they're real.

"Get my stuff?" I say to Meg. "I work here. My mother's place, remember? Now that you nabbed a prince, you want to get rid of me?"

"Shh." Meg puts finger to lips. "Of course not. We'll work it out. But you don't want your mother getting kicked out, do you?"

She has a point. "No."

"Okay, then, you're going to have to lay low awhile. I'll take Philippe up to his sister."

"Be careful," I say. "Sieglinde could still be after him. There could be spies."

"Not to worry," Philippe says. "I will defeat zem all."

"Yeah, 'cause you did such a great job the first time."

"Come on." Meg takes my hand. Her fingers feel so

soft, and again, I can't believe I missed my chance with her. "There's something I have to show you."

I follow her back to the shoe repair. When I get there, she gestures toward the coffee shop. "It's in here."

It's about time the place was open, and sure enough, Sean, one of her brothers, is there, opening up.

"You're back," he says.

"Just got here."

"Who's the stiff?" He gestures at Philippe.

"Oh, him?" Meg looks behind her and beams. "That's Prince Philippe Andrew Claude of Aloria. We're going to be married."

"Yeah, right." Sean smirks. "So you going to take this shift?"

"No such luck for you. I have to show Johnny the stuff. Shove over."

She walks past him, into the pantry, where they keep the coffee and extra sugar and stuff. She throws open the door. "There you go!"

"What's this?"

"Your stuff."

I look. There, from floor to ceiling, are stacks of shoe boxes. And not just any shoe boxes. These are lime green ones with pink lettering. Next to a picture of a palm tree, in fancy script, they say:

Gianni Marco of South Beach

"Gianni?"

"It sounded cooler than Johnny," Meg says.

"So you got me shoe boxes?"

"Not shoe *boxes*, Johnny. Look inside."

I pull out one box. It's heavy, not empty. I open it.

Inside is a pair of sandals. Hot pink metallic leather lining, leather upper with silver crystal detailing, five-inch acrylic heel with glitter inside. My design! "How did you . . . ?"

I can't believe this. I can't believe this. My shoes. My actual real-life shoes I designed are here. And Meg did it—somehow. I turn it over and over and even shake it.

Meg looks at the shoe, then Philippe, and says, "Can you excuse us a moment, darling?"

Philippe looks like he's eaten a bad escargot. "If you must. But do not stray long, my leetle anemone."

I think I see Meg make a face, but when I look again, she's beaming at Philippe. She hands him a shoe box and kisses him (*gag*) before saying, "Each moment is a lifetime, my love." (*Gag*). She leaves him, staring at the shoes.

I'm still staring too, as she pulls me into the closet and shuts the door. When she turns on the light, I see there are dozens, maybe hundreds more shoe boxes. Are they full? Meg whispers, "I guess I can tell you, since you know about the ring. We have brownies."

"Brownies? Sure. You've got an awesome crumb cake too, but what does that have to do with shoes?"

"Brownies are elves, Johnny. It's an Irish thing. They

help clean up. Remember how the place was always a mess at night, and then, it would be clean in the morning?"

"Elves?" *Elves???*

"They clean up after we leave, do the baking, then start the coffee before we come every morning. They don't work during the day. They like to be left alone."

"Elves made these shoes?" I still can't believe what I'm holding in my hand. And what could be in those other boxes.

"Brownies."

"Brownies." But if this is true, I can just get started selling them. Maybe I couldn't get thousands for them, but we'd have money. We wouldn't have to worry. I examine the workmanship of the shoe, and I can see it's top, top quality. I wouldn't have to marry Victoriana. If I could sell these for half what they're worth, it would save the business.

"Anyway," Meg says, "they were bored. It doesn't take them very long to make some muffins. They've been doing the same thing for a long time. They don't want to live at our house because it's too crowded—they like their privacy. So when you left, I got them started on some shoes. I ordered the materials—you can pay me back out of Victoriana's money—and I left out your patterns. They did the rest."

Un-be-stinking-lievable. Meg's solved all my problems, and now, she's going to marry Prince Snottyface. "I can't believe brownies made the shoes." But I can. I can believe anything. "Where are they now?"

"They clear out every morning. It's just their way. After they finished a few dozen samples, they started on a marketing plan. Maybe it's around here somewhere. "Oh!" She spies a folder and hands it to me. "I bet this is it. Anyway, so take the shoes. They should get you started."

"But . . ." I pick up another box. A lime green sandal with a stacked heel and a square-cut brooch on the vamp. Size six. Lovely stitching. I open another, and it's the same shoe, size seven. My dream has come true. It's really happening.

"Sean will help you carry them out. I have to go with Philippe."

Philippe. My dream gets stuck in my throat. Meg understood and made my dream come true. Now she's gone. With Philippe.

"Maybe we can have a double wedding." She throws open the door. "Miss me, darling?"

"But of course, my sweet green mamba." Philippe is still holding the shoe. Only one, like Cinderella's prince. "Zis ees quite lovely. *Ma mère*—my mother—would like zem very much. She will be angry wiz me for disappearing. Perhaps a gift. Do you have eet in size five?"

"I'm sure I do. Let me . . ."

I stop. Across the way, I see Mom, opening our shop. And suddenly, all I want is my mother. My mother to comfort me. I turn to Meg. "Do you mind checking? I need my mom."

42

The fox said, "It is in your power to free me."
                                    —"The Golden Bird"

My mother greets me with a hug, but before I get a chance to tell her the whole story about Caroline, Farnesworth, the swans, Philippe, and Meg, she says, "We had, um, sort of an unusual visitor."

"A visitor? Who was it?"

"Not who, but what." She reaches into the drawer under the register and hands me a scrap of paper smaller than a Post-it. In the smallest writing I've ever seen, it says:

Meet me at the Port at midnight when you get back. Cornelius

"So this visitor, it was a . . . a rat."

She shudders. "Yes. With little sharp teeth and tiny claws. I tried to chase it with a broom, but it wouldn't budge until I took this. I think you have to go, yes? It's important?"

That night, I take Mom's car to the port. I remember the first time, the motorcycle, the shooting. But they won't be there anymore. The prince has been found. I have nothing to do with it. I haven't even tried to contact Victoriana yet. I can't face her. I'm looking for a way to park by the roadside when the gate starts to open. No one's there. I drive the car in. As soon as I reach Terminal C, there's a tiny creature on my windshield. I open the window and allow him to hop into the car. He begins talking right away, but it's all excited squeaks.

"Hold on. I can't understand." I insert the earpiece, and right away, he starts talking again.

"Hoo-boy. You made it. I was worried aboutchoo what wid da witch and dat big guy on da motorcycle. But hey. You made it back. Didya find the fox?"

I nod. "Thanks. He told me where to find the frog, and I found him."

The rat's whiskers droop a bit, and his eyes gleam sideways in the moonlight. "But . . . dat's all he told ya? The fox?"

"That's all I asked him."

"That's all you asked him, but did he ask *you* anything?

Did he ask you to *do* anything?"

Then I remember the fox's strange request, the one I refused.

"Well, he asked me to kill him, but of course, I didn't."

"Of course? You didn't?"

"I'm not going to kill a fox, much less a talking one."

"He wasn't asking you to kill him so he could get dead. He coulda run in traffic if das what he wanted. If he asked you to kill him, den he asked for a reason." He must see the confused look on my face, even in the darkness, because he continues. "We—all us used-to-bes—have things that gotta happen so's we can get transformed back. It could be a kiss or a magic bean, something like that."

"Or making shirts out of flowers?"

"Exactly. Weird, but exactly. I had to find my daughter, but she was killed in an accident before I could, so now, I'll never go back." The rat pauses, and I hear a tiny sniff. "But that fox—if he was asking you to kill him, I guarantee he was doing it for a reason. You gotta go back and do it."

"But I can't go back to Key Largo."

"Why the heck not?"

I struggle to think of an answer. The obvious answer: No magic cloak. The usual answer: Work. The depressing answer:

"I may have to marry a princess."

The rat laughs. "Marry her next week. Do this now."

He's right. I've got a car full of gas. I've been forbidden

to work. Nothing prevents me but a beautiful princess—a princess any guy in the world would want.

Any guy but me.

What I wouldn't give to be in your shoes, said the Baker's Wife to Cinderella.

So I say, "Okay. I'll do it."

Because if I can't help myself, I may as well help the fox.

I drive, radio off, feeling the shake of Mom's old car, the rhythm of rubber on the road. None of it drowns out my thoughts. This should have been the day I got everything, a beautiful princess waiting for me, the shoes, the future. But it means nothing against wanting Meg and having her end up with that jerk. The moon and the streetlights cast white and black shadows across my face, and I want to give in to the beauty of a summer night, but always my thoughts stop me. How could I have been so wrong about what I wanted? Maybe I actually am stupid. And how could Meg not want to be together when we've gone through so much? Doesn't she care? And yet, the shoes in her shop say different. She loves me. She just doesn't love me the way I want her to.

Corrie ten Boom, who helped hide Jews from the Nazis during World War II, said, "If God sends us on strong paths, we are provided strong shoes."

I hope I have strong shoes.

* * *

In two hours I'm in Key Largo. The fox is behind the inn. He holds half a sandwich in his paws. I look around to make sure the place is deserted, that Uncle Sam isn't waiting for me. But the fox is alone. I insert the earbuds and say, "You wanted something from me?"

The fox nods but gives no other acknowledgment. I say, "Is it part of the curse on you?"

"Nah, I'm just tired of eating out of Dumpsters all these years. No one ever thinks to throw away a packet of tartar sauce." He swallows the last bite of sandwich, then licks the grease off his paws with his pink tongue.

"Are you serious?" I can't kill him if that's the reason. It would be hard to kill a fox, harder still, knowing he's a man. What if he's transformed back when he dies? What if there's this corpse in the Dumpster? I could get nabbed for murder.

I picture the headlines: MIAMI DRIFTER WANTED IN KEYS. That's me, Miami Drifter.

The fox finishes cleaning his paws and says, "It's difficult for me to talk about the curse. Difficult. I can only promise that this is what I want and need, and if you do as I ask, there will be no trouble." He looks up at me. The silver moonlight catches in his brown eyes, and they plead with me. I remember Cornelius, his family and his hope gone, doomed always to be a rat. Wouldn't I rather be dead?

Strong shoes.

I nod. "How will I do it?"

He hesitates an instant, then scampers across the shadows and into the bushes. He returns a moment later, a knife gripped in his teeth. It's not a scary knife like a switchblade. It's one of those knives you use to carve a turkey on Thanksgiving. He thrusts it toward me with his teeth.

I take it. "I don't think I can."

"Please. I'm a fox. People kill animals all the time."

I hold the knife straight. What would it feel like to stab someone? Maybe like cutting leather.

He reads my thoughts. "Think of it like cutting up a broken shoe."

"How did you know I work with shoes?"

The fox hesitates, then says, "You told me so."

"I did?"

The fox lifts his neck, and I see his white ruff like snow in the moonlight. "One good cut. I won't bite."

"I don't think I can do this."

"Did you drive here all the way from Miami *not* to kill me?"

He's right. The rat said I should kill the fox, that it was for the best. But I didn't kill the giants, and I didn't even kill the witch. Still, I reach toward the fox, hold his neck in my left hand, close my eyes, and with one motion, slice into his neck.

A bright red pain shoots through my hand. I look down, and it's gushing blood. I press my finger against it, trying to staunch it. But where did the fox go? Where's the fox?

And then, I see him. He's on the ground. His neck wound is not just open, but gaping and getting bigger, spreading out until it's bigger than his body, then bigger than mine. I jump back to avoid being swallowed up by it. But I needn't have worried because when I look back, the hole is filled with something. A man, stepping from the fox's skin. An older man, brown hair streaked gray. He looks familiar somehow, but of course, he isn't. He's the fox.

He's the fox.

I saved him. I will never get used to this.

The fox-man looks at his hands, then puts them to his neck, checking for wounds. Finding none, he stares at his hands again. "I'm human. I'm alive. I'm . . ." He turns his hands from side to side. ". . . old." He touches his face, like he's feeling for wrinkles. "I spent my best years as a fox. Do I look hideous?"

I'm still drinking in the fact that he's a guy. His fox skin lies on the ground, forgotten. I wonder why he got changed in the first place. Could it happen to anyone?

I say, "No, not bad. You don't look old either. Just, you know, middle-aged."

"I was twenty-five when I was changed. Thank good-ness my clothes still fit. Still, my wife won't recognize me. Aw, she's probably married to someone else anyway, prob-ably thinks I walked out on her. How am I ever going to convince her of the truth?"

The truth. I remember playing Four Truths and a Lie

279

with Meg. Does anyone ever really know the truth about anyone?

Meg.

That makes me think of something else. The cleaning. When we played Four Truths and a Lie, I assumed her statement about doing all the cleaning was a true one.

Now, I know that was a lie. *The* lie. The brownies did the cleaning, not Meg. So if that was the lie, all the other statements must be true.

Including the last one.

And five: I am secretly, madly in love with you.

She loves me. At least, she did love me when she said it. She was trying to tell me, but I ignored her. I feel euphoria and despair. Meg loves me. Loved me. But is it too late now? Did I let her slip through my hands?

"Thank you!" The fox interrupts my thoughts and places his hands on my arms. They're rough, probably from years of walking on them, but he's shaking me, hugging me, jumping up and down, happy. "I can't thank you enough."

"You're welcome. I don't mean to be rude, but I need to leave." I have to find Meg. It's after three. If I drive without stopping, maybe I can drive to the hotel, sneak in before Farnesworth gets there and sees me, wait for her at the shop.

If she hasn't left to marry her prince.

But something tells me she hasn't, that she was just pretending to be so happy, to make me jealous. It worked.

280

Meg loves me. She wouldn't have had the elves make the shoes if she didn't. I know it.

It is this thought that propels me away from the fox. "Here." I shove a couple of bills into his hand. "To get you started. I need to go."

"But wait! I have to talk to you."

"I'll see you around, maybe." I start toward the car.

"Wait! Let me—"

The door slams shut. No time for long good-byes. I have to find Meg.

43

In the middle of the night, two little men came and sat at the shoemaker's table. They began to hammer, stitch, and sew.
— "The Elves and the Shoemaker"

I speed down the mostly deserted streets. Halfway back, my needle's near empty, but I hope I have enough gas to make it. I will the car forward. Don't stop. Don't stop now. It starts to rain. Then harder, so all I can see is a blur of red and white light. I feel my car hydroplane out of control. I turn into the skid, right my direction, and keep going. I slow down, but not too much. When you've found out that the person you love loves you, you can't delay. You have to hurry.

I reach the hotel on fumes. When I get to the employee parking lot, the car sighs as it stops.

Four o'clock. The lobby is deserted. The swan area seems oddly shiny and empty. The night clerk doesn't look up. It's too early even for Meg, but I know my only chance is to camp out, wait for her.

I slip back into the shoe shop first, then close the door against Farnesworth's eyes. I sit, considering what I've gained and maybe lost. I wanted so much—romance, adventure. How could I have known that the only adventure worth having was the one I was already in? The only romance was with the girl next door.

I leaf through the marketing plan the brownies made for me. It isn't very thick, and when I open the booklet, there's only one page. It says:

> *Get Princess Victoriana to mention the shoes on television.*
>
> *Get Princess Victoriana to mention the shoes in magazines.*
>
> *Get Princess Victoriana to mention the shoes in the newspaper.*

It goes on like that for a while. I guess a marketing plan was a lot to expect from elves who didn't go to business school.

I hear noises from the hallway, small, high-pitched noises, like voices, but no voices I've ever heard. I open the door and listen.

"Oh no," says a small voice that I can only hear because the hotel is so silent.

"What is it?" says another.

I stay completely still. The voices are definitely coming from the coffee shop. But who's there?

"I'm telling ya, she is gone," says a tiny voice. "Would you want to get him?"

Gone? Do they mean Meg? That the prince has taken her? Or someone else?

"Get him?" says another voice. "We cannot be getting him. We speak to no one."

"But she's only a wee girl, and she is in bleeding danger," says the first voice. "And he knows we are here. She told him."

"Our Meg is a feisty lass," says the other. "She can take care of herself. Best not to meddle."

Meg! It is Meg, and she's in danger. Before I can even think further, I launch myself over the counter and across the hallway. I pound on the door, saying, "Let me in! Please help me! I need to know what happened to Meg."

After that outburst, I'm quiet again, to let them answer. I know who *they* are now. The brownies. They must be in there. Will they answer me? I knock again, more softly so as not to scare them. "Hey, you did a great job on the shoes. Thanks. So much! Will you let me in?"

Then, I realize. I have the key to the coffee shop. It's inside the register at our place. Meg and I exchanged them long ago. I run across the hall and grab it.

It takes precious seconds to open the door and turn on the lights. When I do, the room is empty.

"Are you in here? I heard you before."

I search every counter for evidence of what the brownies have seen, what made them think Meg was in danger. But the counters are so clean I can picture the tiny guys, skidding across them. Even the sugar packets are all turned to face the same direction in their holder.

"Please."

Suddenly, the lights go out. As I fumble for the switch in darkness, I hear something, tiny footsteps like rats in the walls. When I finally find the light switch, I look in the direction of the sound.

What I see is a leg in ragged brown pants disappear around the corner, as quick as a cockroach. He's heading toward my shop.

"Hey!" I follow it. "Hey, you!"

But when I get there, my eyes fall on something that wasn't there before. A note.

I read, in Meg's handwriting:

Help! Johnny! Sieglinde has me in the Bill Baggs Park lighthouse. She'll kill me if you don't come!

Sieglinde! I should have known she wouldn't give up this easily, wouldn't take no for an answer. I know what she's after. She's using Meg to get to the prince.

If only I'd realized earlier how important Meg was to me, that she was what I needed.

For want of a nail the shoe was lost; for want of the shoe
the horse was lost; and for want of a horse the rider was
lost. . . .

—*Poor Richard's Almanack*

Meg is lost. I have to find her. I check my watch. Four thirty. She should be here soon, but she won't be, and it's my fault. I stuff the note into my pocket.

"What am I supposed to do?" I yell across the hallway.

No answer. I turn out the lights. "Will you talk to me in the dark?"

Nothing. I want to leave. I need to leave. But I leave the light out just another moment, and I hear scurrying, then a small voice at my feet.

"You're a good lad, Johnny. You work hard and love your ma. 'Tis why we helped you. You have strength you do not even know about. When the moment is right, you will know what to do."

The footsteps scurry away. When I know the coast is clear, I turn the light back on and rush for the lobby.

I try to sneak out, but it's not my lucky day. Farnesworth's there. He starts toward me, shouting, "Hey, you! You! Boy from the shoe repair!"

I ignore him and run, slipping on the shiny floor, toward the exit.

It's still dark, but slivers of light are starting to peek through the night sky. I dart behind the hibiscus hedge near the driveway, keeping my back against the wall, the better to blend with the morning sky in case Farnesworth has followed me.

But he hasn't. I find Mom's car, unlock it, and put the key in.

The engine won't turn over.

It had seemed like such a good, such a romantic idea, to drive and not stop for gas.

I beat my hand on the soundless horn until it hurts. Then I use my head.

"May I help you?"

I jump at the voice. I turn and see an older man with glasses and neat gray hair. He wears a hotel-parking-lot-attendant uniform.

I find words. He must think I'm vandalizing the car. The last thing I need is to get arrested for destruction of property. "Um, it's okay. It's my car. I mean, my mom's. I was . . . just frustrated it won't start." I stare at the pavement.

I hope this will get rid of him, but it doesn't. I can see his feet, oddly pointed apart from each other on the ground below.

"Was there something else?" I ask.

"I asked if I could *help you*," says the parking attendant. "For example, there's a bicycle which I happen to know is unlocked. Its owner came in late last night. He won't be awake soon, I suspect."

"You want me to steal a bicycle?"

"Borrow it, if there's an emergency."

"There is. But . . ."

"You helped us, my friend. Now I'll help you."

Recognition floods over me. It's Harry, the swan from the lobby. No, wait. He has no wound in his arm. It must be Truman, his twin.

"But how . . . ?"

"Time for explanations later. I suspect you're in a hurry. For now, let me help you find that bicycle."

And, sure enough, it's unlocked.

South Beach to Bill Baggs Park on Key Biscayne is no short ride. The traffic hasn't started, not yet, but it's still dark, hard to see, and after a few blocks, because things aren't rough enough, it starts to rain. Again. Pour, really, that driving predawn rain you get only in Miami, where an entire week's worth of rain falls in fifteen minutes. I keep going, even when it feels more like swimming than biking, even when I realize I don't know what I'll do when I get there. I have no powers. I can't defeat Sieglinde. And yet, if I don't have Meg, I have nothing.

With your head full of brains, and your shoes full of feet, you're too smart to go down any not-so-good street.—Dr. Seuss

I wasn't smart. I went down a road that was not-so-good. I've lost Meg.

I have to find her.

I cross MacArthur Causeway in wind and rain so hard they almost propel me into the water below. I'm not going to drown, not now that I know Meg loves me. I pull the handlebars left and pedal through the wall of wind, barely able to see downtown Miami in the distance. Finally, pedaling is no longer an intentional act but simply something I do, like a motor-driven toy, unthinking, unknowing.

Where is she? What are they doing to her? Don't think about it, I tell myself. Don't think at all. But I know the truth: They took her to get me to bring Philippe back.

Finally, I see the sign that says BILL BAGGS STATE PARK. The lighthouse is there, its light shining against the mostly bright sky. Someone's inside. I reach the mangrove-studded sand and pull my bike until it will go no farther. My legs feel like they're vibrating, and I fall to the ground. The sand is cold, wet against my aching legs. If I wanted, I could stay there forever. It would feel so good just to sleep right now, but I can't. I won't. I push my hands against the sand until I'm standing again, until finally, I can lurch, Frankenstein-like, across the beach, almost falling two more times before I reach the lighthouse.

The lighthouse door is old with black paint stained whitish by salt air. More important: It's locked. I pull at it several times before I accept this fact. Then I pound against it, screaming my lungs out.

Nothing. My voice is lost against the ocean's roar. I try again. Again. But the crashing waves drown out everything but the sound of my own helplessness. I can do nothing. I have no powers, no strengths. I'm just a regular guy, less than regular. If anything happens to Meg, it will be all my fault for involving her.

And that thought makes me feel superhuman despite my aching legs, despite the resistance of the sand against my feet, and the fact that I got no sleep. I back up, crouch, and start to run, to throw myself against the door.

That's when it flies open.

My momentum almost throws me through it, but I stop and collapse against the sand. Black, red, and blue patterns dance before my eyes. When I can focus, I look up.

"I wondered when you would get here," Sieglinde says.

I stumble forward, then back, finally finding a palm tree I can use to pull myself up.

"Where is she? Where's Meg?"

Sieglinde chuckles and glances at the gradually lightening sky. "How dear. You have come for your sweetie."

I try to keep my voice steady. "Give her back. She has nothing to do with this."

"I'll be more than happy to release your Meg."

"Great," I say, even though I realize it's too easy. It must be a trick. But I'm just so tired. "Let me see her." I push against the tree and start toward the lighthouse door.

"Tut, tut." Sieglinde holds up her hand. "I'll give you your Meg, but first, you have to give me what I want. Give me . . ."

A clap of thunder drowns out her words.

"What?" But I know.

"The princess!" she shrieks against the dark morning sky. "Bring me Victoriana, and I will give you back your darling... your beloved Meg!" She raises her arms and laughs at the wind and rain, and I remember the witch in *The Wizard of Oz* who melted in water. I guess that doesn't really happen. "Foolish boy! You could have had her all along, had her and your silly shoes, and all the wonders of your ordinary life. But no. You had to seek out adventure. Now all you have loved is in peril, all for a worthless princess who doesn't care for you, who will never care for you."

Another thunderclap, right on top of the lightning. The whole beach lights up like midafternoon, and I see the palm trees, flapping, propellerlike, hear the sand battering the sea grapes, and see Sieglinde's terrible face as she says, "Bring me the princess before the day is done. Only then shall you have your Meg!"

"No!" With strength I don't possess, I start for the lighthouse door. The wind picks up, pushing me backward into the sand. I hit the door, and it feels almost hot. I look up and see Sieglinde, unaffected, standing straight and tall against the outline of lightning. "The princess!" she shrieks.

Another gust shoves me down again, and when I look up, she's gone. The lighthouse door slams behind her.

Then the wind calms to a breeze. I struggle up with nothing to hold on to but prickly sea grapes that scrape my legs. I rush to the door. It won't budge. I pound it with all my strength, but even as I do, I know it's no use.

I don't know what to do. I guess call the police, like they can do anything about witches.

I stumble away and find my bicycle half buried in sand. My legs ache. I pull at my wet jeans, trying to stretch them out, make them comfortable enough to ride in.

That's when my hand brushes something in my pocket. Is it?

I reach inside and touch it, remembering Meg's words at Mallory Square: "Here. Take the ring. If you need me, you have it."

I have it! It will be my salvation, my salvation and Meg's.

I mount the bicycle, forgetting my aching legs, forgetting everything but riding far enough, getting away from here, from Sieglinde.

The morning traffic has begun now, cars whizzing by on one side, rough water on the other. I concentrate only on my destination. When I reach it, a beach far from the lighthouse, a rocky beach where people go with their dogs, a small beach almost swallowed up by the morning tide, I stop.

I slip Meg's ring onto my finger.

"Hey, what the . . . where are we?"

I look at her. She has on jeans, a blue T-shirt, and the apron she wears to work. She's beautiful, the most wonderful sight I've ever seen. I throw my arms around her. "Oh, Meg! You're okay!"

"Yeah, well, the morning rush is tough on all of us. You're a little wet there, Johnny. Why'd you bring me here?"

"Why?"

"Yeah. I was trying to work. People are going to start talking if I disappear when I'm pouring coffee."

"Pouring coffee? But how could you be at work?"

"Duh. I go every morning, and my idiot brothers didn't consider my impending marriage to the heir to the Alorian throne to be a good reason for missing a shift."

Impending marriage. My stomach gives a jolt.

"But . . . you sent me a note. The brownies brought it. Sieglinde had you in the lighthouse. She was holding you captive."

And slowly, dawn breaks. Sieglinde didn't have Meg at all. She tricked me, knowing I loved Meg, that I'd do anything to get her back, even surrender Victoriana.

I shake my head. "Never mind. It was all a trick."

"Well, that's a load off. Where are we?"

"Hobie Beach?"

"*Hobie* Beach?" She glances around, her eyes falling on the bicycle I'm holding. "Do you have your mom's car?"

I look around, stupidly. "No. Only this bike."

"Perfect. So I'll have to find a cab back. Like that's easy around here." She searches in her pockets for money. "Can you do me a favor and not use that thing if it's not an emergency?"

"I thought it was an emergency! I rode through pounding

rain, thunder, and lightning to rescue you, and you say it's not an emergency? It *was* an emergency!"

She stares at me, saying nothing.

I say what I've been wanting to say since I left Key Largo. "I love you, Meg."

"What?"

"I love you!" I yell it over the whoosh of cars. "And I know you love me too. You were trying to tell me, that day we played Four Truths and a Lie, but I ignored you. I didn't know."

She shakes her head. "The game's over, Johnny." She walks closer to the street, looking frantically for her money.

"But it couldn't be the way you said. That would mean there were *two* lies."

She stops walking and turns to face me. "I got mixed up. They were both lies. How could I be in love with you, Johnny? You said yourself we're just friends."

She's found her money, and she turns and walks the rest of the way to the roadside, looking for an opening to cross. She's tapping her foot, and I know she wants to run, wants to dart into traffic, anything to get out of my life.

"I was wrong, Meg!" I yell after her.

She turns again. I can see she's shaking, and not from the cold and rain. Maybe I should let her go. Maybe it's too late. Maybe she's rather be with Philippe now.

"Wrong about what?"

"Wrong about being friends, or *only* friends anyway. I

love you, Meg. I didn't realize it until I started losing you, but I love you, and I hope you weren't lying when you said you loved me."

She doesn't answer for a long time, just stares at me, and I hear the voices of seagulls, the growl of waves against shore, the roar of cars, and finally, Meg.

"You jerk."

"What?" Not the answer I expected.

"Oh yeah, you think you're funny, messing with me, playing with my feelings. Well, no more. I've spent half my life crushing on you. I even tried to help you find the frog, just to spend time with you. Stupid. And now when I finally give up and find someone else—"

"Someone else? That goofball!"

"Philippe loves me."

"And do you love him? If you do, I'll leave you alone. But if you don't, and if you're willing to be with the dumbest guy in South Beach—and that's saying a lot—then I want to be with you. So do you love him?"

I'm shaking, waiting for her answer. She looks at me, and I know she sees it, know she sees me holding my breath too.

Finally, she laughs. "Of course not. How could I love someone who calls me his 'leetle sea urchin'?"

I breathe out. This, at least, is good.

"But the kiss? You kissed him, and it broke the spell. If you didn't love him, how did it work?"

She shakes her head like she's dealing with an ignorant child. "You never listen well. The spell said it could be broken by the kiss of one *with love in her heart*."

"So?"

"Love in her *heart*. I have love in my heart, so when I kissed the prince, it broke the spell. I didn't have to love Philippe. It's what they call a loophole."

"So the love in your heart . . . ?"

"You, stupid. I never loved anyone else. Does that make you happy?"

That's all I need to hear. "Yeah, it makes me happy."

There, in the wet morning, with cars whizzing by in front of us and waves crashing behind us, like some kind of weird romance where the soundtrack's off, I take her in my arms and kiss her.

44

After a few minutes of that, when motorists start honking at us and yelling that we should get a room, and other sweet things people say to teenagers in love, we come up for air. Meg says, "So what are you going to do about Princess Barbie?"

I shrug. "Guess I'll have to let her down easy. It'll be tough for her, losing out on the hottest stud muffin on South Beach, but she'll get over it eventually."

Meg laughs and pushes some hair off my forehead, prompting another motorist to lean on his horn. "But what about the money?"

"I don't know. I think it's important to make sacrifices for your family, but I can't make this one, and Victoriana shouldn't have to either. It's too important. We should both be allowed to choose who we want."

Meg sees a cab heading down the opposite side of the causeway. She waves it down, stepping into traffic to do so and setting off another medley of horns. "Well then, we'll have to tell them. Both of them."

At the hotel, we're lucky to get into the elevator without incident. But I know getting into the princess's room will be another story. Even on the elevator, when I press the penthouse button, a chambermaid who's riding with us gives me a funny look, like she knows I don't belong there. I nod, to show her I'm okay. She's a new maid I don't know.

"Hey," she says when I nod. "Don't you recognize me?"

I look at her, and now that she mentions it, she does look familiar, with red hair in a ponytail that winds almost to her waist. "I don't know. Should I?"

She laughs. "Probably not. I've changed a lot lately. You might even say transformed." She cranes her neck to one side.

And then, I get it. "You're a swan."

"Former swan. I'm Mallory. Good to see you."

"You . . . work here?"

She nods happily. "Farnesworth offered us all jobs once he accepted what had happened. After he finished being mad, he was happy about us all being human. He's just a lonely guy. But Truman pointed out that we could be better friends as people. A couple of the guys, Ernest and Harry, went back to Key West with Caroline. But the rest of us are bunking with Farnie until we find an apartment, and working at the hotel. Margarita's a bartender. Jimmy's a bellman, and Truman's a valet."

"Yeah. I saw him earlier."

"He hasn't driven a car in years, but really, who knows this place better than us?"

The elevator reaches the penthouse. The door opens. I say, "Wow. That's great. Any way you could do us a favor?"

"Sure. You've done so much for us."

But when she finds out what it is, she's less sure. "I don't know if I can get you in with the princess."

"Just tell her we're out here. She'll let us in."

A few minutes later, I'm being led into the Penthouse B suite.

45

As soon as the sitting room door closes, Victoriana hugs me. "Oh, Johnny! Dear boy, you have saved everyzing! My bruzzer—he is home! I do not have to marry Volfgang!"

I look down. "Yeah, about that . . ." Then, something catches my eye. She's looking very hot in a pink-and-white sundress with matching . . . "Hey, where'd you get those shoes?"

"You like zem?" She twists her foot flirtatiously, glancing at the closet. "Zey were a gift from Philippe. My darling bruzzer was so grateful zat I send you to him. Zey are a new designer, Gianni Marco. You know him, maybe?"

"Know him? I *am* him."

Victoriana's blue eyes widen. "A hero *and* a shoe designer? I am beside myself." She props herself up against my shoulder, then lifts first one foot, then the other. "Zese, zey are quite lovely."

"Thanks." I stare at her hand on my shoulder. There's something intoxicating about being with her, even now. Maybe it's just that she's wearing my shoes. Still, it's hypnotic.

Meg clears her throat. "You can thank *me* later for giving them to Philippe. But isn't there something you want to tell the princess?"

I step away from Victoriana, almost causing her to stumble. After she rights herself, I say, "Um, yeah. I can't marry you."

"Not marry me? *Pourquoi?*" She glances at the closet again.

I look at her shoes. It would be so perfect if I could persuade her to mention them in public, as some kind of alternate reward. I remember the brownies' marketing plan. But after what I'm about to say, she never will. "Um, it's just . . . I'm kind of in love with someone else."

The princess's mouth forms a surprised O. Her blue eyes flick from me to Meg, then back. "Ah, I see."

"I'm sorry," I say.

Her face breaks into a humongous grin. "Sorry? Oh no. I

am quite relieved. I did not want to marry either."

"Relieved?" Even though I am too, I feel a little insulted.

She glances at the closet again. What is up with that—some kind of nervous tic? "Of course. I was desperate. I needed my bruzzer back, and what uzzer reward would be suitable for a princess's quest?"

"Oh, I don't know?" Meg pipes up. "Money?"

"Money?" Victoriana looks taken aback. "You would have done zis zing for money?"

I nod. Vigorously. "It's pretty important to a lot of people, particularly people who need to pay electric bills."

"I do not even know what an electric bill is." Victoriana breaks out in a big teeth-flashing smile. "But I have money. I have very much money! It only seemed too little payment for such a great debt. But tell me how much you need."

Meg clears her throat, and I'm about to say that, if Victoriana wants, she could just tell a few magazines about my shoes, and we'll call it even, when suddenly, there's a huge crash from inside the closet.

"Aw darn!" says a male voice.

"I think someone's in there," I say.

"Could be dangerous," Meg adds, and without even waiting for Victoriana to agree, she strides toward the closet and throws open the door.

A pile of dresses, skirts, and about ten shoe boxes falls out. On top of it all is a man.

"Ryan!" Meg exclaims.

"Ryan?" I say at the same time.

The princess crosses the room on her teetery shoes. "You two know each uzzer?"

"Sure. We were together when you met me." I feel more than a little peeved. I mean, I went on this whole big quest, ran all over the Keys looking for a frog, practically got buried alive by a witch, and the whole time, she's had Ryan in the closet? "You're in love with Ryan?"

Ryan grins. "Them's the breaks, Johnny boy."

But Victoriana laughs. "*Non, non, non.* You misunderstand me. I have a little—'ow you say—dalliance wiz Ryan. But I do not love him. I do not wish to marry *anyone.* I am too young. My bruzzer, Philippe, swears on his honor zat now zis roller coaster ride is over, he will return to Aloria, settle down wiz ze girl who has kissed him, and rule the country in a responsible manner, and we will beware of Sieglinde and ze witches."

Settle down.

"Um," Meg says.

"So you see, I am free. In fact, I am returning to Aloria as soon as Philippe can contact the young lady. Do you know where she is?"

Now, it's my turn to look at Meg. She laughs a little, staring down at her apron. "Um, that's me, and you see, I don't want to marry Philippe either."

The door to the room flies open. "Do you mean it, my leetle wombat?"

"Yeah." Meg winces a little at the wombat thing. "I'm

afraid we're going to have to break off the engagement."

"Break it off? I am not understanding."

Victoriana shakes her head. "In zis country, people do not wish to marry ze princes and princesses. It is mystifying."

Meg shakes her head. "I'm not in love with you, Philippe."

"Mon dieu!" Philippe raises his eyes to the heavens, or the ceiling anyway. "Thank goodness." Then, collecting himself, he says, "I only mean we do not know each uzzer so well."

"It's all right," Meg says. "I'm sure it would have been . . . interesting, but I'm not exactly princess material, am I?"

"No." Philippe shudders. "I mean, yes. I mean, I want you to be happy, my darling mole rat."

Meg smiles, not at Philippe, but at me. "I am. It was nice, saving you."

Philippe takes Meg's hand and brings it to his lips. "A pleasure. You and my dear, sweet sister have my eternal gratitude."

"And mine as well," Victoriana says. "But I do wish zere was something more I could do for you zan . . . money." She says the word like it's something you wouldn't say in front of a teacher.

Meg prods me.

"Since you ask," I say, "there is something."

46

A few minutes later, it's all settled: I'll send her ten pairs of shoes, and she'll wear them, mentioning that they were made by "an exciting new designer" she met in South Beach.

"Sort of a princess product placement," Meg says.

"Zis is not trouble," Victoriana says. "But now zat we have settled zis, we really must go." She walks to the door. "Bruno!"

The mountainous guard appears. Victoriana says, "Can you please alert ze limo driver and ze pilot." She gazes at Philippe. "Now zat my bruzzer is safe, we need to go home."

"Have a great trip," I say, "and beware of Sieglinde."

Victoriana nods. "I will always be aware."

Fifteen minutes later, we're on our way down to the lobby. It's a little crowded because Bruno insists on standing in the center, holding Victoriana's hand, and I'm stuck between him and Ryan. It's like being pinned under two fallen oaks. Another treelike guard backs up Philippe.

"Listen, man," Ryan whispers. "I'm sorry about . . . I know you liked her, but it was just, Vicky and I have so much in common. We like the beach, partying . . . it's like it was meant to be."

Yeah, it's hard to find girls with those interests in South Beach. But I say, "Don't worry about it." I suck in my stomach to avoid Bruno's elbow.

We reach the lobby, and Bruno tugs Victoriana out past me.

"Ouch!" she yells. "Zat is not necessary!"

"Eet is my job!" Bruno looks around as if expecting a mob attack at any moment. But other than the usual guests on their way to the pool, the lobby's pretty uneventful. If anything, it looks empty without the swans.

"Ze limousine?" Philippe says. "Where is it?"

Bruno says something in French to the other guard. The guard starts toward the front doors. "He ees checking." Bruno glances around again.

"But you called down for the limo. They said it was

ready." Meg, too, looks at the doors and whispers, "I don't like this, Johnny. You know Farnesworth would have her limo here."

She's right.

"Maybe you should go back to your room," I say to Victoriana. She nods and starts back toward the elevator.

"Eet is not necessary." Bruno takes her arm. "Gerard, he is checking."

Victoriana stares at his hand, which is tightly around her wrist. "Please, Bruno. You are hurting me."

"Eet is for your own protection."

The elevator door beside ours opens, and a woman with two little girls exits. When she sees Victoriana, she shrieks. "It's really her! It's the princess!"

The two little girls run over to Victoriana. "Can we take our picture with you?" the older one begs.

"Samantha, that's very rude!" the mother snaps, but she doesn't pull her away. Victoriana has gotten free of Bruno and is talking to the girls, but their shrieks have alerted other guests, who run over and start snapping cell phone photos.

"Can I try on your tiara?" asks one woman.

"Mira, José! Mira!"

They're all shoving, poking, touching. Victoriana's trying to be gracious, saying, "Wait! Please! I will speak wiz you all." Her eyes seek out Bruno, but he's glancing around like he's searching for something. The other guard is talking to the valet, arguing with him. Victoriana's car is still nowhere in sight.

"Bruno!" Victoriana cries as a big guy steps on her open-toed shoe.

"Hey, watch it!" Ryan tries to shove the guy out of the way. "You don't treat girls like that."

Bruno's still looking around, searching for something. Or someone.

And suddenly, I know why the limo isn't here. Bruno didn't call for it. He called someone else.

I reach for Victoriana's hand through the crowd of people. "Come on, Princess. We have to go."

Victoriana looks around, unaccustomed to going anywhere without her bodyguard. "But Bruno—"

"Johnny's right." Meg, who's been staring at Bruno too, nods agreement. "You should go." She leans over to Ryan. "Maybe you could get your car for Victoriana and Philippe."

"It's a two-seater."

"It's an emergency," I say, trying to extricate Victoriana.

Ryan starts out toward the employee lot. Victoriana tries to follow, but the crowd is relentless.

"Wait! Wait!" a woman says. "I need a picture!"

"Can you give me some money?" a boy asks.

Finally, Victoriana's through. She tries to make eye contact with Philippe, who's oblivious. But the crowd has alerted Bruno that his charge is escaping.

"Your Highness!" Bruno's voice penetrates the crowd. He shoves past them, knocking one of the little girls on her rear end. She starts to bawl. "You should not have done zat!"

He grabs Victoriana again.

Victoriana tries to pull away, but he holds fast. I see tears in the princess's eyes.

I try to look calm, even though I know now that I'm dealing with a spy. I signal to Ryan to get his phone, call a cop. "Aren't you supposed to be working for her?" I ask Bruno.

"Stay out of zis, peasant!"

Ryan comes back and tries to step between Bruno and Victoriana. "Hey, buddy, leave her alone." He's almost as big as Bruno, and much younger, so he grabs Bruno's arm. But Bruno's trained in self-defense. In an instant, Ryan's on the floor. Bruno wrenches Victoriana's arm behind her back. She screams.

Her shrieks alert the masses in the lobby. Until then, they were listening to the voice of authority. Now, they're realizing something's wrong.

"What's he doing?" A woman points at them.

"He's trying to kidnap the princess!"

A buzz goes through the crowd. The information gets translated into several languages. Someone calls for hotel security. Other cell phones come out. People rush toward Victoriana. In the melee, she breaks away from Bruno's grasp again. I find myself between them, among the pressing bodies. It's a mass of flesh, and Victoriana's trying to get to the parking lot with Ryan, who has struggled up. "Please! Let me through!"

Suddenly, everything freezes, everything and everyone. The room goes silent. And then, people start to move

309

in lockstep, clearing a path to let Victoriana, Philippe, and Ryan through.

What's happening? I try to speak the thought, but I, too, am frozen. My tongue won't move. In the silence, I can feel my pulse pounding, so I know I'm still alive. The only other thing I can move is my eyes, and through them, I see Victoriana, Philippe, and Ryan walking through the parted crowd. I shift my gaze to the left, to Meg. I try to make eye contact. Does she see what I see?

But Meg's eyes are moving rapidly back and forth, back and forth to Bruno, to the crowd, to Victoriana, Philippe, and the other silent people.

Meg's doing it. She's the one who froze the crowd. Somehow, she got Bruno to unhand Victoriana too. She made them all give way.

I was never the best at math, but at some point, even a guy with a C in trig can add one plus one. Plus one. Plus one.

The brownies. The magic ring. The way the swan got healed when Meg laid hands on it, and I started feeling better after the scorpion bite. The graveyard. And now, this.

Meg's a witch.

But what does this mean? What does it mean for me? For us? Did she cast a spell on me? Is that why I fell for her, not Victoriana?

And what else has she done to me? To everyone?

Now what she's doing is she's saving the princess.

Victoriana's gone. She'll return home, to her friends, to her family.

To her shoes!

But suddenly, there's a gust of wind. It knocks people over, and everything unfreezes.

In the middle of the room appears Sieglinde. Siegfried too.

"Can you do nothing right?" she demands of Bruno.

Bruno cowers before her. "*Bitte.* I could not get to her. There vas another vitch. She stopped me. She let them go."

"Go where?" Sieglinde shrieks.

Bruno gestures mutely toward the door to the employee lot.

"Fool!" Sieglinde stomps her foot. "How could you let her get away?"

"I didn't . . . I couldn't. There was . . ." He looks at Meg, who's staring at her feet. "A witch."

Sieglinde turns to Meg. "You? Here?"

Meg faces her. "Where'd you think I was? Trapped in a lighthouse? That's just the lie you told Johnny."

"I vill put you there now!" She looks at her son. "Siegfried! After them! Now! You vill succeed this time!"

"Yes, Mama." Siegfried gulps but runs to the door. When he gets there, it's locked. He pulls at it, shakes it. It won't open. Sieglinde raises her hand as if she's about to release a lightning bolt or something to blast it open. But suddenly, her feet are knocked from under her, and she's on the floor.

"Go the other way!" she screams at Siegfried.

He runs off toward the front entrance, knocking through the crowds and the doormen. Sieglinde struggles to get to her feet, but it's like she's stuck in something, chewing gum that binds her to the ground, and as I watch her, I know I have to go after them too. I began this quest to help the princess. I have to see it through to the end.

I start to run after Siegfried.

"No, Johnny!" Meg is still staring down Sieglinde. "Try the door again!"

I slide to a stop and go toward the door I know is locked. It opens easily. I run down a dark passage and see Victoriana and Philippe, struggling to squeeze into Ryan's two-seater convertible. The princess stops to pick up a fallen sandal.

"Go!" I yell. "Go quickly! They're coming for you! Ryan, just take them anywhere. The witch will find you if you go to the airport! And Bruno probably didn't call for the plane."

They hear me, and slam the door, leaving the shoe just lying there, abandoned, Victoriana in Philippe's lap. The motor starts. They're going to make it. They're going to make it.

Suddenly, I feel a hand on my chest. Then, something cold against my neck.

It's the blade of a knife.

"You vill make them stop now," Siegfried's voice says.

"No!" But I don't want to die, and Victoriana is gesturing

toward me, telling Ryan to stop. Ryan hesitates.

Siegfried digs the knife into my throat. I feel blood. His breath comes in short bursts. "You go, he dies. Give me . . . give me the princess, and no one vill . . . get hurt."

I can feel Siegfried shaking as he says it, his breath hot in my ear. He's as scared as I am.

"Please," Victoriana tells Ryan. "He is a hero. He saved my bruzzer. I cannot allow zis."

Philippe nods agreement. He opens the door, and both he and Victoriana stumble out.

Against my back, I can feel Siegfried's heart racing, as hard as my own. He's panting almost like he's about to have a seizure. But when he sees Victoriana, he loosens his grip a bit.

"Ja!" he exclaims.

"No!" I shout at the same time. "Victoriana, no!"

"Shut up!" His voice is raw. "Now you . . ." He gestures toward the princess, and I can see he's shaking like he just came out of a cold pool. "You come here."

"No!" I repeat. I twist, trying to meet his eyes, but it's hard with a knife at my throat. "Is this really what you want?"

"Johnny, I am going wiz him." Victoriana goes to Siegfried. He grabs her arm, loosening his grip on me at the same time. In one fluid movement, he has Victoriana in his clutches, the knife at her throat. He kicks me away.

"No!" I scream. It can't end like this. I can't have done all this work just to have him take her away.

"It is okay," Victoriana says. "You did your best."

"No." I stare at Siegfried and remember how he let me go in the graveyard, remember his mother screaming at him. "Is this really what you want? Or are you just doing it because of your mother?"

"Vat are you talking about?"

"About you." I gesture at Victoriana. "Are you like this, a kidnapper, a killer? I understand all about family and wanting to do what your parents want. I've done my best for my own family. But sometimes, Siegfried, you have to make your own decisions."

"I am brave." He holds Victoriana closer. "She must come with me." But there's doubt in his voice.

"You let me go in the graveyard," I say. "You're twice my size. I couldn't overpower you."

He laughs shakily. "Of course not. I . . ." He stops. "I did not let you go."

"You did. And in Zalkenbourg. You let me go that time too."

"I messed up those times. I have no powers, no magic." He says it in a trembling voice. "My mother, she says I mess up alvays."

"Maybe you messed up because you knew you were doing the wrong thing."

He loosens his grip on Victoriana a bit, and I hear her take a deep breath.

"Let her go," I say.

The hand holding the knife trembles. "But . . . she vill be so angry with me if I do not bring her the princess."

I know he's considering it. There's uncertainty in his eyes. "The police will be mad if you take the princess. If they catch you, I bet you get the death penalty for that. That's worse than your mother being mad."

I hear him breathing, hard. The hand holding the knife wavers.

"Is it worth it?" I ask. "Your mother's a witch. She'll get away with it. But you'll be caught. Will she be able to get you out?"

He shakes his head. "It is true."

I gesture toward the cowering princess. "Is this what you want? To hurt people? To make them do things they don't want to do? Your mother's looking for power. She wants to be the one who helped the king. But what's in it for you? Don't you want to be the good guy?"

Siegfried looks at Victoriana. A slight breeze riffles her golden hair, and she nods.

"If you release me," she says in a strangled voice, "I will make sure nuzzing happens to you. I only want to be wiz my own family as you wish to be wiz yours."

Siegfried shakes his head. "I do not know what to do."

"Do the right thing," I say, "the thing you know in your heart is right."

Siegfried stares at Victoriana a long time. We all do. She's so beautiful, as startling as the day I first met her, but more now, because I know she's sweet and kind as well.

Finally, with a sigh, Siegfried releases his grip on her.

"You are right. I cannot do this thing. I cannot." He holds the knife out.

I don't want to take the knife, don't want to touch it. But Siegfried holds it in a shaking hand. It has a streak of blood, my blood on the blade. I take it gingerly between my fingers and wrap it in my shirt.

"Go," he says to Victoriana. "I know my mother vill be here soon, to see that I have failed again. You must go. Now."

Victoriana nods. "You have not failed."

"Now!" Siegfried yells. "Go now!"

Victoriana nods. She takes Philippe's hand and runs to the car, pausing only to scoop up the sandal.

Ryan has the top up, but Victoriana rolls down the window. As Ryan pulls out of the parking lot, she yells, "Zank you, Johnny! I will never forget you. And I will wear ze shoes!"

And then, she's gone.

We stand a long moment, me and the scary motorcycle guy. Two mama's boys.

Finally, he says, "I knew you vere under the bar that time too." He sighs, and I can tell he's trying hard not to bawl. "I am a vuss. She vill kill me. It vill not matter if I go to jail because she vill kill me."

I actually feel sorry for the guy. It's not his fault that his mother's an evil witch bent on Zalkenbourgian domination.

"You did the right thing," I say, even though it doesn't seem like enough.

That's when Sieglinde shows up, followed by Meg. They burst through the back door. Meg runs up to me and embraces me. "You're all right!"

Sieglinde spreads her arms. "Your police are here, but they are too late. My son has taken them! My son—" She sees Siegfried. She says, "You are here. Vere are they?"

I look at Siegfried. He says nothing for a long moment, but finally, he gestures toward me and the gun. "I let them go, *Mutter.*"

"You what? How could you?"

He shakes his head.

That's when the cops catch up with Sieglinde. One grabs her while the other takes out the cuffs. The third is reading Sieglinde her rights.

"How could you?" she screams. "You fool!"

"I am sorry, Mama." Siegfried is bawling. "I could not do it."

"I cannot believe this! I disown you!"

And then, just as the handcuffs slip onto her wrists, Sieglinde disappears.

47

"I held her at bay as long as I could," Meg explains in her shop an hour later. We called the airport when we got into the hotel lobby, and a few minutes before, we received word that Victoriana's plane had taken off. "I wanted to come help you."

"Like you helped me in the graveyard?"

She shakes her head. "No, that was all you."

I'm not sure whether to believe her, so I say, "But you healed me from the scorpion bite? It really was poisonous." She's nodding, so I add, "And the swan. You fixed him too."

Meg nods. "Yes, I'm a healer. It will come in handy some-day when we have kids. In fact . . ." She touches the small cut on my neck, the one my mother covered with a Band-Aid. In an instant, it doesn't hurt at all. "But you were the one who got Siegfried to surrender. What did you do to him?"

"Just . . . talked, told him it was a bad idea and stuff." I can still feel the knife against my neck, and I shiver. It amazes me that I even *could* talk, like people who develop superhuman strength and lift a car off their kid or something. "It was weird. I mean, I don't even know why I went after him. I don't have . . . powers like you."

Meg pats my arm. "You have powers."

I laugh. "Right. Faster than a loose heel. Able to repair soles in a single stitch."

Meg laughs. "They're just a different kind of powers. You're decent and you're honest. That's why Victoriana asked you to help her in the first place, and that's what made Siegfried see the light. There're all kinds of magic in the world."

"All kinds of magic." I touch her hair, then run my hand down her cheek. "It'd still be cool to be able to make a room freeze."

"I'll do it for you."

"That's why you wanted to come along with me, to pro-tect me with your magic powers because you thought I was a wuss."

"Because I love you," she says, gripping my hand. "I

wanted to be with you. I knew you were doing something dangerous, or you wouldn't have lied, and I didn't want to have to wonder what happened to you like . . ."

"Like my mom," I say.

"Right. So I gave you the ring, and I told you to wear it if you ever needed luck, *knowing* you'd put it on if you were in a tough spot, that it would bring me to you."

"Even though that would put you in that same tough spot."

"Especially because of that. And then, I tried to always be ready. I told my mom I might be going suddenly, and she understood."

"I . . . wow." My head hurts from thinking, but I want to keep talking, so Meg doesn't get the idea I should go home and rest or something. "So if you've been a witch all this time, why couldn't magic have saved us from the dungeon in Zalkenbourg?" When Meg narrows her eyes at me, I say, "I mean, not that you haven't done a lot of cool stuff."

"It was too dark. My family's magic is in our eyes. To use it, there has to be eye contact."

I nod and get to what I've really been wondering about. "So did you make me fall in love with you with magic too, then?" I'm not sure if I care, really, I just want to know.

But Meg shakes her head. "Of course not."

"Would you tell me if you did?"

"Probably not. But think about it. I've had a crush on you for years. If I could just cast a spell and make you love me back, that would have been a lot easier than trying to make you jealous with Philippe. It's not that I didn't think about it, but I wanted it to be real."

"I want that too."

"My family pledged decades ago to only use our powers in case of emergency, not for taking tests or making money."

"How about housework? You use the elves for that."

"The brownies are free to go whenever they want. They just stay out of, I don't know, tradition."

"Oh, okay."

"So are you mad I didn't tell you?"

I look up at her, and it's like everything I know about her is different now, is changed. But everything about me is changed too. A few weeks ago, I was some poor slob, repairing shoes with no hope of a future. But now I've fought two giants and won, been engaged to a princess and given her up, changed six swans into humans, and found the love of my life. Who wants things to be the same?

I shake my head. "Could I just kiss you now?"

She nods, and I do.

"Johnny, come quick!" Across the way, in the shoe repair, my mother's watching television. She's pointing to the screen, and when we go to look, I see it's Victoriana, filmed just before boarding her private plane, safe at Miami International.

"We had a wonderful time in Florida," she tells the

reporters. She looks at a reporter who's asked her a question I didn't hear. "Oh, no special reason. Just ze sun, and ze shopping. In fact . . ." She holds up her foot, the one with my shoe on it.

"My shoe's on television!" I say.

"While I have you all here, I want to show you ze thing I love very much. And zat is zis shoe. It is a very special shoe from a new designer, Gianni Marco, who is right here on South Beach. But I am very certain zat his shoes will soon be on ze runways of Europe."

The reporters *ooh* and *ahh*, and I hear cameras snapping, everyone taking photos of the princess and my shoe.

48

*Oh, flounder in the sea, come come, here to me. My wife
wants me to make a wish. Come to me, oh, magic fish.*
— "The Fisherman and His Wife"

Mom tells me to bring Meg back to the apartment tonight for
dinner, to celebrate the fact that we have electricity to cook
it. And some other stuff. But when we get there, my mother's
on the floor. There's a man crouched over her.

I cannot handle this today.

"Hey!" I rush toward her, signaling to Meg to call the
police. "What are you . . . ?"

The man looks up. "She fainted. I was just . . ."

Our eyes meet. I know him from . . . somewhere.

"I just came here to find my wife," the man says. His
nose twitches.

Twitches. That's when I realize where I know him from. It's the first time I've seen him in daylight, at least in human form.

"Your wife?" I say.

He nods. "I guess she was a little shocked. I don't blame her. It's been fifteen years."

"You're saying this is your wife?"

"Unbelievable, right? She probably thought I was dead."

"Cornelius said that all the used-to-bes have families who think they're dead," I say, because the man I'm talking to is the fox. Todd. "So you mean to say you're my . . .?"

"Your father," says my mother's voice from the floor. "But how can it be? Where have you been all this time? And why did you come back now?"

I look at the fox who is now my father, then back at Mom. "I think, maybe, you ought to sit down."

Meg, who knows the story, agrees. "Why don't I get you some water, Mrs. Marco?"

We walk over to the sofa, and after Mom can breathe right, Todd, the former fox, begins to speak. Meg holds my hand, and I squeeze hers, glad she's here.

"Many, many years ago, I had an argument with my wife." He nods at Mom. "At this point, I don't even remember what it was about."

"Work," Mom says.

Todd nods. "Work. I was young, and I was proud, and

while I should have apologized to my dear wife, who was always right about everything, I didn't want to. So the next morning, instead of going to work, I went fishing."

"Fishing?" Mom says, and I remember the rat saying that the fox had been a fisherman.

"Yes, fishing," Todd says. "I went early, four in the morning. I stood on the MacArthur Causeway like an idiot. I didn't catch anything, and just as the sun was rising, and I was about to give up, I felt a tug.

"I was happy because, by that time, I had realized the error of my ways, and I thought I'd return home with a huge fish for dinner, so my wife would forgive me. When I reeled the fish in, it was better than I expected—a beautiful, big snapper with fine fins and red scales. But just as I was rejoicing, the fish spoke to me."

Mom gasps. Me, I'm not surprised at all.

My father continues. "'Please do not kill me,' the fish said very clearly, 'for I am a magic fish, with the power to grant all your wishes.'

"'All my wishes?' I asked. I didn't believe it, of course. 'I'm just overtired.' But the fish said, 'Why don't you give it a try?'

"So I did. I wished for the first thing that came to mind, a boat, since I'd been feeling sorry for myself for not having one. And almost as soon as I said the word, I was standing in a twenty-foot open fisherman.

"And that should have been the end of that but I was

young and stupid, and I said, 'What? This boat's too small. If you're such a magic fish, I want a bigger boat, a huge boat.'"

"Let me guess," I say. "He got mad."

"No. In fact, he smiled in a way you wouldn't think a snapper could smile and said, 'Fisherman, you drive a hard bargain.' The next thing I knew, I was standing on a yacht, sixty-four feet, twin engines, and steps leading down to what I'm sure were extremely luxurious cabins."

"You had a wish, and you used it for a yacht?" my mother says.

"That's exactly what I thought! As soon as I saw it, I realized I'd made a huge mistake. Here I was on a yacht fit for a billionaire, but I wasn't a billionaire. How was I going to explain it to my wife, you, who would be upset because we had so many things we needed? So I said to the fish, 'Wait! There's one more thing. I'd like a big house, a mansion.'"

"The fish rolled his eyes, but finally, he inclined his head toward the right. 'Look over there, on Hibiscus Island. That big pink house is yours now.' And I looked down and saw a set of keys by my feet."

"And we're not living in a big mansion because . . . ?" My mother shakes her head. "I don't believe this."

"Give him a chance, Mom," I say, still amazed that this is my father, my for-real father I thought I'd never see. I grin at Meg, and she grins back.

"We're not living in a big pink mansion," my father says, "because I was young and stupid, and in the moment the fish made the house mine, I realized I couldn't even afford the taxes on a place like that. Better the money, I thought, an annuity, maybe. 'Could I win the lottery?' I asked the fish.

"And the next thing I knew, I was standing on MacArthur Causeway with nothing but a fishing pole, and the fish spoke to me.

"'You have asked too much,' he said, 'So you get nothing.' Well, needless to say, I was pretty mad about that. So I said that if he didn't give back what he'd taken, I was going to kill him, and stuff him, and hang him on the wall."

"Oh, boy," I said.

"Exactly. I'd forgotten that he was a magic fish. Next thing I knew, the air was filled with the stench of garbage, an odor surprisingly pungent to me. I was in a place I'd never been before, and everything was very big because I was very small. I now know I was at the Port of Miami. I ran to the water's edge, and there, I saw the fish.

"'You have done too little,' he said, 'and asked too much. You have threatened someone who did you a kindness. Now you will pay the price. You will remain in this form until you find the feather of a golden bird. Once you do, you must ask the person who brings it to you to cut your throat with a knife, but you must not tell him why. Only when you have done this will you be human again.'

"'Human again'? I asked. 'What do you mean?'

"The fish flipped his tail in the water, and beside it, I saw a reflection. But it wasn't my face I saw. Rather, the face was red and whiskered with sharp teeth and a pointed nose, a nose with a rather strong sense of smell.

"'You've turned me into an animal?' I yelled at the fish, and I lunged without thought into the water. But when I went beneath the surface, there was no fish to be found. I would have thought that it was my imagination, but since that day, I have been a fox. I called myself Todd, which means 'fox.' I lived on garbage and avoided dogs and waited for the day when someone would come to save me. How could I know that that someone would be my own wonderful son?"

My mother takes a long drink of water, fans herself, then looks from my father to me. "You expect me to believe this?"

My father shakes his head. "I wouldn't have believed it if it hadn't happened to me. But you can ask your son—*our* son. He was the one who found me, the hero who saved me."

She places her hand to her forehead. "This can't be happening."

"You were the one," I say, "who believed all along he wasn't dead, that he wouldn't leave you. You were the one who believed in magic."

"But I didn't think he was a fox!"

"I saw him as a fox, Mom. It's true."

My father moves closer to her, carefully, and places his hand on her arm. "I never forgot you, either of you."

I say, "Stranger things have happened—and recently too."

My mother takes my father's face in her hands and gazes at him a very long time. "I thought you had left because of our fight. I looked everywhere." There are tears in her eyes. "We've lost so many years."

My father takes her in his arms. "But we have so many years left."

"You know your son, then?" my mother asks.

Todd—my father—nods. "Fine boy, even if he did kill me. He kept his promise to me, though it was hard to do. Those are the type of values I'd have wanted him to learn, and you taught him."

My mother nods. "He's like that."

"I'm glad." My father stands and holds out his arms to me. I step into them. This has been a crazy day, a crazy week, a crazy world.

49

That night, I go to the beach with Meg because I need to relax, to get my mind off what happened, to be with Meg. When we get there, we take off our shoes. I notice she has a pedicure, a silly one with flowers on her toes, and I wonder if that was for Philippe. "I'll have to get the brownies to make you some special shoes," I say. "Victoriana shouldn't be the only one with Gianni Marco originals."

She squints at her toes but doesn't smile. "Are you going to regret it?"

"Regret what?" I grasp her wrist as we start toward the water.

She follows but slowly. "You know what. Giving it up—the chance to marry the princess, the most beautiful woman in the world, and one of the richest."

"Are you kidding? I'd hate that."

"Hate being rich?"

"Hate being stuck in a glass tower. If I were with Victoriana, there'd be a hundred paparazzi on this beach. And I'd hate . . ." I stop, listening to the waves as they hit the sand.

"Hate what?"

"Hate not being with you." I pull her toward me and try to kiss her. "You are literally magical."

She smiles but says, "Won't it be boring, being with the same old girl you've known your whole life?"

I pretend to think about it, then I do. All my life, women, my mom and Meg, then girls I wanted to make out with, have been dragging me to these chick flick movies. You know the ones, where you know from the first minute that the couple's going to end up together. But first, they have to overcome some obstacle, like a hurricane, or one of them being engaged to someone else, or having a horrible secret, or needing to meet at the top of the Empire State Building on Valentine's Day, or—my personal favorite—the one where the woman's in a coma, but her *ghost* is walking around the guy's apartment anyway. I always thought those movies were a little predictable and a *lot* unrealistic. But after what's happened, I'm less sure. Maybe you actually do need to face obstacles with someone to know that they're the one you'd sacrifice for.

I shake my head and say, "I've got a quote for you."

She groans. "When did you have time to look one up?"

"I just remembered it. It's by Victor Hugo. He said, 'I met in the street a very poor young man who was in love. His hat was old, his coat worn, his cloak was out at the elbows, the water passed through his shoes—and the stars through his soul.'"

50

As long as the shoemaker lived all went well with him, and all his undertakings prospered.

—"The Elves and the Shoemaker"

When I open my exclusive shoe shop in the lobby of the Coral Reef Grand, Princess Victoriana returns to South Beach for a visit, which means the press comes too. Paparazzi swarm the lobby, and I pretend it's because of me.

"So you've been okay?" I ask her as she models a yellow-and-white T-strap sandal with a Louis heel, yet another pair of shoes she's buying.

"Better zan okay," she says. "I am starting college in ze fall—wiz proper bodyguards, of course, so my parents will no longer worry about me being kidnapped *or* disgracing zem."

She turns her foot to display the heel, and there are at least a dozen flashes.

Behind the counter, I hear Meg saying, "Gianni. That's G-I-A-N-N-I."

"Who's that?" a reporter asks her.

"That's the designer, the reason you're all here. Have you looked at the shoes?"

"Excuse me," Victoriana says, and she walks over to the reporter and lifts her foot onto the counter, just like she did the day she asked me to meet her. "Zese shoes, you can say zey are ze favorite of ze princess of Aloria."

More flashes, and the reporter says, "How did you say that was spelled again?"

"G-I-A-N-N-I," Meg repeats. "When he's a household word, you'll be able to say you broke the story."

"*Exactement*," Victoriana says. "My future sister-in-law, she will wear his shoes on her wedding day."

This is news. Philippe's fiancée is an American actress. Philippe had met her before his transformation, but they kept their romance secret. Victoriana told us that her parents would never have approved of the match, but after what happened, they thought it best to get Philippe married off as quickly as possible so he wouldn't be caught in any more witches' snares.

"*Oui*," Victoriana says. "Ze shoes, zey are in Hollywood too now!"

Mom and Dad come in. My father surveys the reporters

334

and the customers and laughs. "To think, a few weeks ago, I was living in a Dumpster!"

My parents closed the shoe repair to do shoe sales instead. Parents. It's weird to think of them that way. They're taking care of the money part of the shop now. When I finish high school, I'll be able to go to college and learn to run the business myself. It will be hard work, but I'm used to that.

Our first order of business has been finding a factory to make the shoes. It was too much work for the brownies, and we don't have them anymore anyway.

That's Mom's fault. When I told her about the brownies, she was really grateful. But when I described the one I'd seen, I mentioned his ragged clothing, and she felt bad. "We should make them some clothes, sort of a thank-you gift."

So, all week, while my father ran the shoe repair, Mom sewed little outfits out of scraps of fabric. Saturday night, she left them in Meg's coffee shop.

Sunday morning, the clothes were gone, and the place was a mess.

"I don't understand what happened," Meg said.

Mom shook her head. "I thought they'd be so grateful for the new clothes."

"Clothes?" Meg said. "You gave them new clothes?"

Then, she explained that it's okay to leave food out for the brownies, but never any kind of payment, and that when brownies are given clothes, they always leave. "No one knows if they get offended, or if they think they're too grand to work. No brownie has ever stuck around to explain."

My mother was very apologetic, but Meg brushed it off. "Oh, it's okay. My brothers can do some work for once. I never felt right about having the brownies."

The press has been covering the princess's visit, and the reason for it, like crazy, so it's no surprise that the phone's been ringing with calls from socialites, wanting to own a pair of Marco originals, and boutiques wanting to carry them. We even got a call from Wendell, the park ranger, congratulating us on our success and telling us about his own: He just booked the giants as a featured act with the circus. As their manager, he gets ten percent of the take, which is way more than he could have gotten for the frog on eBay.

Mom's been kind of enjoying taking all the calls, so I'm surprised when she hands me the phone. "I think you should take this one yourself."

"Hello?"

"Hello, is this Mr. Marco?"

"Yeah, this is Johnny. I mean, Gianni."

"This is Carol Ellert. I'm a buyer for Saks Fifth Avenue."

My mouth goes dry. Still I manage to choke out, "I'm sorry. I'm having trouble hearing you." I motion to Meg, to anyone, to please get me some water. "Where'd you say you're from?"

"Saks Fifth Avenue. We'd like to set up a meeting with you about stocking your shoes in our store."

Meg's back with the water. She mouths, "Who is it?"

I mouth back, "Saks," and we do a little happy dance right there.

"Hello?" the voice on the other end says. "Hello? Did I lose you?"

"Oh no. I'm sorry. I just . . . there was a customer."

"I understand. Soon, you'll have a lot of customers. Now, as I was saying, we'd like to meet. Is next Thursday good for you?"

I come from a long line of shoe people. My grandpa called us cobblers, but that sounds more like a dessert than a person. My family has run the shoe repair at the Coral Reef Grand, the fanciest hotel on South Beach, since before I was born, first my grandparents, then my parents, now my mother and I. And my father too. So I've seen the famous and the infamous, the rich and the poor, wearers of Gucci, Bruno Magli, Manolo Blahnik, and Converse. I know the beautiful people. Or, at least, I know their feet.

But until this summer, I'd never have imagined that they'd be wearing my shoes, or that I'd be involved in an adventure with a witch, six swans who used to be people and are again, and a beautiful princess who offered to marry me, or that I'd find my father. I certainly never thought I'd turn that princess down to be with the girl who works across the hall.

I wink at Meg. Into the phone, I say, "Let me check my schedule. I think I can definitely fit you in."

AUTHOR'S NOTE

My book *Beastly*, published in 2007, contained references to several traditional fairy tales. Since its publication, I have received quite a bit of mail from readers, indicating that they were unfamiliar with these tales (such as "Snow White and Rose Red"), if they hadn't been made into a movie. As I always loved Grimms' fairy tales, I decided to write a book based upon several traditional tales that have not been made into movies, the better to bring them to modern audiences. Some, such as "The Elves and the Shoemaker," were favorites of mine as a child, while other lesser-known stories, I discovered in my research.

These are the tales I chose:

- "The Elves and the Shoemaker": A shoemaker leaves leather out and finds finished shoes in the morning. When he finds out that elves have made the shoes, his wife tries to repay them with fine clothing. The elves leave and never return.

- "The Frog Prince": A princess loses an item and begs a frog to retrieve it, promising to allow him to come into her house and be her friend if he does. Her father, the king, forces her to keep her promise. She is disgusted and throws the frog at the wall, at which point, he turns into a handsome prince.

  Readers may note that there is now a movie version of this tale. It did not exist when I began or, indeed, finished writing this book. At this writing, I have not yet seen Disney's *The Princess and the Frog*. However, from what I have seen of the previews, it is as different from the traditional tale as is my version.

- "The Six Swans": A man's children are enchanted to become swans. Their sister eventually finds them and turns them into humans by remaining silent for a year and making shirts out of flowers.

- "The Golden Bird": Three sons try to find a bird that has been eating their father's apples. The first two fail. The third listens to the directions of a fox (or wolf) who tells him to stay at a poor inn, steal the bird but not its golden cage, and to perform several other tasks. The son eventually gets the bird, a horse, and the hand of a princess, but the fox asks a final favor: that the son kill him. When the son does, the fox transforms into a man.

This story is originally from Russia, where it is called "The Firebird and the Gray Wolf." It was adapted by Russian composer Igor Stravinsky for a ballet, *The Firebird*.

- "The Valiant Tailor": A tailor kills seven flies and makes a jacket bragging about this achievement. People believe he has killed seven men and ask him to kill two giants. He tricks them into killing each other.

  This was actually made into a short film, *The Brave Little Tailor*, starring Mickey Mouse as the tailor. However, I loved the story and believed the movie to be obscure enough that most teens would still be unfamiliar with it.

- "The Salad": In exchange for a kindness, an old woman gives a huntsman a magical cloak that takes him where he wishes and a bird's heart that produces gold. A lady and her daughter trick him out of them, so he changes them to donkeys with the help of a magical salad. He eventually relents and marries the daughter.

- "The Fisherman and His Wife": A man catches a magic fish and does not kill it but asks it to grant his wishes. His wife asks for more and more extravagant items until the fish takes everything away.

May you enjoy discovering these and other tales. A good first place to look is on the web at www.surlalunefairytales. com, which includes most of the fairy tales I've mentioned here, and many others.